The Club

By the same author

Novels

Landscape with Dead Dons
The Conspiracy
Bad Dreams

Pieces

Inside Robert Robinson
The Dog Chairman
Prescriptions of a Pox Doctor's Clerk

Editor

The Everyman Book of Light Verse

Memoirs

Skip All That

The Club

Robert Robinson

ROBERT HALE · LONDON

First published in Great Britain 2000

ISBN 0 7090 6731 3

Robert Hale Limited
Clerkenwell House
Clerkenwell Green
London EC1R 0HT

2 4 6 8 10 9 7 5 3 1

Typeset by
Derek Doyle & Associates, Liverpool.
Printed in Great Britain by
St Edmundsbury Press Ltd, Bury St Edmunds, Suffolk.
Bound by Woolnough Bookbinding Ltd.

ONE

What made all that money so interesting to the world outside was little different from what made it interesting to the people actually involved. The idea of an unexpected windfall is a fantasy entertained by everyone, and when it happens no one is really surprised: seeing it happen to others simply shows you that it *does* happen, and all you have to do is wait your turn. The members of the Club, of course, had an obvious and particular interest, but at the beginning this was scarcely perceptible beneath a general feeling that though you didn't run across this sort of thing very often, when you did you realized you had never doubted that you might – it was a natural phenomenon, and the satisfaction aroused by seeing it demonstrated extinguished narrower considerations. But just as the initial response to the discovery of fire, the coming of the wheel, or the invention of the steam engine may have been a general murmur of agreement on the lines of man being a noble piece of work – a view of the matter later promoted in classrooms – this would quickly have been followed by more particular questions about how to turn it to advantage.

In these days of lotteries which dole out millions, the idea of coming up with an individual prize of anything less would have people calculating the odds against winning such a sum, and might not sell many tickets. But bear in mind that in the members' case no tickets had to be bought, and there were no odds to consider: the cash simply fell out of the sky, and you only had to bend down and pick it up. What you did with it then became your affair – put it on a plain number at roulette, perhaps, or give it to the poor. I take it that the significance of money is at the same time both relative and absolute: that is, if you have got some, having more is just as pleasing to you as it is to someone who has little or none – that is money's absolute condition, its universal agreeability. But in its relative dimension it will always mean more to some than to others, and the two categories do not always divide on what might be assumed to be rational grounds – some poor men aren't terribly interested in having more, and some rich men cannot bear life on any other terms. So money is something that people invest themselves in.

In clubs, one seldom knows who has it or who has not. You may see that your neighbour across the road lives much as you would expect him to, but in clubs there is nothing to go by. Knowing a man in a club means no more than knowing his conversation and his face. Meet him in the street and you realize you don't know his name, and from the hugeness of the relief with which he shakes your companion's hand – whose identity you roar out as though he were some favourite historical figure beside whom the mention of all other names is rendered superfluous – you recognize that he doesn't know your name either. You have some idea he is a barrister or a publisher, or are you thinking of someone else? That he is a member means – well, that another member must have put him up, and two other members will have supported him, and members at large who either know him or have met him at lunch will have signed the book, and after due consideration the committee of the day will elect him, and that means – what does that mean?

That from the moment of his election he is perceived to be a member of the same tribe. Oligarchies have always absorbed outsiders whose desire to belong endorses the oligarchy's suzerainty. This adoption process might seem to be casual, but it never is, since those who have it in their power to adopt are so conscious of the frailty of their own bona fides that they are immensely sensitive to the possibility of the stock being watered.

But it is no more than a matter of presentation, style, behaviour: you don't have to produce the deeds to your land or your houses, if you are known to the people who put you up then it is assumed you *can* be known. The relationships of members are entirely at face value, conventional behaviour is all that is required and since this is instinctive for many and easily counterfeited by others, the climate is a temperate one.

But when a question of money arises – money that is to descend upon the club itself – do the members know enough about each other to devise a policy? They know nothing of each other's individual finances, since conversation that seems likely to encroach upon this particular area will be scarcely less reserved than if private sexual fantasies were in question: should talk seem to be coming too close, someone's facetious comment will act like a warning notice that a trespasser may suddenly observe as he is about to touch an electrified fence. Simple good manners, of course, but there is a special requirement. In a club, there is parity: membership itself has already done the singling-out; anyone putting on the dog will have no audience, for where all are dogs there is no need to bark. A more than ordinarily fraudulent politician saw fit to enter as a jocular topic over lunch the fact that he had been caught with his pants down, rather as if his fellow members at the table were Rotarians he was in the habit of condescending to. She'd cure anyone of being over-sexed,' he guffawed, mentioning the name of his unhappy mistress. Nobody seemed disposed to take this up, and then a member who was already on the point of leaving, rose and smiled pleasantly. 'There may be a cure for being over-sexed,' he said. 'There is no cure for being under-bred.'

Members are only rude deliberately, and this is very rare. There are those who get it wrong, of course, but this usually happens 'after dinner' and again, not often. But small infringements of the prevailing style show that even though as I have said it is easy to bear the markings of the tribe, the real trick is to make sure that what the markings conceal never peeps out. Where are you coming from, as the Americans say, and in a club only so much of the answer as a member is willing to offer is ever on view.

Your financial status is the inviolable redoubt, and when there was a preliminary vote on what to do with the cash, I was not surprised to find the members opting overwhelmingly for giving it away – one or two hands were raised a trifle more slowly than others, perhaps, but at a general meeting and in full view of one's fellow members, who would wish to appear other than open-handed, since open-handedness would be an indication that as far as money went, it was as little of a problem to you as it appeared to be to the others? But bear in mind that it was a meeting at which no binding decision was being made, so the general disinterestedness was not something that would immediately be put to the test. And to begin with, the actual figures were a bit vague. One member alone ran against the crowd and, standing up, made the point that assets belonging to each member individually could not properly be disposed of by any other member or members in a general vote. But there was a murmur to the effect that this was a legal nicety and had yet to be determined, and anyway all that the present proceedings did was to give the committee a mandate to deliberate further. Nonetheless, I thought it was rather engaging when the members, having voted pretty well *nem con* to give the loot away, roundly applauded the dissident as he sat down.

My name is Owlish – Richard Owlish – and I'm aware there may be an element of the 'owlish' in these preliminary remarks of mine: I'm not at all sure what the word as an adjective precisely means – some hint of the solemn, perhaps, a habit of diagnosis, an inclination to offer a perspective on things – but my friends have always told me my name is apt (that they are able to tell me to my face is a comfort, for it suggests they don't think they are being unduly malicious). I once thought they were referring to the spectacles I wear, for whatever style I choose they always seem too big, but I think it goes further than that, and while it isn't a very flattering adjective, have come to feel over the years that they could have chosen others that were much worse. Some inclination to treat experience as a tableau at which I am an onlooker, some habit of observation, seems part of my temperament, and although I was involved in the events I'm describing I all along felt that I was a spectator, close to the action, and able to tell the story.

But back to the money. We'd had the general meeting, and while this had given the committee a free hand to suggest a variety of dispositions, more specific proposals would be solicited from the members themselves before the way forward could be agreed in detail.

What the world outside liked about the whole affair was the way it showed that magic could happen, and even readers who knew little or nothing about art had heard of the painter in question. The papers played the fairy-tale element for all it was worth – I can't say for more than it was worth because here was a story you didn't need to improve. In 1897 a member of the Club died and made certain bequests: his books were to go to the club library, and though he gave the trustees freedom to sell whichever of his pictures they had no wish to keep, he made it a condition that certain named items were to be retained and hung on the walls of the club. This was a small price to pay, since the sale of the good pictures reduced the club subscription for the ensuing ten years, and many of the indifferent canvases did well enough at auction to knock the price of a dish of boiled mutton down from a shilling to tenpence. The stuff they had to keep was hung haphazardly, for the members didn't notice pictures, and indeed we have never had an art committee. There were three canvases, a couple from the brush of the Victorian painter William Langley who specialized in cowscapes, and another much larger affair which exhibited a whiskery model of a much earlier day in the role of John the Baptist. The Langleys were cherished by the benefactor because they offered views of his estate in Scotland, and though the trees and the cows and the hills and the river had a doggy look, by which I mean the artist might have dipped a dog in his paintbox and keeping hold of its lead allowed it the freedom of the canvas, they were felt by the members, as indeed they had been by the original owner, to be homely and inoffensive.

The John the Baptist item was about eight feet by four feet and though the model is recognizable from other pictures of the same period, many felt the man – who had been painted so often you felt he could hardly have ventured into the street without someone saying 'Didn't I see you on the telly last night?' (I thought this was quite a good joke, but when I tried it on men they tended to look blank) – had never been done such justice. However, good as the characterization was, its impact was always diminished by the signature in the lower right-hand corner. Discounting the signature, members discounted the picture. It hung in the dining-room and became in time indistinguishable from the wallpaper.

That is until a man from an institute that wasn't the Courtauld but was certainly quite as respectable, was being given a tour of the club by his host. We don't go in for pictures very much since the feeling has always been that members have pictures at home and only need something to stop the walls looking bare when they come to the club. We have some landscapes that are nice enough without being at all special, mostly 'British school' or Italian *capriccios*, and a few portraits, a couple of good ones by Reynolds, but we've never plastered the walls with them, and I must say when I am taken to the Garrick and see all those ancient actors hanging up in their awful costumes I can't help thinking they make the place look like a mouldy copy of *Spotlight*.

The man from the institute was nodding politely enough at the stuff he was being shown, no doubt wondering when he could get back to the office. But as his host pointed out the big John the Baptist and laughed about the signature, he lingered a little, then looked a bit closer.

'Not very well lit, is it?

'Lit? No one looks at it.'

The pundit climbed on a chair – the place was now empty – and studied the signature. Took out some sort of pocket magnifying glass, and looked through it.

'Odd about the signature.'

'Rather absurd.'

'Well, it doesn't seem to have much to do with the rest of the picture, no, and the paint behind it – just the bit in the corner where the letters have been inscribed – is of quite a different quality, isn't it? I can't make out whether there is a small tear or a join in the canvas at that point.'

'I don't think anyone's ever looked that hard.'

'Wouldn't mind seeing it in workshop conditions.'

'You'd have to take it down.'

'Yes, but you said nobody looks at it.'

'They don't. But if it wasn't there, they might.'

The institute man said he had a feeling it could be to the Club's advantage. Would his host suggest it to the committee? His host thought the art-fancier was probably wanting to make work – indeed, the man said he would undertake the scrutiny personally, do it in his own time – but the point was put to the committee, and the picture came down under the eye of two men in dungarees who wore collars and ties as well. It was away for several months and I don't think anyone remarked on the gap, or if they noticed it, could recall what it was that used to fill it. Then there was a call from the art man, and, as he listened to what he was being told, the club secretary said, 'I will have to ask the chairman to speak to you. Will you please hold on.' And when the chairman came out of the morning-room to the secretary's office and took the phone, he showed that the news he received was well within his worldly competence, for the first thing he said was 'Damn. We can't afford to insure it.'

The institute man, a picture restorer and art historian called Firethorne, had found it wasn't one picture but two, the top one being racked into the frame of the bottom one, but in such a way that it looked as though the two frames were integral: you could hook the top one out – if you had the knack of it – as easily as you might peel the plastic off the back of a parking permit. It was a method of concealing the value of the picture underneath, perhaps because some earlier owner had come to it by means he wouldn't want anyone to know about, and had the perfectly workmanlike top canvas framed over it so the real thing was only ever on view when he felt like it. This method of concealment was not uncommon, according to Firethorne, and it had been the little corner of the concealed picture bearing the signature which had alerted him to the possibility.

'Of course, I'll have the top one relined and reframed – the little tear which revealed the signature actually seems to have been deliberate, very neatly cut, but that makes it all the easier to repair. And the members can go on not looking at it,' he added, somewhat facetiously.

'Oh please do,' said the club chairman. 'And, of course, let us have your invoice.'

'Thank you, I will.'

The ingenuity of a man who makes certain everyone is put off the scent by allowing the signature of Leonardo to seem to have been applied to a picture manifestly not his work is surely to be admired: in drawing attention to the possibility, he effectively dissipates it. Everyone loved the story and, of course, for most people the cash rather than the genius was the bewitching ingredient. The business of putting a value on the picture – a full-length *Leda and the Swan* of which only copies had hitherto been known – was, as I indicated earlier, rather uncoordinated to begin with: the secretary rang round the insurance companies, and none of them was prepared to take a position; they would contact the museums, of course, and get back to us. One or two syndicates at Lloyd's said they'd be pleased to take the picture on but quoted prohibitive rates, admitting the figures were pulled out of the air because they had no real idea. Meanwhile, speculation was rife. Of course, it would be sold – no one would wish to keep such a masterpiece in private hands, who could think of denying the world access to such an unduplicatable treasure? And, as the chairman had clearly seen, what institution outside the great public art collections of the world, with their sophisticated security, could afford to insure such a trophy?

'We'll put some of the money towards paying off any club debts, then I should be very surprised if members wouldn't want a variety of worthy causes to benefit. Perhaps we should have a party to mark the event.'

But first we had the general meeting, with the voting going as I have described, and although everyone seemed in favour of giving the money away, in the week or two which followed there were certain developments. The committee itself always met in the library, an elegant oval room recently decorated in cream and gold, where the bookcases, and the alcoves with comfortable chairs, were separated by marble pilasters and columns, and in the centre of the room there was one of those circular William IV mahogany tables that have curved leaves you can put in to enlarge the circumference and seat about twenty or more, if need be.

'Where is the picture now?'

'Eating its head off at the bank. We really must get on with it.'

The chairman was a man called Ledward and yes, he was chairman also of Borchgrave, and if you want to rank the company as a merchant bank you have to remember such old-fashioned institutions as Warburg and Kleinwort and Ansbacher before they vanished into the whirlpools of the international conglomerates, leaving only their names on the blotting paper which had absorbed them. Borchgrave was a rarity among merchant banks, privately capitalized and with a client list of such quality and quantity that it could not fail perennially to attract predators, none of whom ever got closer to Ledward than lunch.

Why Ledward wanted to spend time being chairman of the Club is as mysterious as the question why anyone would volunteer for a job no one else wants, and to which there attaches neither emolument nor kudos. You might imagine there could be advantage, but if Ledward's knighthood had so far been withheld, his charitable activities would do more for him than his position as chairman of the Club, and I've never heard anyone at a dinner-party boast of doing something which sounds so distinctly a couple of notches below being a mayor. I concluded that Ledward suffered, as I have always suspected members of voluntary committees suffer, from a profound conviction that he was in essence a nonentity.

'No news on price, yet?'

'Well, news, yes. What was it we talked about?'

'Any figure you like. Five million? God knows. We're still waiting to test the market.'

'Let me give you the gist of a note that Eric has over there.'

Ledward looked across at the secretary who took a sheet of paper from a folder and slightly waved it. He sat at the diagonal opposite Ledward, and there was a space between him on either flank to show that he was the one who was paid.

'And have you got the other thing – the invoice?'

The secretary laid the first sheet of paper down, then pulled another from the folder, held it up, then placed it on top of the first.

'A Japanese called Ihara writes from Pacific Rand of which he is the president to ask if the picture is for sale.'

'How much?'

Ledward said, 'Ten million.'

'Good lord.'

'He says it's his opening bid. He may go higher.'

'I thought Japan was out of money.'

'They're still pushing it around among themselves,' said Ledward, 'some of them, anyway. Though who will be left with the parcel when the music stops is anyone's guess.'

'The banks,' said Calderstone, a professor of haematology, 'have a knack of lending money to people they hope are crooks, but who always turn out to have been the village idiot.' And then more or less remembering that Ledward was something to do with banks added, 'I mean, you know, the banks you see in the street.' Calderstone smoked a pipe, which was a sufficiently unusual thing in the club to make members wonder whether it was a bid for singularity; the fact that he was a Nobel prize-winner does not altogether discount the possibility, since small vanities are by no means confined to the undistinguished.

'I must say everyone is taking this very coolly. Ten million pounds and possibly more. I suppose this O'Hara is on the up and up?'

'Ihara,' said Ledward, turning to the man who'd spoken, the

Earl of Olney, who, in his pin-striped double-breasted suit, not only looked like anyone's idea of an estate agent, but actually was one.

'You mean trustworthy? That rather depends on where you're standing. Over here, he might be in gaol, over there he's highly respected. Runs one of the top six construction companies in Japan, and since the bidding system is routinely rigged by ministers who are handsomely paid by the interested parties, contracts for public building come to each of the six, and to nobody else, in strict rotation. But that's only one of his interests. His company, Pacific Rand, has tentacles all over the Rim.'

Besides Ledward and Calderstone and Olney there were two other members of the committee. One was Prince, the ageing scion of a Lloyd's' firm of underwriters whose Names had come through the disaster of the first two years of the Nineties comparatively unscathed – they'd been in the red the first year, but Prince, who had steered as clear of the London excess-of-loss spiral as any old lady who kept her money in the post office, had sniffed the wind the year before, 1989, he always said he had left it late, and underwrote to a fraction of stamp until the débâcle was over, turning a small profit. He had done the commonsense thing – it was what in hindsight everyone should have done, and had they done it Lloyd's, like Munich Re, would have made their eight billion instead of losing it. Forbes was the fifth committee member, a permanent secretary and one of the eminences of the home Civil Service and (it was sometimes felt) complacently aware of the fact. He would hunch his shoulders as he strolled from the club with you, his hands in his trouser pockets, staring ruminatively at the ground with the ghost of a smile on his face, as though whatever opinion you were expressing was only what he would have expected, for how could you be expected to know? Men found this irritating.

'When he says he'll pay more,' Forbes interposed, 'he means he'll top any other bids.'

'No, he doesn't go so far. But he indicates he expects an auction.'

'High rollers only, of course,' Olney said.

'Oh, the rich museums. There are quite a number. But before we dwell on those possibilities, this other matter arises: the invoice.'

As Ledward spoke, the secretary slid the top paper to one side.

'From the chap who discovered, uncovered, the thing. Our benefactor, in a sense.'

'Round of applause for the man who invited him to lunch. Barrington, wasn't it?'

'Well, he's sent us his invoice as I invited him to do.'

'Can't expect a man to work for nothing, especially when his labours turn out to be so productive.'

'He had, I believe, no intention of working for nothing,' said Ledward, waiting as the secretary half stood, the better to slide the paper across to him. He picked it up and scrutinized it impassively. 'Very reasonable. To reframing the John the Baptist, and to relining it, the figure is two hundred and fifty punds plus VAT.'

Calderstone said, 'I was rather pleased to see it back. I didn't actually miss it, but all change is for the worse.' And the sentiment and the way he drew on his pipe were faultlessly at one.

Prince said drily, 'And, of course, he has thrown in his discovery of the Leonardo for nothing.'

'Not quite,' said Ledward.

'Shouldn't he get a little something for that?' asked Olney.

'I think in your business you call it commission, Olney,' said Ledward, nodding. 'Yes. Well, at all events, he thinks he should.'

'He mentions it?

'Specifically.'

Prince said, 'And the figure?'

Ledward pursed his lips. 'Ten per cent of the sum realized.'

Prince put back his head and let out a loud laugh. There was a silence. Then Forbes said, 'Handsome.'

'Oh dear me,' said Calderstone, at length. 'Money!' The disdain with which Calderstone managed to invest the word may have sounded to members of the committee a trifle disingenuous – the distinction of the Nobel is by no means mitigated by the £600,000 which comes with it.

'But of course, without him,' said Olney, perhaps sensitive to the possibility of commission as a concept being treated too lightly, 'we wouldn't have known what we'd got.' Olney was a large pear-shaped individual who had the air of listening hard, as though reception in his area was poor and he caught what other people said only sporadically.

There was a pause.

'But,' said Ledward, 'taking Ihara's figure as a base, it means our friend gets a million.'

'And charity is the loser,' said Forbes, somewhat abstractedly.

'Among others,' smiled Prince, 'since I do not expect the general endorsement which we got at the Extraordinary General Meeting to remain unmodified.'

'Isn't that a touch cynical, Prince?' asked Forbes, as though taking the broader view – a freehold to which he held the deeds.

'I think sceptical was the word that eluded you,' Prince replied, matching Forbes' complacency. 'But even if it were more apt, it would not have been correct. When a general matter becomes particular, the crowd resolves itself into individuals, and individuals cannot be predicted.'

'Yes, yes,' said Ledward, 'that was a further point. The man who spoke against the motion at the EGM – Routh, isn't it? – points out' – the secretary held up a third sheet of paper – 'that he has polled fifteen members of the Club who are unsatisfied by the outcome of the last meeting and thus another EGM must be called. The rules are perfectly clear.'

Forbes was always prompt to concede a point – to give it, rather than have it taken away.

'Perhaps Prince was not so far out.'

'Thank you.'

'What people say about money is not always what they really feel.'

'You put it so much more succinctly than I, Forbes,' said Prince. 'I suppose I was thinking that because so few declared themselves against the resolution it didn't mean there mightn't be those among the majority who were holding up their hands by way of camouflage. Routh cannot be accused of that – if it be an accusation.'

Olney said, tuning in momentarily, 'You give Routh marks?'

'That would be schoolmasterly. He's an awkward devil, but he made some cogent points, and made them coolly, despite knowing he was running against what looked like the sense of the meeting.'

'Yet when he'd finished they applauded him,' said Calderstone.

'And those who applauded him had already voted in favour of a resolution that he was telling them to resist. You see what I mean by camouflage?'

The door of the library opened and one of the ladies who worked in the office put her head round it. The secretary rose and conferred briefly, taking from her a sheet of paper. He walked round the circular table and placed the paper in front of the chairman.

Ledward, who was really rather a humourless man, although not without a sense of timing, actually smiled.

'This is from the Frick, gentlemen,' he announced. 'They too would like to buy our picture.'

'*They* won't get it for nothing,' Calderstone said.

'No, no, that aspect doesn't arise,' Ledward went on. 'They offer – well, as a banker, I should be used to figures with a troop of noughts after them – they offer fifteen million.'

'That is pounds not dollars, Chairman,' said the secretary, as he made the note.

'Ah – yes.'

A chorus of nods, all silent ones. The millions mentioned had now become a presence, as though someone unexpected had entered the room, and those already there had looked up and wondered how cordial their welcome ought to be – and whether it might have to be extended more than once.

TWO

Routh was a courtier, and had an office at St James's Palace, also a flat, a grace and favour apartment. So that when he came out of his front door, he turned left, left again, crossed the road in front of the sentry, went up St James's and in fifty yards or so he was at the Club. With his glossy black hair, skinny moustache and tight little double-breasted suit – a world away from the flowing garments Olney wore – he looked as abrupt as he sounded.

I glanced at the board as I came in and saw there was a notice setting a date for Routh's EGM for a month ahead, by which time the committee hoped that a clearer idea of the picture's value would have been gained from interested parties. Meanwhile, suggestions from members as to charities that might be suitable as beneficiaries could be made in writing to the committee.

Routh was the only person in the bar as I walked in, and I greeted him. I knew there was no point in offering him a drink, since he drank one small glass of dry sherry – La Ina – before lunch and it was already in front of him. The possibility of Routh offering anyone else a drink never arose – he would have felt it to be an irrelevant gesture, and even faintly coarse.

'You had no difficulty in raising a quorum, I see.'

Immediately I spoke, the idea of Routh approaching anyone for their support struck me as unthinkable. Of course, the bolshie fifteen would have approached *him*. After I had made my remark

Routh looked at me as though waiting to hear something to which he could reasonably respond, and if we hadn't been alone I should have nodded and taken my drink with me and spoken to someone else. The barman gave me my glass of white wine and I tried again.

'I should think they're rather taking it for granted that the charities are going to get it, aren't they?'

'They are beyond their remit,' Routh said.

'I suppose they were given liberty to think about it when the motion was carried.'

'They were to consider whether charities should benefit. To invite suggestions as to *which* charities should benefit is to treat the question as though it had been answered.'

'I see what you mean.'

Routh nodded, which for him was almost fulsome. I once asked a man who had been a member of the Club years before I was elected whether Routh had always been like this. 'Oh no,' said the man, 'much worse.' I should have liked to have talked to Routh about why he was mounting this rearguard action – I could hardly believe it was self-interest, though I do not even know whether courtiers are paid, is it a job taken on by the well-born as a kind of duty, welfare work of a sort? But one felt a little uneasy even talking about the weather with Routh. Then he asked me a question which would have been unremarkable from anyone else, but from Routh sounded almost like an advance.

'Where do you stand. Owlish?'

Um.

'Do you know, I simply haven't thought.'

Routh finished his sherry. Nodded again. Left.

Had I thought about it? Did I stand anywhere? To allow the reader to assess my own degree of detachment – if that isn't a euphemism for having no view – I shall have to offer a few personal details that would be impermissible in any circumstances other than those in which one is dispassionately describing a sequence of events. I live in Kew, and Kew has always been the sort of suburb no one is shy about owning up to.

Good houses were built in the eighteenth century, followed by large comfortable ones with big gardens in the Victorian and Edwardian time, and some perfectly all right semi-detached terraces and mansion blocks in the twenties and thirties. I live in a house that was put up in 1745. It's a nice, roomy, red-brick place with a garden at the front and the back, and within a stone's throw of the main gates of the Gardens. Parking's a bit of a problem sometimes, especially at the weekends when families come to Kew, but other than that I can't think of any disadvantage in living where I do. The place has a villagey feel, it's quiet, and my neighbours are rather like me – there's an architect and a doctor and a man who is in advertising, and a journalist, people like that. Professional people I suppose you'd call them, but that doesn't really tell you everything: the architect designed the parliament house in Tripoli (I see the Representatives as a sort of screen-print by Warhol, each one a snapshot of Colonel Gadaffi) as well as the controversial new cathedral on the site of the old fever hospital in Venice (coals to Newcastle, no doubt, but in braving the inevitable comparisons he surely gets marks); the doctor is a cardiac surgeon who built his own private hospital; the advertising man has an agency with branches in Europe and the United States; and the journalist – well, that's perhaps rather a deceptive way of describing him, since he owns the paper, more than one, in fact.

You see, what I'm a little shy about saying too baldly is that they all have money, and so do I. They are all like me, yes, but in one respect they are not: they all earn the money they have, one way or another, whereas I inherited mine. My father was a lawyer, a solicitor who went into the family firm and energized it, turning it into the foremost corporate practice of its day, a position which has sometimes been challenged, but not successfully. I was his only child, and after my mother's death his estate, not only intact but considerably enhanced, undiminished by death duties, thanks to the trusts in which it had been held, passed to me. I am now head of the firm that he created, enjoying the work and the contacts it generates, but my involvement owes nothing to material necessity.

Once again, in my owlish way, I may have sounded a little pedantic in rehearsing these facts, and I can only hope that owlishness has not come too close to complacency: I am well aware of that danger, but it seemed right to make it clear that if I had not taken a view about the money and the picture it may have been because I didn't feel it necessary. A thought (I realized as soon as it came to me) that might indeed be complacent.

As I was reflecting in the bar on what Routh had asked me before he left, the hall-porter came in and told me Randolph Wells was on the telephone. Wells is my brother-in-law, and I went out to the booth in the corridor.

'Richard,' he said, 'I'm in a bit of a fix. I wonder if you could drop round after lunch? Like to consult you.'

I said, 'What's it about?'

He said, 'An office thing, but don't worry. I want to talk to you.'

Already I felt myself paying the bill, and wondered vaguely how much it would be this time.

'No panic,' he said. 'Have lunch, then come and see us.'

I walked into the dining-room and took a seat at the end of the long table next to Ledward. Usually with Randolph it was investments that went wrong – it happened quite often, and each time he could never quite believe it, telling me with the hurt look of someone who has just been bitten in the hand by his favourite Dalmatian that it was entirely unforeseen. 'I can't understand it; I know business has been bad,' he would say, 'but there's all the underlying equity, and that should have brought in a pretty penny if properly handled, but they rush into a fire-sale and after the liquidator's taken his whack there's tuppence left for the shareholders.' I always see his point, convinced as I am that investment is exposed to so many uncertainties that he never surprises me – a bet on a share is almost as random as a bet on a lottery. I keep away from the stock market and stay with land and farms and property which, over the long term, are what money is only talking about.

'Just the man,' Ledward said as I sat down. 'Everything looks like plain sailing, and then the unforeseen.'

'Events, dear boy, events,' I said, thinking of Macmillan who coined the phrase.

'What?'

'You do plans and make arrangements, but then something actually happens.'

'Well it has,' said Ledward. 'Letter from solicitors in Ipswich saying the family, the descendants, whoever they may be, of the chap who left us the bloody picture are questioning whether we have good title.'

'The will?'

'Oh yes, it's on file in the archives. I think Eric has dug it out, and anything else which might have a bearing, but, there's a good chap, can you get your office to give it a look?'

'Nothing easier.'

'It's not what one expects. And Routh's meeting coming up. A contentious atmosphere.'

'It's only money.'

Ledward looked at me. I had spoken captiously.

'Money,' he said, 'is never only.'

I dug into my sausages. Then Ledward spoke again, musingly.

'Men who are members of this club are perceived to be affluent, but it is known – as the committee from time to time has cause to know – that some find it difficult to meet their subscriptions.'

This prompted me to say something that had been in my mind since the vote had been taken.

'I wonder if those for whom money is not a problem may not be perceived by those who do have difficulties to be a little free and easy.'

A man across the table said, 'When it comes to disbursing money that is not their own, people can behave quite cavalierly.'

'It's what I had in mind, Carr. Of course, it all goes by vote, finally.'

Ledward leaned across to him. 'You said you wouldn't know what to do with the thing.'

Carr was perhaps the most knowledgeable of the Old Master

dealers whose galleries crowd the rather stand-offish little streets that run behind Christie's.

'Things are relative. You give me a picture by Pieter de Hooch and another by van Hoogstraten and I'll sell each of them at the right price. But what's to compare Leonardo with? We shall get something astronomical from one of the big museums, and I suppose that's just it. I find the charming assumption that we are in some way bound to give the cash away rather cool.'

Ledward and I nodded in the serious way people do when hearing the side of an argument they do not support. Carr was one of Routh's fifteen dissidents.

'Will you pick up the documents from the office?' Ledward asked, as I rose.

'I'll get them now.'

Miss Mornington, who runs our office, gave them to me in a folder, and I looked through them as the cab took me to Lincoln's Inn Fields, where I would drop them off before going on to my brother-in-law's place.

The proposition was a very simple one: that the Club's benefactor – the Hon. Thomas Percy Anstruther – willed all his books and certain of his pictures to the Club, leaving the residue of his estate (after certain other charitable bequests) to his wife in the first instance, and since she had predeceased him, and by the terms of the same will, thence to the remaining heirs in equal portions. The descendant of these heirs, some sort of collateral great-great granddaughter of the residual legatees, laid claim to such of Anstruther's property as was not specifically excluded from the family's inheritance by the terms of his will, and in consequence was the legal owner of the picture by Leonardo, at present in possession of the Club. Huntercombe and Co would be pleased to hear from the Club at an early date, whereupon the detail of the matter might be more closely examined, and were, yours faithfully.

Balderdash, I thought, before riffling through the rest of the papers. These included an inventory of the stuff Anstruther had left to us, all the books and a list of the pictures, and then there was a copy of the will, a copious document running to eight or nine pages, which I decided our chief clerk could get to grips with. Scanning a page or two, I noted there was a reference to the inventory, so that would be all right. Country lawyers, I thought, getting a steady income from the conveyancing trade and drawing up a will or two, and now wanting to keep on the right side of a barmy old lady who'd seen it all in the papers and had put some weird personal spin on it. And there were fees in it for them as well.

I told our man what the situation was and gave him the papers. He had a haircut shaved to the bone and one of those baggy suits that look like tents. I often said in my head, as he told me which QC he'd put on to a case, 'You don't look like a lawyer's chief clerk to me', but I knew what he would have replied if I'd said it out loud: 'Well, if I was Edmund Gwenn, you'd have to be Charles Laughton.' These fancies of mine with their theatrical overtones were close to the mark, because if a barrister's clerk is like an actor's agent, a solicitor's clerk is like the man who's producing the show. He was twenty-nine years old, and as sharp as a tin-tack.

Then I walked over to Holborn, and took the tube to Turnham Green which is the nearest stop to my brother-in-law's house in Bedford Park. I've never liked Norman Shaw, his houses seem to me to take hold of the suburban way a lot of people of modest means live, with the intention of turning it into a genteelized version to be sold to the carriage trade – all architecture is imitation, but not all that is imitated is worth imitating. Angela let me in, kissed me on the cheek, then went back into the kitchen as Randolph himself emerged in his shirt sleeves.

'Not at work?'

'Gardening leave. They've suspended me.'

His house is what estate agents a rung or two down from the Earl of Olney's lot would describe as double-fronted, there being a room either side of the front door. The one we went into is what Randolph insists on calling the sitting-room. I am perfectly certain he was brought up in a house where this term was never used, and to my ear it is only slightly less affected than 'parlour' would be; though I have to admit that small details of a social or anthropological nature do sometimes beseige me, like the floaters I have in my eyes – no good trying to swat them, they are permanent, though I can go for days without noticing them.

What he'd done seemed to me to be the equivalent of something they called in the army 'signing in blank'. I'd done it myself once during my National Service – rushing off on leave and telling the orderly-room clerk to fill in the letter above my signature. A note came back from the brigadier to the company commander wondering what sort of schools the second-lieutenants he was getting could have come from – 'I know they can't be expected to spell *separate* or *Mediterranean*, but what does he mean by the phrase "nevertheless the fact remains is"?'

'You see,' Randolph said, 'we have a private client who sold some shares. Right?' This football-speak was another of his tics, at first intended to irritate, but now merely habitual. 'The wife held an equal number of shares and after he'd sold his lot he realized that from the tax point of view it would have been better if she'd sold hers – she lived in Barbados, or at any rate that was her address, and her bill for CGT would have been far less – biggish numbers, perhaps a million and a half. So he asked us to alter the thing, switch the names. Stockbroker didn't mind, just a paper thing. But as accountants, we shouldn't have done it. Clerks just logged it into the system; paper put in front of me; for once I didn't read it, just signed. Interviewed by the Revenue and – as they say in old detective stories – the rest you know. They think I was in collusion with the client.

Detective stories. Who tipped off the Revenue? I asked him.

'Tipped off? But they had the paperwork.'

'Yes, but what would draw their attention to it? Why would they think anything was wrong?'

Randolph was silent awhile. I cast my head back, looking up into the veins that stood out in the plaster of the ceiling, momentarily recognizing that Shaw's sin had been the greater in that he, along with such as C.F.A. Voysey and Bailly Scott, had identified the faint-heartedness which lies at the core of the suburban idyll, marketing it as a cult.

'Stockbrokers, perhaps? They might have been asked; probably were. Don't know. But since you ask, I wondered about that myself.'

'No one in the firm? I mean, you hadn't got up someone's nose?'

Randolph shook his head.

'It's down to me. And the annoying thing is if the bloody client had got it right in the first instance we could have devised something perfectly legal.'

'They won't prosecute. Cost a ton of public money, and they wouldn't win.'

'Glad to hear you say it, I was hoping you would, but that's not the immediate point. It looks as though I may be fired.'

He was a partner in a respectable firm of accountants, Crawfords, and of course they wouldn't want anything to rub off on them, more especially since they'd recently been taken into the massive embrace of the Pacific Rand Corporation whose writ runs from Vancouver to the Pacific Rim.

'The damnedest bit of it is I'm supposed to be piloting the top honcho round when he comes to tour his new European fief next week. They tried to put someone else on to it, natch, but my name and CV having been sent in early his office wouldn't have it, and our people didn't dare insist. Taking his bloody overcoat in restaurants and whistling up his chauffeur, and me with all this hanging round my neck – all I need.'

I noticed how miserable Shaw's narrow windows were, as if he couldn't afford to let too much light in, or perhaps he didn't want the people inside to get too much of a look out in case they started feeling like hostages.

'May give you a chance, though. He could take such a liking to you they wouldn't be able to fire you.'

Randolph looked surprised.

'You know, I hadn't thought of that.'

'Well, keep me in touch,' I said.

'I'll butter the bastard up. Good idea.'

'Haven't seen you at the club, lately.'

'What's happening about the money? Wouldn't mind laying hands on some of it.'

'Never know. They want to give it away, but there's a chap – know him? Routh? – who thinks otherwise. Better come to the EGM he's calling.'

I liked Randolph. I kept trying to think of him as an idiot, but he never quite was. His own worst enemy, as they say.

'Bye, Ange,' I called as I went out into the street, and that was another thing I liked about both of them, no ceremony – I mean, I like ceremony when it's toward, but relatives should feel easy with each other. Though, for a special reason, I could never be finally easy with Angela, and she knew it. She was my wife's sister, and my wife had died, and when I saw Ange that all came back. I do not intend to encumber anyone with the details of my emotional life except where they impinge on the story I am telling, so I will say once and for all that my wife had been my dearest friend and the love of my life, and her death in a car smash had broken my heart. I should add, since I hope not to have to advert to these matters again, that our children, Tom and Adelaide, are away at school, and a good woman called Pilbrow, I call her Margery, looks after the house.

As I reached the end of Ranfurly Gardens my mobile phone rang. It was our chief clerk. Was this a moment to talk through what he and others had made of the documents I'd left with him? I stood at the corner with the thing to my ear.

'Of course, the trick of it is that they claim the Club was never left the picture in the first place,' said Ted Mirfield, who told me he'd made a precis of what the partners had advised. 'Common sense suggests they may have something.'

What the people from Suffolk had latched on to was the fact – and it seemed to be a fact, though Ted thought it might be worth getting counsel's opinion here – that the picture the Club had been left was the John the Baptist one; the top layer, so to speak, and not anything else the top layer concealed.

'Because our friends in Ipswich have it that this is what Thomas Percy Anstruther willed to the Club, and the inventory seems to bear this out.'

'No hint in the will or the other papers that Anstruther knew what he was doing – I mean, knew he was slipping us the Leonardo as well?'

'Can't see it. The thing turns on whether what he hands over by way of bequest is what he *says* he's handing over, or whether what he hands over *is* the bequest, whether he knew about it or not.'

'Who'd have a look at it for us?'

'Oh, I think Purefoy, don't you? He'd do it anyway, he's one of our silks, and he's a member of your club, I think.'

'Right, Ted. By the by, who's the claimant?'

'Party of the name of – got it here, what is it? – yes, Letitia Mary Barlow.'

'I wonder if the people in Ipswich went to her or she to them? Fragrant old ladies get bees in their bonnets. And lawyers read the papers.'

'Wouldn't do to bank on her being a nut case.'

'Quite right. Let's see what Purefoy thinks.'

'And then,' said Ted Mirfield, who would have had a chance to make a better lawyer than many, if his father hadn't been a bus conductor and his mother a cleaner, 'assuming Thomas Percy Anstruther didn't know he'd got a Leonardo, where did he come by it? And then where did *that* party come by it?'

'Nothing's simple.'

'Never supposed it was. What I'm wondering is, how long before the party who sold it to Anstruther is picked out as having questionable title?'

'Could happen.'

'Hope your club isn't counting its chickens.'

Ted sounded amused, but I couldn't help hearing the note of satisfaction that was there as well. What if we lost the lot? *Schadenfreude*. Ted wouldn't be the only one laughing.

THREE

The Earl of Olney walked out of the Belmont Sporting Club and made his way down Mount Street to the restaurant he favoured. He liked the food and he liked the staff, and it was close to his office, and they gave him credit.

This evening at the restaurant he was the guest.

'Olney, how good to see you,' Prince said. 'Shall we sit here?'

Both men were accustomed to letting others know what their requirements were. The head waiter showed them to the places the host had indicated – a corner by a window, at a table laid for four. The greeter wafted an underling forward, who swiftly gathered up the superfluous place settings.

'Did you hear we've had another offer?'

'Haven't been in the club,' said Olney.

'The Kunsthistorischemuseum. Twenty million.'

Olney brought out something he felt met the case in a thoughtful general way. 'National Gallery won't get a look in.'

Prince said, 'No, no, not on.'

'Miserly budget,' Olney said, not wanting anyone to think he wasn't culturally aware.

'That wouldn't matter, they're up for Lottery money. The snag for them is they've just had some – thirty million to buy the Van Gogh, another one of those cornfields, and now they're back of the queue. I mean who could defend them getting seconds? Especially to blue on a – well, I accept it's got to be good, being a Leonardo, but you know I can't help thinking of it as a *trophy*. Trophy in the sense of something a film star buys his wife.'

Olney ordered oysters, Prince had smoked eel.

'No cap in hand for the others. They've got access to unlimited supplies of old private money. The robber barons. We don't have that sort of culture here.'

Then Olney said, 'Export licence. Would that be difficult? Might be, don't you think?'

'Could be a hitch there. Not that there's any commonsense reason why there should be; after all it's not as though he was born in the Royal Borough or somewhere, is it?'

Olney was squeezing lemon on the oysters, then shaking red pepper over them.

'Wasn't he born—'

'Where was it?'

Olney wondered why Prince didn't know it was Italy.

'Well – da Vinci, I suppose,' Prince said. 'Wherever that may be.'

'It's in Italy,' nodded Olney, whose conversational tread tended to the literal.

Prince was taking small forkfuls of his smoked eel, carefully avoiding the onion. Then he said, 'How did you get into the estate agent business?'

'Oh, you know. Something to do.'

Prince nodded, as though the answer was comprehensive. They'd both ordered partridge, and it arrived.

'Nice place. Glad you suggested it.'

Olney was wondering when Price would get to the point. What this was all about.

'Mustn't make cabals, I know that, but we are after all fellow members of the committee, and I thought I'd take you into my confidence.'

Being an earl, Olney had come in for this kind of opening gambit often enough, usually from people who were trying to sell him something.

'You're likely to be disinterested, which is why I thought we might talk. Not a word against anyone else, all good chaps, but you need to be sure that someone is in a position to take an objective view.'

This sounded so like a man who had once tried to interest him in a bankrupt garden centre that for a moment the phrase, 'Don't sign anything', something of a watchword with Olney, came into his mind. Perhaps the business of buying and selling houses, though it was conducted in ritual terms by polite men wearing good shoes – at least, at his end of the market – sometimes had elements of the devious which would naturally sharpen anyone's sense of caution to the point where it could become a sort of suspiciousness.

'It's a couple of things, really. I've found myself coming round to Routh's view, largely because Routh is the sort of man who always operates on principle. Rather too inflexibly, as we know – that business of wanting them to cancel our subscription to the *Telegraph* because some wag in it had said the Archbishop of Canterbury looked like a goldfish if you turned the sound down on the telly – really too absurd.'

'And, anyway, he does,' Olney said.

'Silly fellow. I don't mean the archbishop, I mean Routh. He's so rigid. But this time I think he's got a point.'

They'd been drinking a bottle of Mâcon-Lugny, and now they'd started on some Chambolle-Musigny les Amoureuses. The waiter came forward to replenish their glasses and Prince said to him, 'Leave it, please.'

Olney, sawing away at his partridge, said, 'Routh's just doing it because he thinks the members should get the money, isn't he? Don't see much principle in that.'

'He thinks you can't dispose of individual shares of a windfall payout by general vote unless it's a joint equity company. I dare-say Owlish is the man to find out about that for us. But I think Routh is very attracted by rules, doing things by the book. Anyway, at a purely practical level what he says rings a bell with me. At Lloyd's you trade for yourself and for no one else – no mutualizing losses, no mutualizing gains. Probably telling you what you already know. You a Name?'

Olney nodded.

'An optimist. Well, we've got two flat years ahead of us, then we'll be all right.'

'*If* the individual Name survives, and the whole place isn't turned into some high street insurance company.'

'You're right. Distinct chance that's going to happen. But some of us still beat the drum for unlimited liability. Only way to make money. And lose it, of course.'

Olney knew that Prince had seen his Names through the disaster time.

'My father had always been in Lloyd's,' Olney said. 'Like something everyone did. Everyone who could. I mean, he'd say I'll give up hunting this pack of hounds if I have a bad year at Lloyd's – as though there was no such thing as a bad year – or perhaps one in a very long time. So I went in as a matter of course.'

Prince had pushed the remains of his partridge aside and was pouring Olney more of the Chambolle. He said, 'But it was like that for three hundred years. Nothing went wrong, a hiccup a few times, but would any of us have backed it to the tune of everything we possessed if we ever thought it would come to that?'

Olney nodded.

'I think you were very clever, drawing your horns in before the typhoon struck. Wish my agent had put me on your syndicates.'

'Well, let's be sensible,' Prince said. 'Since I *was* drawing my horns in, I wouldn't have had you. I was reducing stamp, you've got to remember. I didn't want anyone else's money, there was enough, and more than enough, to be looking after. Were you all right?'

Perhaps Prince recognized the wine was warming his guest's responses.

'Absolutely not. You said about doing the estate agent thing. Had to do something. I took a punch in the face. The land and the house, such as they were, and the trust funds – well, nearly all. Had enough to continue membership, only just, though.'

'Last couple of years, you should have done pretty well.'

'Well enough. And tax-free, considering the losses the profits were set against.'

But Olney did not seem cheered by the thought.

'We must all look to the future,' Prince said, as the waiter brought them small dark grapes in grappa. Then he said, 'So, anyway, that's where I stand *vis-à-vis* Routh – I increasingly feel that whatever we realize from the sale of the picture should be divided between the members, not simply because Routh may be right about the joint equity thing, but because – face it, and I must say I hadn't, until recent days – whatever is done with the money it should be the individual member's responsibility to use it as he thinks fit. Not an original thought, it was what Routh put to me when I tackled him about the thing – like drawing teeth from the man, to get him to say anything, but that's what he did say.'

Olney chewed the keenly flavoured grapes, sucking up the grappa from his spoon.

'And some members might just buy winegums with their slice.'

'If that makes them feel easy. It doesn't affect Routh's principle. *You* decide what ought to be done with the money; you don't ask anyone else, you just do it. However. Now then. All I'm doing is getting you to consider the thing in the light – well, it's Routh's idea, I've just come round to it. But it isn't the only thing I want to put to you. I said there were two things.'

The waiter brought their coffee.

'The other is this. Closer to home. Am I right in supposing you have some people from Japan coming tomorrow to look for a place for their boss?'

Olney sat up straight. He was surprised, even startled.

'Your intelligence is pretty good.'

But Prince simply shrugged, put a lump of brown sugar into the cup of black coffee in front of him and said, 'I have a bunch of Names outside the UK, one of them mentioned this, and I thought it would be a good idea to be in touch with you. Can't be sure who's turning up, whether it's the boss or who it might be, but he's certainly from the group whose top man made the first offer for the Leonardo.'

'Ah,' Olney said, not quite clear where this left him.

'And if you are showing them some properties, I thought – and I suppose this comes in tandem with my updated feelings about Routh's EGM – it might not be a bad idea to get a clearer idea about the man. What sort of party he turns out to be.'

'I suppose so,' Olney agreed.

'And also it might be a thing to get a notion of what he might be willing to pay – finally. We can't just leave it to chance. That's why I thought I'd speak to you, since you're going to be the one who will actually be the first to encounter a willing buyer. My feeling is we should arrange contacts with all the possible bidders, but you're first in the ring. Do you see what I mean?'

Olney's first reaction was one of alarm. Would he do it right?

'Not very good at this sort of thing. Er – you know, getting people to tell me things.'

'And you an estate agent? Too modest! Anyway, it's not nearly as important as being at the point of contact. Do what you can. No one thinks you're MI5. Just lend an ear. Can't do any of us any harm.'

Prince paid and they went out.

'Nice meal.'

'They do one pretty well.'

'Hope you didn't mind me sharing my thoughts.'

Prince hailed a cab for Lord North Street, Olney raised a hand. Then turned back up the street towards the Belmont Sporting Club.

The Earl of Olney's name looked well on the agency's writing-paper, and even though the title might in some cases be counter-productive, in that it could overawe certain of the clients, it was very useful when dealing with the big guns. He wasn't wheeled out for bread and butter deals, but when it was heavy business he was the natural front man. Olney had put it about that he could do with a job, and the title got him this one. Nothing too strenuous, other people took care of the figures, and Olney did the escorting: his suits, his accent, his physical largeness made him seem part of the decor when he threw open the heavy doors of Mayfair apartments or the sugar-pink conservatories of wedding-cake mansions in The Boltons. Indeed he often gave the impression of being the spirit of the places he was showing, and clients had the obscure sensation that if they bought the freehold or the lease they would become like him – large, lofty, well born, titled, secure.

On the other hand, when he was not in professional mode, when he was doing his shopping in Wandsworth which was where he actually lived, or playing baccarat at the Belmont, he might have been one of those earls nobody quite believes in, as though earlness had been somehow laid over him, like a transfer, which you felt you could probably get a supply of at Selfridges. There was something instant about Olney, as though he had sprung, not from a long line of aristocrats, but from just behind the letterhead on his firm's stationery. The accent was impeccable, but if you left that aside, or assumed it had been carefully manufactured, you could have taken him for one of those noblemen who might have been a forest ranger or a life-guard, in Australia, and had become by accident an earl via the death of a distant cousin.

But he wasn't, he was the genuine article and like other genuine articles in other walks of life – politicians and High Court judges, public servants in the higher ranks of the Civil Service and here and there a bishop or an industrial tycoon – would most of the time conduct his life with instinctive regard to principle, and equally instinctively would find from time to time that the rules did not apply to him. There is a shady little corner of the estate-agency business, even in its more exalted reaches, that very few within the firm itself and certainly no one outside it ever comes to hear about. Now and again, when a house has been hanging about on the books for much longer than the owner, who is desperate to sell, or the agents, who are anxious for their commission, find comfortable, an offer may be received which is not passed on to the client.

Instead, a member of the firm steps round and invents a bid comfortably below the genuine offer which has been tucked away, but attractive enough for the eager client to accept. And when the contracts are exchanged, the deed is done. And a little later on the house changes hands for the higher bid, and the difference is shared discreetly by the partners. There had been guarded references, delicate hints, and, of course, nothing had been written down, but Olney had been quite clear – such free-trading was part of the package he was being offered. It didn't, it couldn't, happen often, it was far from regular, but it went some way to finance his losses at the Belmont.

As he strolled into the Connaught to meet the Japanese, he wondered vaguely if there wasn't a sniff of the free-trade in this little caper. The agency ads would make them feel they were abreast of prices, but the actual numbers were often very vague – POA and IRO gave you some idea, but the selling strategy was only to pull the line taut when the fish was on the hook.

Slightly to his surprise the two men were taller than he'd expected, spoke perfect English, though occasionally missing the idiom, and while they smiled all the time, did no bowing. Ironed out of them at business school, Olney thought.

'Lord Olney, this is James Akisura and I am Hari Moto. Shall we sit down for a moment?'

They went into the small room to the left of the lobby.

'Coffee? Though I find it makes me restive,' said Moto. 'Perhaps a glass of champagne? Waiter – some Louis Roederer Cristal. Do you have the '93?'

They sat by the window and the wine was brought.

'You know, I find a glass, or two glasses, pleasantly refreshing,' said Moto as he tasted it, nodding at the waiter. 'But any more than that, I am reminded of green apples.'

He opened his floppy briefcase and pulled out the schedule Olney had sent to the Tokyo office.

'Getting down to tin-tacks, there are three properties that seem very much the right sort of thing, but one of them is favourite, as I think they say at your public schools.'

Wonder how they got that wrong, thought Olney, 'favourite' being a word you heard on a builder's site. Picked it up second-hand from the London office, probably. Do they have one though? Steering them towards properties, you had to be wary of the London office, though if the buyer was from the Orient the local man watched the light in the boss's eye and took care not to be a smart arse by running counter to it.

All the properties Olney had sent to Japan had locations that were irreproachable and it was no surprise to him that their in-house web-site man had OK'd them; he'd have been scanning all the give-away ad-mags that estate agents circulated to the upmarket London postal districts, together with pieces he'd have picked out of *Country Life* and *The Field*, along with the property sections from the broadsheet Sundays. Was Akisura the one who'd done the sifting? Moto led the talk, and his enamelled manner suggested a flunkey who felt he had his master's confidence; would his asssurance come with the same gloss if the master were present?

'Did you say who it's to be for?' Olney asked, languidly.

'It will be the company's place. It must have prestige for two reasons: it will provide our chief executive with accommodation suitable to his standing and meet his entertainment requirements, and it will function also as our London base.'

Tax-deductible, Olney translated. And not being the boss's real home he had better things to do than mess about looking for it himself.

'Pacific Rand's interests as you know, Lord Olney, are located principally in the Pacific region, but it has a direct interest in the UK now that it has purchased the equity in one of your leading accountancy firms.'

Not only tax-deductible, the bean-counters were on the payroll.

Moto went through the three properties he'd said were in the frame, and while Olney nodded, profoundly understanding of the enthusiasm of prospective buyers, he mentally logged the disadvantages. Addison Road was 'exclusive' but the inside of the house had made him think buyers might feel what will we do in these tall, sad rooms while the traffic thunders by? The flat in Hans Place was spacious, six bedrooms, but the permanently parked cars, petrified by the wand of some passing mink-clad fairy bound for Harrods, not to mention the effect of the abundant soft furnishings gave the interior a stuffed look, which might deter those of a claustrophobic turn; though space being at a premium in Japan, Olney reminded himself, the constrictions might be comforting to them.

'But I am really keen on this one.' Moto produced the brochure in question. 'So very British, and in an area of great authenticity, overlooking old Mother Thames, and the Father of Parliaments.'

Olney gazed at the coloured pictures. They gave an ingratiating impression of something like Hampton Court Palace, as conceived by a Texas oil man. The owner had built the place, opposite Lambeth Bridge, for his wife, but she had run away with a computer repair agent who had knocked at the front door asking to renew a driving-licence (this last bit wasn't verifiable, for though he was of an entirely unimaginative temper, Olney sometimes allowed snobbery to get the better of him. He said the salesman must have mistaken the house for the town hall). Gables and turrets abounded, and all over the façade there were brightly gilded escutcheons which Olney said did credit to British Home Stores.

'And the appeal is enhanced,' he said earnestly to his two companions, 'in that it is only three years old. The very best of an ancient tradition, with the highest possible contemporary specification.'

Moto suggested the key might be sent round, and Olney raised the office on his mobile phone.

'We need not trouble you further, Lord Olney,' Moto said, when the messenger had brought the key. 'We shall consult you very shortly. Our chief executive, Mr Ihara, regrets another appointment has robbed him of the pleasure of making your acquaintance in person.'

So it *was* Ihara. He'd pass that on to Prince. Not the time to talk about the picture – they probably didn't know about it, anyway. He handed them the key, all shook hands, and the two

Japanese walked out into Carlos Place where they climbed into the back of a stretch limo. Olney himself went off like a busy executive anxious to resume the rest of the day's work, and hurrying up Mount Street knew what his first phone call must be.

'Jarred, that figure you were asking for the Happy Eater on the Embankment? Yes. But what would the creditors let you take? Got a sort of offer here from an outfit I don't know much about, but still. These people would be in at one point seven-five. I know you've been after two point seven, you just told me, but this is cash money. Let me know.'

And Olney was pretty certain that two would be the come-back number, that 1.9 would be what they'd take, and that if all went well the difference when it was sold to the Japs would be 0.8. Eight hundred thousand pounds wouldn't be a bad return for a glass of champagne. And they'd paid for that as well.

Over the brow of the downland, with the sea wrinkling in a leaden haze behind it, a golf-buggy bumped into view and came to a halt. Out of it climbed the driver, and then a second figure loomed up against the skyline and hauled out a bag of golf-clubs from the back of the vehicle.

'A number five, would you say?'

'So sorry, haven't the slightest idea.'

The player was a short square figure with bow legs. He wore a white cap.

'You are no great help.'

'Perhaps you should have hired a caddy.'

'Why didn't you say that before we started out?'

'It is not for me to give advice to expert golfers.'

Randolph had no objection to doing what the situation demanded, namely buttle for the man and try and get him on his side. He'd hired the clubs and paid the green fee and said yes, they'd have a buggy. But his wonderfully polite style had worn off when it became clear that between the holes, his employer was going to ride and he was to walk briskly along beside him, on foot. In the offhand way he piled money into shares – they might just as well have been horses – he finally didn't give a damn about his own security if it conflicted with the way he felt. Ihara seemed OK and looked very Japanese, which is what any reasonable man would have expected, but a reasonable man wasn't going to stop being the sort of person he'd always been just because someone else was Japanese.

He sat down on the grass as Mr Ihara swung at the ball and when Randolph saw it soar into the sky he felt annoyed he hadn't been the one to hit it, an unreasonable reaction since he'd never played golf in his life.

'A great joy. A great joy.'

Mr Ihara made after the ball, down the fairway, and Randolph climbed into the buggy and chugged over the grass, coming to a halt behind Mr Ihara and waited to be asked what iron to hand him.

'Seven. No, eight.'

Randolph slid out of the side of the cart and walked up to Ihara with the eight iron, and took the five from him. The player chunked under the ball and it landed neatly on the green.

'Something wrong with a man who doesn't play golf,' Ihara said, as Randolph dragged the putter out of the bag.

'I'd sooner play ludo.'

When Mr Ihara holed his putt, he said to Randolph, 'Oh no you wouldn't.'

It was a nine-hole course, because that's what Mr Ihara had specified, and they finished about midday. No question of Randolph giving him a game – even if he could have done because Mr Ihara liked to play solo.

'We'll want to be in good time for lunch. I'll drive, and you sit on the back step,' Randolph said. 'The clubs will go in beside me.'

Randolph wondered if Mr Ihara had noticed the golf club wasn't private. It wasn't a club, it was a restaurant, part of a chain, and the nine-hole course was an adjunct, the only one he had been able to locate. It had been made clear to him that Mr Ihara liked a nine-hole course and was not happy on an eighteen-hole one, although a reasonable man – always Randolph's assessment of himself – could surely content himself with the first nine of however many holes. Or even – Randolph further reflected – the last nine.

He'd booked a table and was hoping the conventional menu might appeal to Mr Ihara as typically British.

'There's steak and fish. Dover sole and plaice,' he explained.

Mr Ihara said, 'I'll have sushi.'

Randolph said, 'You can't, they don't do it.' Then added, 'It's not quite the thing to ask for what isn't on the card.' To his surprise, Mr Ihara laughed. The waitress came up to them and Mr Ihara said he'd have the fillet steak with onion rings. Randolph approved of the way his guest now seemed willing to fit in. 'Dover sole,' he said.

'What are you going to drink, sir?' Randolph put in the sir because he felt he hadn't indicated recently that he was well aware of where they both stood.

'Tizer,' Mr Ihara replied.

'It's some special beer? They may not have it.'

'It's a famous English beverage,' Mr Ihara said, 'and I am somewhat put about that you do not recognize it.'

The waitress had no Tizer and brought Mr Ihara a diet Coke. Randolph ordered a bottle of Muscadet de Sèvres et Maine for himself, pouring a glass for the boss as well. Randolph had a forkful of fish moving towards his mouth when Mr Ihara said, 'Unfortunate thing, you putting your name to that crooked deal.'

Randolph closed his mouth, but it fell open again. He laid down the fork, then toyed with his glass and took a big drink.

'And such a petty scheme.'

'I had no idea—'

'I like to keep my slitty eye on things, Mr Wells. Where were you at school?'

Randolph was knocked sideways by the revelation that Ihara knew about his transgression.

'I was at school at Stowe. Have you heard of it, sir?' The sir came out with great punctilio this time.

'Not really. I was at Winchester.'

Ah. Oh. The carpet was being rolled up behind him.

'But I suppose you had sneaks at – where was it? – boys who were useful to the authorities. At Winchester it was a positive cult. So I learned early that if one was to be kept abreast of information it might not be in others' interests to disclose, it was important to have someone in place who answers to me and to me alone. A sneak in every office, Mr Wells.'

Randolph had been annoyed about the golf-buggy, and now the present revelations struck him as unreasonable – he'd brought it on himself, of course, but he'd managed to start thinking of his act of carelessness as no more than evidence of a trusting nature.

'I'm very sorry that you should have felt it necessary to conceal your knowledge from me. As your host—'

'You are not my host,' said Mr Ihara, 'and you are sorry for nothing except yourself.'

The waitress cleared the plates.

'I would like a knickerbocker glory served in a tall glass, with a straw,' said Ihara to the waitress.

'They all come with straws as well as a spoon, sir,' the waitress said, 'and little green umbrellas stuck in the bananas.'

'Perfect.'

Randolph ordered coffee for them both. He was, at last, a little abashed.

'Of one thing I should like you to feel convinced, Mr Ihara. I had no knowledge of the client's intent, and no idea of abetting it.'

'Yes,' Mr Ihara said, 'you do not strike me as having the necessary guile to make a crook. And you have assurance, but the wrong sort.'

Randolph wondered where all this was meant to end. And why Ihara's office had insisted he should be the one to steer the boss around when Ihara knew he was likely to be fired.

'It's the Leonardo I'm interested in, Mr Wells,' Ihara said, as they drank their coffee. 'That's why you're here. Your sin was a venial one and is of no importance. You will return to the office tomorrow, the partners will welcome you back, not only because they have been in receipt of a brusque memo from HQ for so casually imputing base motives to one of their senior men, but because I shall walk in with you, my arm round your shoulder, at least metaphorically.'

Had some prize suddenly come his way? Randolph felt as he felt when he bet on a share. Would it, for once, romp home?

'In return, you will keep me posted on the state of the auction, of any movement in the bids. I am willing to pay what I must for the picture, I am not willing to pay more. I need a member of your club to assist me in this. Since I have been candid with you on the subject of sneaks, it must be clear that what I ask in no way breaches – where was it, Stowe? – your Stoic principles, for all I require is first access to what will become public knowledge anyway, and if the information benefits me it most certainly also benefits you and the members of your club.'

For a moment Randolph looked serious. He felt his serious look took care of any scruples. Then he reached across the table and shook Mr Ihara's hand.

'I am very grateful to you, sir,' he said.

'Good,' said Mr Ihara, rising. 'Now pay.'

FOUR

Something happened. 'It was *dreadful*!' I heard one member's wife say to another as they were walking up to the ladies' cloakroom. She gave the word the horrified intonation it usually gets, and could have been describing a road accident. But the element of enjoyment in her voice let you know that whatever the accident was, it was of the indoor variety.

I had put my name down for the Leonardo dinner which Ledward had proposed, since my evenings were never so full that general occasions were the secondary consideration they are for most people. I go to private views at art galleries (I wonder how private they really are since those present drink the warm white wine in a compensatory way, as though they had been dragged in off the street by time-share salesmen), and when publishers have a party to launch a book, or I get an invitation to a second-night or there's something on at the Law Society, I usually go because I can read the books I get out of the London Library on any other evening; and when it's a *vin d'honneur* put on by a local lady in aid of those brought low by 'experimenting' with drugs or in support of the 'victims' of AIDS, I pay my twenty-five quid and turn up and buy my raffle ticket because it's something to do: the wounds such occasions seek to staunch are often self-inflicted, and I have to admit that the impossibility of my own condition ever being alleviated makes me feel a resentment that is quite hard to contain, especially when the charity is for the benefit of 'single' parents.

When the Club has a party, the old silver comes out, and the mahogany glows in the candle-light. That evening, as on many another, the women wandered through the place with smiles on their faces, like an army reconnoitering a citadel it has already decided is not worth beseiging. The wives of members have an air of importing, without revealing, something private and domestic that is at odds with a place whose style is a cross between a bus-station and a college hall. They smile and nod, but some have met at other times and in other places and hoot merrily at each other, and this seems to make the expression on the faces of other wives by contrast more distinct: an expression, as of one who is withholding an opinion until some later date.

There are wives who make you feel for a moment they are not men's wives but men's grandmothers, and there are others so unlike anyone you could imagine the member getting to marry him that they seem to be wives-for-the-evening, hired from a wife-agency. There are good-looking animated wives with whom men chuckle and flirt, and buxom, grey-haired wives whose jolly style make members feel younger, as though nanny has become frolicsome. The good will, the good cheer, is abundant, but there is an abiding impression that when everyone gets back home to Holland Park or Carlyle Square, East Grinstead or Henley-on-Thames, the husbands will have a vague feeling they are going back into hibernation and the wives will feel they are waking up. Perhaps my own solitary state makes me a little jaundiced.

As I see the names of the places I've cited above, I'm reminded the unpleasantness began with talk about where people lived. We sat a dozen at each round table and now, at this stage of the evening, there was a lot of talking and a sense that thc occasion was generating its own momentum, and people were feeling easy and relaxed. A man I had hardly seen more than once or twice (an idiosyncrasy of club life is thinking a man is never there because he is never there when you are there) was detaining the waitress in a way that caught my eye and ear (I think I have already noted the way small instances of aberrant social behaviour seem to snag my attention like a bramble catching a sleeve). On the menu for the evening there was little choice, but I heard this man say to the waitress 'What's nice?' Our staff are reticent. The waitress looked pleasant but blank: no member had ever sought to ingratiate himself before. 'I don't know' she said finally. The man then said, 'You choose for me.' I turned so abruptly to the lady on my left that I practically ducked under her armpit. Then I heard a female voice across the table saying, 'Sidney. Sidney. Don't you always say it's East Dulwich?'

'Dulwich? Lovely. So beautifully kept.'

'Oh, that eighteenth-century terrace along from the big pub. Opposite Pickwick Gardens, isn't it? And the art gallery. How I envy you.'

These were voices chiming in. But – 'Sidney,' said the first female, 'East Dulwich. Isn't that what you always say?'

And now it was plain that Sidney was the one who had attempted to colonize the waitress, and it was plain because of his discomfiture. No doubt about it, the lady who was speaking was his wife. I hadn't taken note of her until her voice rang out across the table, and I saw she was a small, round-faced woman with curiously ruddy cheeks, as though she had spent many years in the open, possibly as a shepherdess. But the vehemence of her enquiry may have heightened her colour, and she now turned to the lady next but one to her, with whom she'd had the conversation preliminary to her question, and said – and her voice was loud – 'If you lived in Streatham you wouldn't say you lived in Wimbledon.'

'But we do live in Wimbledon. Wimbledon Park.'

'That's not the point. What I'm saying is if you lived in Streatham you'd say so.'

'I've never lived in Streatham.'

'No, but if you did.'

Another lady leaned forward and said, 'Did you know the Thrales lived there?'

'Sidney,' said this unfortunate man's wife, 'did you hear?'

Sidney was affecting to entrance the lady next to him with a largeness of manner that would not permit him to hear his wife's by now strident query. But the absence of a response was no damper, quite the reverse. Speaking not just to the lady from Wimbledon Park, she addressed the whole table.

'Now East Dulwich isn't even Dulwich. But there *is* an actual East Dulwich, it's a place you can address your letters to, *if you live there*. But we don't live in East Dulwich, we live in Peckham, and Sidney pretends we don't.'

There was no way in which anyone could behave as though they didn't understand. If you hear from a wife that she lives in a place her husband won't admit to, you only make it worse if you start giving it marks. Sidney, of course, did a big laugh.

'She'll tell you she takes in washing, next.'

This made it worse still, since the titters it induced did not conceal that those present had not quite got the hang of what he meant, though the woman who'd referred to the Thrales said with the jolliest air of carrying it all into the literary realm, 'Dickens – *marvellous*!'

Then someone did start getting it on for Peckham, nice terraces of between-the-wars houses, wonderful restaurants and so forth, but I saw the look in the eye of Sidney's wife, and what burned there did not suggest her fires were banked.

'I don't say there's anything wrong with Peckham, it's Sidney who seems ashamed of it.'

'God,' said the woman she'd been talking to, 'have you any idea how lace-curtain Wimbledon can be? People trying to pinch your gardener.'

'Wish I had a gardener to pinch. Chance'd be a fine thing.'

There was a tendency to smile or even chuckle, as though the word 'pinch' had been deployed ambiguously by the speaker to raise a laugh. I think the feeling was that if we could all treat the woman as though she were coming on as a card or character we could pretend the thing had been kept within the bounds of good humour. But her weatherbeaten face gave the impression of zeal, as of rough tasks encountered in adverse conditions, and once embarked on a course of action you couldn't imagine her wavering.

'There's a patch in front of the house where the bins are, and a bit of concrete at the back. Gardener! Be all right if we got some of that money you're going to give away. Divvy it up among the members, let's all have a share. Charity begins at home – isn't that what you say, Sidney?'

This was going to be hard to contain since the other women, unlike the speaker, knew instinctively that club matters weren't for general conversation. I don't think I'm a snob (of course, everyone says that) but I did wonder how Sidney had become a member – who'd put him up, and why. On the other hand, can you blame a man for his wife? But she would insist on talking about the money.

'I suppose most of you don't need it.'

One of the women, fearing a total silence, said, 'Go a long way towards a new conservatory. Those builders' prices!' And another said something like, 'Rip you off, my goodness', and there was a general murmur. But they didn't want to talk about this sort of thing, they only wanted to avoid leaving Sidney's wife more exposed than she already was. But she wasn't having any.

'I'm talking about *bills*. Household stuff, unpaid, they run on from month to month—'

'Come on, Mu, nobody wants to hear all this.' The wretched Sidney was forced into reacting, though any intervention on his part simply made it all the more difficult for the rest of us to pretend nothing was happening. One of the men began, as though something had reminded him, 'I say, did you see that marvellous play last night? BBC2, wasn't it? That wonderful – what's her name – you know—' It is a hazard of club life that men who have no conversation tell you the plots of plays they've seen on television, and it's absolutely no use lying and saying yes when they ask you if you saw it too, because far from stopping them before they get started it seems to encourage them to go into even greater detail. The truly teeth-grinding part of the interchange is the collaboration they force on you by insisting you know the names of the principle actors they have forgotten. The worst offenders snap their fingers at you petulantly, as though their forgetfulness was somehow your fault. However, on this occasion I responded with gusto.

'Oh lord yes, that wonderful actress – Janet – Janet—'

'Yes, yes, Janet, of course,' – he was true to form in brushing aside the assistance he had importuned – 'of course that's her first name. But the other—'

I tried to get it going round the table. '*You* know, come on, help us out—' But before the others could rally round, Mu had her head out of the way of the heavy blanket we were trying to drop on the embers of the earlier stuff and said, 'I bet no one here has a black and white set.'

One of the men said, 'That's very interesting. They say there's something about black and white that makes a picture more authentic. My father kept his old Box Brownie. . . .' It was a nice try, but I could see what was coming.

'That's not why we have a black and white set,' Mu went on, 'we've got one because the licence was cheaper.'

Throughout all this I couldn't fathom whether she was revenging herself on Sidney for some fearful hurt he had put upon her, or whether it was some sort of natural ill-will, something poisonous in her because she'd never had a good enough time, or had it for long enough, to make her feel like getting the better of. She might even have been the wonderful actress whose name we couldn't remember, performing. Or doing it for a bet. I don't think it was the wine, though it might have helped. And she'd actually married the man so the presumption must be that she can't have objected to his style – at least in the beginning – which, the little I'd seen of it that evening, wasn't attractive. But poor Sidney's face didn't permit such easy exits. Whatever was going on, I think she simply couldn't help it.

'Money isn't that important, when you've got it. Though perhaps there are more members of this club than anyone knows of who need it as badly as Sidney and me.'

Sidney was almost green. 'Mu, why do you like to exaggerate everything?'

He'd given up pretending; it wasn't possible for any of us to go on doing that. I felt what had been said couldn't any longer be laughed off, as we'd in all decency been trying to, and that if it was now taken seriously for a moment, that might be another way of wrapping it up, getting rid of it. And I said – for no one else at our silent table took the lead, some glancing round as though pleasantly registering the amiable hubbub of the rest of the room – 'I think it's a curious thing about money – I agree with you, there is an awful lot of concealment.'

'Only a branch of manners, isn't it?' said a man who I don't remember having spoken until now.

'Not necessarily. It may just be a branch of deceit.'

I could see Mu was not going to join in. She seemed not to be listening. My ploy was doomed.

'Very difficult to determine who's in what category – rich or poor,' said the same man, somewhat vaguely.

'Ah,' I said. 'Yes indeed. And there may be people with enough who are pretending to have more, and people who have less pretending it's enough.'

'Isn't that the same thing?'

'Quite probably.'

'One doesn't want to pry.'

'And thus one never knows.'

Mu got up. Sidney looked at his watch.

'Have to leave if we're to get the last bus,' she said.

Was that to be her final assault? It was mild enough, and perhaps it wasn't meant to wound. Though in the light of all the other things she'd said, that didn't seem very likely.

'Lovely evening. Don't get so many. And we wouldn't be here at all if Sidney's office didn't pay his subscription.'

As they left, I could see that last sentence sticking out of Sidney's back, between his shoulder blades. I found it hard to imagine what would happen when they got home. My guess would be that he would be silent – though he was richly entitled to murder her I suspected he would take it out in an extended silence. Would it reach her? But now everyone was making a move. No remarks were made as our table got up to go, though looks were exchanged. And as I say, it was a woman, who, having retrieved her coat, said the words, 'It was *dreadful*!' Of course, she may have been talking about something else.

But Sidney didn't go home with Mu. To my astonishment I saw him when I came down to breakfast the following morning; I keep a suitcase at the Club and had stayed over so I could walk to the office the next day. All the finery of the previous evening had been put away and the dining-room had returned to its daytime chastity. No one speaks in the morning, and I took a table in a corner and read the paper, glancing over it now and then to look at Sidney – after the celebration I'd asked someone what his name was, but though two men knew who I meant, neither of them could tell me. But the cashier said it was Spalding. He was not alone. Sitting with him across the long room was Routh. An unlikely duo. They were adjacent to each other at a small table and though I can't say for certain that actual words were being exchanged, some sort of conversation, however meagre, must have been generated otherwise they wouldn't have chosen to sit together. The austere Routh, the uneasy Spalding. I pondered: Routh would scarcely have bothered to take breakfast with a member merely because he was supportive of the dissident motion he was going to put before the club, and anyway Spalding would already have joined his caucus – something his wife had implied. But what other community of interest joined them? What feasible link could there be between the taciturn courtier and a man like Spalding?

And then I thought of Spalding's wife making her way back to Peckham all alone on the bus, and the picture made me gloomy. No doubt the separation had been caused by what she'd said, and the phrase came to mind, 'I shall sleep at my club tonight!' I've never actually found the words in any Edwardian novel, but I used to say I was waiting for the chance of uttering them, and my wife would laugh: it was one of many ways we had of rejoicing in our own felicity.

At the office there was a message to telephone Ledward.

'The thing is, these people in Ipswich. Another damned letter, wanting our response. I've held off writing to them until we had some guidance. Did you say you'd talked to your QC?'

Purefoy had been too busy to go into the matter in the depth it required, but at first glance he thought there was something to be said on both sides. The cases, which he'd had someone devil out for him, could support both ways of looking at it: that the bequest included everything that the legatee discovered it to include, even items the donor might have been unaware were being passed on – it might be a desk which held share certificates, even though the desk alone had been specifically bequeathed – and conversely, that the legacy was limited to what was designated in the will.

'And,' I said to Ledward, 'it won't come as a surprise to you that there are two cases, one of which went one way and one of which went the other.'

'Like stockbrokers' so-called advice,' Ledward said bitterly. ' "On the one hand this, on the other hand that".'

'But at this stage Purefoy thinks we'd have the better of it.'

'The question is, how serious they are,' Ledward mused. 'Costly business, if they take us to court. Not to mention the publicity. Bloody nuisance. Plus the wrangle that's coming up at the club. Honestly, that picture's a millstone.'

'Soon be rid of it, one way or another.' I thought of Mrs Spalding. Wouldn't be a millstone to her. But then she went home by bus, and Ledward was driven in his Rolls.

'Here's a thought. Don't mean to impose, Owlish, but if one of your staff could go down to Ipswich and take on the lawyers face to face—'

'You don't impose, not a bit. But wouldn't it be better to meet the litigant herself? Then we'd know how much of a loony she is. Get an idea whether she's likely to cave in or whether she really means to stick it to us. *Then* drop in on the lawyers and see what their end of it looks like – they could be humouring her. Pay their bill, and we're off cheaply.'

I'd already decided to do it myself.

*

Prince was in his counting-house, counting out his money. He sat in a glass eyrie on top of the Lloyd's building, the one which has Mammon's guts spread over its façade, and was reading through the projections he had cast for the results of the 1997 year of account. He saw that in the event – there was of course a three-year time-lag – he was out by scarcely a hair's breadth: there would be a profit rather better than marginal, say three per cent, and in a soft market that was an achievement. But he could have done with more.

He, personally, could have done with more. Required more. And why was that? George Prince was a canny old party, had steered all his clients through the storm of the early nineties, had not made a single error and had received many offers from money men who envied the profits such surefootedness brings in a lean time – from the Cayman Islands, from Bermuda, from Saloman Brothers and the Thundering Herd in New York, from the great Soros himself, from the gnomes and gargoyles on the glass spires of Zurich, even an offer of the deputy's job (so people said) from the Bank of England; they'd all been after him. But nothing could match a mineshaft of your own, something that went deep down into the great money seams where the huge raw deposits were brought to the surface glittering with the ammonites of power and satisfaction.

But he needed more. No, it wasn't that he was mysteriously short of the stuff, as one might be if one were being leached on by a blackmailer, or would be if wild extra-mural speculations had swung back like a cannon ball demolishing a tower of money, or dishonourable dealings long concealed had floated up like bodies to the surface, or Revenue narks making one of their cryptic forays had found a cache of loot naked and undeclared. None of these things; no practical consideration of save or spend came into it; there was no entail, no mortgage on the houses he owned – the one in Lord North Street, the Sussex manor in its mellow acres, the Tuscan farmhouse in Fornacci, high in the spiky hills that look over the plain, north of Lucca. There were commercial properties that bordered ring-roads whose brick and mortar had been raised on his capital, the vaults of Coutts were crammed with his stocks and bonds, and the large personal lines he wrote on his own syndicates at Lloyd's – in this age of transparency, all open to the view in his yearly reports – inspired the respectful confidence of all his Names. These amenities furnished a material life he lived without noticing that he lived it – the air he breathed was money-crammed, a given that was as absolute as the three dimensions of existence itself. But there was never enough.

Never enough, in the way a man who collects stamps ever feels his collection is complete, or someone who explores the far places of the world is ever satisfied except in contemplation of the expedition he has not yet made. If there was the possibility of money, Prince reached towards it by instinct, not because he was miserly but because it was the product which validated his ability to produce it. He was not the entrepreneur, he was the manufacturer: what he did was to make money appear in season, sometimes in places where it hadn't appeared before. He grew it; he planted its seed; it was a crop. And when he harvested it his satisfaction was tinged with melancholy that he had not produced more. No doubt there was a touch of the obsessional in all this, but then neither Newton nor Einstein would really have been satisfied until all the laws of physics had been reconciled, and were under their command – until they'd got the lot.

Smart young men hurried through the streets, eighteen storeys below. Prince saw them as he stood behind the tinted glass speaking into the telephone.

'It seems to have no down side. We are both risk-averse. I want to be sure of that. The figures will have to be very, very carefully assessed.'

What he heard from his correspondent seemed to meet with his approval. He nodded as he spoke.

'That seems appropriate. I can't appear in the thing myself, obviously.' He waited. Then he said, 'Ah – good point.'

What he had heard gave him pause.

'Yes. Yes.' Prince deliberated. 'But the matter of domicile should settle it. Don't you agree? The strike price will have to be played against that possibility and I shall concern myself with it. We'll be in touch as necessary.'

Planning ahead. When Prince took his seat again at his desk the expression on his face might have been that of a farmer who had done his part, and who knew the rest must be left to nature. And was thinking: can she be relied on?

FIVE

There was a hard frost the day I drove down to Suffolk. An orange sun hung close to the horizon in the pale glittering blue sky above fields covered in rime. Mulgrave Hall – I'd got out of the car and asked them at the last pub. A mile or so further on, they'd said, so I left the car and took the air, swinging along a lane that threaded its way downhill through the crisp frosty acres and the dark stands of trees. A fox sneaked through the hedgerow as my feet rang on the tarmac of the icy lane. Good houses in Suffolk, lath and lattice in the plasterwork, pink and cream wash. Those big gables. Rich men building early and well. Money enough and to spare, the Hansa, the wool people. The image of a widow rose up in my mind – Letitia Mary Barlow. No mention of a spouse. Relict – dreadful word – alone in an empty house. I began to wish I'd telephoned, but then I'd have been fobbed off with the Ipswich lawyers.

I heard the *juck* of a pheasant from a neighbouring wood. Rare in the shooting season, it's as if they knew. Day before shooting starts, they're perched in multitudes on posts and fences, the day after, they vanish. I could hear the distant echo of voices rolling across the fields. Bang bang. The guns were out, probably the last stand of the day, the light was beginning to mellow. I had a place near Chichester, but I didn't preserve. Sometimes neighbours invited me, but I was never much of a shot, and there was a man with a farm in Surrey, almost within earshot of Leatherhead town centre – one stand for the guns was actually at the edge of the by-pass, if you missed a bird you could bag a motorist – and when he asked me to shoot with him one afternoon I downed a brace; unfortunately one was a hen, and they were only shooting cocks. 'Well done, Richard,' said my host, who'd stationed a man behind me to polish off any unhappy pheasant I'd winged. '*Your* bird, Richard,' this chap cried, as he had to fire behind him to give the second one its quietus.

At a bend in the lane I saw a substantial house across the fields with a grassy terrace in front of it sloping down to the pasture. It was the one the people at the pub had described. The country day was in my nostrils, and I climbed over a gate thinking to come up to the house across the fields, passing a spinney of hardwood to the right, coming round on its flank, the icy grass tickling my ankles, and running suddenly into men with guns standing at their pegs. Felt rather a fathead, as one always does when one isn't dressed the way everyone else is. I wasn't exactly done up in a pinstripe suit, but I might well have been. As they turned to look at me I thought they stared as if I was a gryphon or a unicorn. How could I let them know I wasn't Kipps or Mr Polly? I remembered a ghost story, I think it was by Maugham, where a stranger on a cross-channel steamer begs another to share his cabin, being fearful of apparitions, and in order to reassure his fellow traveller says 'I am a member of White's.' At the memory a smile came to my face before I could quench it and I felt they must think I was the village idiot. Very difficult either to engage with them or ignore them, or go straight on across the meadow to the house. Then the birds came over and they all fired in their turn, and the tension was broken because they went about collecting what they'd shot and I was able to carry on beyond them, deciding my best chance was to assume the character of an absent-minded professor. But when I got to the house and swarmed up the slope on to the terrace, I realized I might be taken for a member of the Swell Mob come to lift the spoons. Daft of me to have encroached in this way. I put my hands in my pockets and lounged airily round the side of the house and found the main entrance. Should have driven up in the car, could at least have sat in it until someone appeared. When they did, I should have to bumble, for which I think I'm probably well fitted.

The guns were trudging towards the house, the light was waning. I heard them clatter on to the terrace, then the noise faded away as I realized they'd turned to the other side of the house where I assumed the cars were parked, to leave their guns and brogues and put on the shoes they'd brought with them in the boot. What to do? Rang the bell, rapped at the knocker. After a bit the door opened and a cheerful fellow in breeches said, 'Yes?' I was now rather fervently wishing I hadn't pitched up like this, without warning.

'Letitia Barlow?'

'Oh, you've come about the radiators, haven't you?'

'No. I'm a lawyer. I tried to telephone but something seemed to be wrong. I mean, I couldn't get through. My name is Owlish.'

'Well you might as well come in. I'll call her.'

She came in still glowing from the bright cold day outside, a comely figure in her late thirties with brown hair streaked blonde and wearing a dark-green cashmere sweater above her houndstooth breeches.

'Has something happened? You're from Huntercombe's? Do sit down.'

'I tried to phone. I couldn't get through.'

'Really? I don't think there's anything wrong here.'

'No, I mean it's my telephone, my mobile, that's probably wonky. I've come at the wrong moment. Very awkward. And no, not Huntercombe's. I'm Richard Owlish and – I'm not actually retained by the people who've got the Leonardo, but in a way I am because I'm a member of the Club—'

I was certainly doing my bumbling. Though her face retained its attractive glow it took on something else from outside – a chill. The day was closing in and the light in the room, which was a library, was darkening so that it looked a bit like a room in an old cross-hatch engraving. The woman walked over and turned on a lamp. I could see the busts sitting behind the pediments of the bookcases.

'And what can I do for you?'

It was more than stupid, it was clownish to have promoted an encounter which I hadn't thought through, which I'd barged into in the vague belief that I'd find an old lady who would sit and nod while I assessed her intentions.

'It only happens in stories,' I said, looking round at the books. 'I'm sorry, I beg your pardon. What I mean is, I came here thinking I'd find an old lady and discover she wanted the picture because she was barmy.' The woman laughed, suddenly. 'It's an awfully crude way of putting it, and I couldn't imagine saying it a minute ago, but it's the truth.'

'Do sit down.' She laughed again. '*What* did you say your name was?'

I sat down and said, 'Owlish. Yes, that's true too. Oh dear.'

She crossed the legs in the elegant breeches – I noticed the action, distinctly.

'Well I'm not, am I?' she said. 'Not yet. That old. Or barmy. So you hoped to talk some poor old creature out of her rights. *I* want the picture because you know, honestly, I think it's mine.'

'It certainly could be, it certainly could be.' I found myself trying to stifle an impulse to agree with anything she said. 'I mean, I wouldn't be here unless, would I?' I'd come into her house like a pea brain and now I'd I'd started doing another sort of foolishness – what did she need with *my* reassurance? Why was I offering it?

'No, no, I didn't want to talk her out of anything, I just thought I'd find out how serious she was, whether it wasn't some fantasy she had about the thing.'

'Well, I'm serious.'

'Of course you are. But,' I said, nodding sagely for no reason at all, except that I was trying to recover a position where if I wasn't the village idiot I'd been doing a pretty good imitation of him, 'you see, it's likely to go against you. They'd say the bequest was whatever the bequest contained. And the case would be awfully expensive.'

She got up and moved over to the chimney piece, opened a box and said, 'That's what I thought. Would you like a cigarette?'

My sails sagged. Her ingenuous response removed what little wind I'd been trying to whistle up. I was back into a sort of homified gentle remonstrance.

'Oh, goodness, you mustn't take my word for it.'

'I wouldn't do that. It was really a cousin of mine. He knows a lot about art, but I don't think he knows much about anything else.' She held the box out to me, and I'm damned if I didn't take one. Hadn't smoked for years.

'You see,' she said, 'what appealed was the way it could all be paid for out of the absolutely monstrous huge sum of money the picture would fetch.'

'I quite see that.' I spoke like a wise old person not wanting to bear down too heavily on a promising pupil. 'But the odds are so long.'

'Yes, they are. Long odds are so seductive. Come and have a drink.'

My God, I felt I could do with one. I'm not sure why, but I felt more like a drink than I've felt for a long time. I followed her out of the library and into a room where three of the guns were sitting at a card table and playing what looked like ha'penny nap for cartridges.

'He's come to diddle me out of my inheritance,' said Letitia Mary Barlow, pouring me a large whisky, and then one for herself.

The men looked up. 'Hello.'

We sat in a corner away from them. As she sat down, she pushed up the sleeves of her cashmere sweater and the plump rounded curve of her forearm seemed almost indelicately on view. When I was in my teens, I would stand outside a house and imagine a window being opened and a girl leaning out and saying, 'We're having a party. Won't you come in?' My dreadful mismanagement of the day's events seemed almost to have brought it about.

'We're off, Letty. Great day.' The men swept their cartridges into their pockets.

'Harker's got a brace each for you.'

'Good man.' And they were gone.

I got up. 'What relation are you to Thomas Percy Anstruther?'

'Oh, you're going?' She got up too. 'Relation? God knows. Some great-great-great. My mother's side.'

I said, 'Funny not knowing much about a man who gives you a Leonardo. I mean me not knowing.'

'Well, he gives you a Leonardo, but did he know he was? Giving it to you? I mean, that's really the thing.'

'Of course it is. I shouldn't think it belongs to anyone better than it belongs to you. Morally.'

Dry sort of word. Non-committal, too, of course. But somehow the Club's initial gesture about giving the thing away seemed to me for the first time to be particularly empty.

'Have you ever seen it?' she asked, as we moved across the room to the door.

'As a matter of fact, no. I wonder if it's any good?' She laughed. 'Silly of me, what I mean is—'

'I know what you mean,' she said.

We were in the corridor and she took my elbow to guide me.

'No, they've got it in the strong room of some bank. I must have a look. Very remiss not to.'

We got to the side door, there was a mist rising. I said, 'If anyone ought to see it, it should be you. Are you ever in London?'

She said, 'Good lord, I know it's Suffolk but people go on as though it was some asteroid.'

'Well, but it's a long haul. Why not have a look? Since you have an interest, I mean. Wouldn't mind clapping eyes on it myself. I could, um, I could get them to open the place up and – er—'

On the step I said, 'If you gave me your number—'

She said, 'It's the same one you couldn't get through to.' But she gave it to me, anyway.

'Perhaps you ought to write it down.'

'No, no,' I said. 'I'll remember it.'

When you're driving your car down The Mall at the time the offices close and you pull up at the set of traffic lights before

Admiralty Arch, you think idly of the men crossing in front of you, and assume them to be civil servants. Whitehall seems to take up all the other side of the road, and what with it being HQ, you feel the staff must be quite high up in the hierarchy; Permanent Secretaries, that sort of thing. But as you wait for the lights to change, it's doubtful if 'mandarin' springs immediately to mind as a way of describing them.

Forbes was at first glance indistinguishable from the rest, and perhaps that was the condition all civil servants aspired to; since the fiction is that governments run the country, it was as well that those who actually did run it drew no attention to the fact, and thus as mandarins were always subfusc. But there was a little something about Forbes that couldn't be suppressed – an air of command which was as ineradicably part of the man's nature as the vanity of his style when speaking with his equals.

In the corridors of the ministry everyone had the same calm preoccupied air, to which was added a pleasant extra inflection that suggested no one was ever too busy to stop and give ear to a colleague; busyness would be the mark of one having to keep up, and in a society where 'able' was the adjective that distinguished a man, keeping up was the wrong signal. Relationships in the office were apparently relaxed and easy, there was no proclaimed deference, no evident subordination; but no mark was ever overstepped. Everyone knew not only the gradations of the hierarchy, but also the gradations within those gradations – who welcomed assistance, who resented it, who welcomed dissent and who did not, who might always be approached and who might never be. It was a civilized way of running what was essentially a rule-ridden environment, where someone's way could almost always be got if the methods of intra-personal negotiation continued to be what they had always been. This suited everyone; they would not have been the sort of men they were if it had not.

Salaries were, of course, known. These were good if not extravagantly good, as measured against inflated standards outside the Service. And then there was money that could be anticipated, after retirement: executive and non-executive positions, chairmanships and directorships, sometimes of companies the ministry had had dealings with, which would give the retiring secretary a distinct edge – for a time at least he would be exactly the man to mark the cards of his new employers, privy to the current climate within the ministry, and with a fine sense of the right approach. The understanding that civil servants would defer taking up positions for three months after they'd left could in no way impede their future employers seeking their advice before that period had elapsed. But, of course, all this was only money to look forward to, a little harvest for the future.

Meanwhile, people such as Forbes could enjoy the exercise of power, though their mandarin's robes were never in evidence. Forbes lived near Godalming, in a house built in the 1920s, a good house with polished hardwood floors and big windows, sitting in an acre and a half of ground, with a handsome garden and a tennis court where he played vigorous singles with the nephew he had taken in when (as it was understood) he had been left an orphan. It was with this young man that, having crossed The Mall by Admiralty Arch, he was now stepping briskly across Trafalgar Square in the dusk towards Piccadilly and then to Aquascutum in Regent Street. Edward was to have a suit.

Under the eye of the man with the tape-measure round his neck, Edward paraded for his uncle. 'I like the chalk-stripe, don't you, Rupe?' Rupert Forbes nodded. He was a tall man with glacial blue eyes and thick white hair which fell in a cowlick over his brow. Perhaps again he wasn't quite like his colleagues, in that his air of decision made him actually look the high-flyer he was: in the final stretch, the last lap before the top job was in his grasp, this would have helped him, but on the way up he may have tried to keep it out of sight. In the Service, ambition is not announced.

He bought the suit, signed the credit-card slip, and they walked out. 'I'm back to the office for an hour. See you at home.' Edward thanked him for the suit and waved goodbye and Forbes made his way towards the ministry, across Piccadilly and into Jermyn Street, down the side of Waterstone's great book palace, then into Lower Regent Street which was dense with traffic. It was dark now as he passed Her Majesty's Theatre, crossed Pall Mall and made for the Duke of Yorks steps. This brought him out a little along The Mall, by the ICA, and all the time he'd been walking he'd been thinking about money. There'd always been enough for the comfortable life he led, but not a great deal more, and buying Edward's suit, one of sundry items that from time to time both felt were necessary to the young man's comfort as well as his position in life, had reminded him of this. The sale of the Club's picture, which in a way he viewed as a sort of comedy or farce, might be worth taking seriously after all. He hadn't joined Routh's insurgents yet, but it was a perfectly respectable thing to do. Which was more than what was about to happen would be.

He glanced down the road towards Horse Guards Parade, but the lights of the ministry had gone off at 5.30. Forbes crossed The Mall, and walked into St James's Park. When he did this sort of thing it wasn't that the stringent appraisals of action he used in his work were in abeyance, it was simply that his mind was a blank, he did not reflect or consider. It might be imagined that what he was going to do was such anathema to his daylight self that thought had to be suspended. The infantility of the proceedings, their essential grossness, would have shamed him if he'd given them the slightest thought. But he never did. A man on a seat got up and walked with Forbes into the neighbouring bushes and in five minutes they were out again. The man walked one way, Forbes another and, as he estimated how long it would take him to get to Waterloo by bus, his mind turned itself on again. But in the minutes of white time that had just elapsed, any difficulties he'd had about money had increased. A third party had witnessed the initial encounter, had lingered at a distance while it was consummated, and as Forbes walked away, had recognized him. This third figure then followed the other man and engaged him in conversation. The two seemed to come to an agreement.

Mr Ihara sat on something that looked like a hairy throne at the end of a salon one hundred feet long, whose walls were painted with *trompe l'oeil* scenes of the Mojave desert under a bright blue sky. The scenes on the walls were the Texas oil baron's notion of lightening up the place, and to give it added class he'd got the artist to paint in classical columns as a frame for the whole, so the effect would be that you were looking out at a scene familiar from Western movies, but from the inside of a Greek temple.

The throne was in the Indian taste, as far as the cowman had determined it, being adorned with large cattle horns and feathers that stuck up vertically from the backrest; it was one of half a dozen others in the room, and in case anyone hadn't caught on, a massive mirror some eight metres across, of the type regularly smashed by patrons of bars in the same films which featured the desert and its rock formations, hung on chains from the ceiling, glitteringly engraved with the word 'Pow-wow' to indicate you were in the drawing-room.

Ihara said to Olney, 'Do you not warm to the innocence of the place?'

Olney wasn't at all sure that this was the word he would have used, but attributed it to Ihara's provincial origins; as far as Olney was concerned, anyone who wasn't a Londoner came from Warrington. It was this essential simple-mindedness which gave him an initial charge, it allowed him to come off his blocks as brisk as you please, and in the opening stages of any negotiation made other parties doubt the certainty of their own positions. And though the primary freshness of this impression did not survive, it never entirely evaporated; there was something in Olney's preliminaries which left the people he was dealing with under a lingering doubt. It was not something he calculated, his native stupidity wouldn't have allowed him to, it was simply the way he was.

The scam, the free-trade he'd initiated when the Pacific Rand Corporation had opted for the Texas man's Tudor ranch opposite Lambeth Bridge, proceeded according to plan – plan was a grand sort of word for something so simple. The sweetness of the deal lay in its size: sell a flat or house in Islington for a few hundred thousand, and the vendor was after his cash pretty well the day following, but where the equity involved was a couple of million or more there'd be a time lag, perhaps as much as a fortnight – the beauty of it was that the upfront money needed for the free-trade wouldn't be called in until the money from the secondary deal was safely there to cover it. There could be snags, but if either of the deals fell through, you simply walked away – here was the force of Olney's great slogan, Don't sign anything.

Jarred Ranson, the man who acted for the liquidators, had come across finally at the figure Olney had predicted – 1.9; the front company, called Mondo Real Estate, set up by the house agents, had acted as purchaser, and the Japs to whom it was being sold on had agreed at 2.6 – they'd knocked him down a hundred thousand as a matter of face, but Olney had had to keep *his* face straight. He'd settle with the Belmont, of course, but it wasn't a lot, and then he was left with – it was pleasant not to finish the sentence, to leave the prospect as an agreeable scenario until bingo! it became hard cash. The negotiations for both deals were close to completion. Property lawyers in Hong Kong and Malaysia and Japan were just as cute as anywhere else, but there was an awful lot of slack between Connaught Road HK and Mayfair that you couldn't put on hard disk.

'And the place had been hanging fire on the market – not everyone's taste,' Mr Ihara said.

If it had been Moto talking Olney might have said something about waiting for the discerning buyer, but Ihara's style warned him he shouldn't try it. So he said, 'Of course, the location being what it is, it was going to sell at any price, eventually. In these latitudes—' was someone from the Land of the Midnight Sun going to understand he meant 'district'? – 'it's top dollar, whatever's going on at the lower end of the market.'

'Where do you live, Lord Olney?'

'Oh – now. Now I live in Wandsworth. Nice enough, Mr Ihara, but Lloyd's, you know. Perhaps he didn't know. 'Lloyd's,' Olney went on, 'the great insurance market where many of us came a cropper.' Lloyd's was a trump card which you could play very modestly – you were a loser, but only because you were a winner. Olney was pretty good at seeming to defer when the client was grand enough. 'Came a cropper. Funny word. Means, um, means—'

'Means you fucked up,' Mr Ihara nodded understandingly.

Like many foreigners, perhaps he used the word to show he was *au fait* with the demotic. But there was something in Ihara's tone which brought Olney up short.

'Failed for eight hundred pounds. You know your Dickens?'

Olney had no idea what the man was talking about.

'Pickwick. Mr Solomon Pell. The shyster lawyer. Said his brother-in-law had failed for eight hundred pounds. And boasted of the figure, as though losing so great a sum was as distinguished as making it. Came a cropper.'

'Yes.' Olney nodded. But where was all this coming from? It sounded off-message.

'Now that figure would be – well, what would you say? Some tens of thousands, perhaps.'

Olney didn't want to say You've got me there, because talk of cash in the abstract got on his nerves. He liked the property to be bought, the price paid, the papers got shot of. Analytic money-talk always felt like holes being dug under him, opening up not chasms exactly, but potholes in which he could catch his foot and twist his ankle. So he nodded.

'You met our Mr Moto, I think,' said Ihara. 'What did you make of him?'

The phrase Me no likee sprang into Olney's head. He didn't utter the words, but it was only after he'd left Mr Ihara's new house that it came slowly wreathing through his brain like smoke from a distant bonfire that there was something about the expression which would have been offensive, anyway.

'I'd say he gives good discussion.' Then Olney, not wanting his affectation of trans-Atlantic style to be mistaken by a foreigner for a vulgarism, added, 'Head screwed on pretty well, I'd say.'

'So long as his task is very plainly laid out for him – so long as he does not encounter ambiguities, Mr Moto has no equal. When his path is clear he is indefatigable. He is dogged. And as Trollope puts it in *The Last Chronicle of Barset*, "It's dogged as does it!" '

Olney had heard of Trollope, and had thought the name was unfortunate without being certain why. He was fairly sure the man was an English author, and for a moment wondered how anyone called Ihara was in a position to pray him in aid. But it didn't matter what was being said, something was up – he could hear it.

'And so it was simply a matter of telling him to winkle out who the vendors actually were – who, indeed, were Mondo Real Estate. What alerted me to the possibility that there was an entrepreneur was the very short interval between Mondo's purchase and their willingness to sell.'

Olney said, 'I pointed out, I believe, that it had been bought by them as a speculation at a knockdown price. They were after a quick turn—'

'Don't come the old soldier with me,' Ihara said. 'It was a nominee company. Moto devoted a little time and a little money and found out who their sponsors were.'

All rear-guard action now, Olney thought. When Moto came in with a folder of papers, he faced Mr Ihara and bowed; they only ironed out superfluous bows at business-school, Olney fleetingly thought, Moto still had the hang of the indispensable sort. Moto left and Ihara went through all the documents, the sale to Mondo Real Estate, the sell-on to Pacific Rand, and the papers detailing those who were behind the nominees, bribed out of whoever it was at the Registrars. No face-saving possible. Olney had to sit and listen.

Ihara said, 'I'll split it with you – after all, if I can't join an English devil in robbing my own company the world is really upside down.'

'I don't believe anything is yet signed,' Olney managed to bring out, rallying, if rather feebly, behind the old formula; and then Ihara's words were so utterly unexpected he was rather bewildered, not at all clear in his own mind whether he should feel thankful for the bizarre accommodation that was being offered, or put out at having his pocket picked by the man he'd been hoping to rob.

'Come, come,' Mr Ihara said with the gentleness of tone a man uses when the upper hand is his in a matter that is of no great moment to him, 'a hundred per cent of nothing is still nothing. Take the money and run. As for me, I think this palace of kitsch is an excellent investment even at the price you and your partners ask, and though as you may imagine the measly three hundred and fifty thousand is scarcely of account to me, it is reasonable commission. More importantly, it makes us colleagues, and the more colleagues I have the more secure I feel. You're on board, Lord Olney, and cheap at the price.'

To be treated so contemptuously was a novelty to Olney. He could muster no adequate response. His suits, his size, his title – their resource had vanished.

'The more you dwell upon it, Lord Olney, the clearer it will become to you that you have been hoist with your own petar – the final 'd' is added only by those who do not know their Shakespeare – and that with the documents in my possession, the deal, I should say, the two deals, the *joint* deals, will now go through. Give your partners my warmest regards, I have them on toast, as they will surely recognize – it is not in the Asian temperament to gloat, but it's better than cutting people's heads off with those big swords as we used to do. And should Pacific Rand at any future date decide to invest in a London estate agency, I shall consider the down-payment to have been made. Let them make out their cheque – Mondo Real Estate's cheque – to me in person, three hundred and fifty thousand pounds to which must be added a further thousand to cover the necessary disbursements made by Mr Moto in the course of his enquiries.'

Mr Moto entered, bearing a cheque in completion of the sale. When he handed it over, he bowed to the earl, but very slightly. Olney felt he was closer to being a Warringtonian at that moment than he could ever have imagined.

SIX

Something rather sensational happened. I have a habit of categorizing things (I may have mentioned it) and when I say 'sensational' I don't believe I am overstating the case.

I dropped into the club to pay a bill and saw Prince in the lobby and asked him where the picture was held. He said it was in a strongroom at the Law Courts end of Fetter Lane.

'Someone else just rang to ask. Do you know a Carter?'

'There's a Carterton. Oh, and there's Carr.'

'Must have been one of them. When are you going?'

I told Prince I was picking up the claimant that morning, since she was naturally curious about the picture, and I gave him a quick run-down of who she was. Then I telephoned the bank which rented the place. They'd verify my membership, and I would identify myself on arrival. I explained there'd be someone with me and the bank said they'd get the club to vouch for her. That meant Ledward, as chairman. He'd already had an edited account of my meeting with Letty Barlow, rang the bank on her behalf, and the way was clear.

'She's an extremely civilized woman who was advised by a relative, and in my opinion,' I had told him, 'she has no intention of carrying the thing further. I can't say for sure, of course, but that's the distinct impression I came away with. Mind you, if anyone has a right to a slice of the loot I think she must be high up the list. I more and more come round to Routh's view of the matter, and feel members should each decide what they do with their share of whatever comes out of all this.'

'And you'll be handing her some of yours, will you?' Ledward sounded rather dry.

'Not a question of that, not at all,' I replied, and his remark rather ruffled me. 'There may well be a case for part of the total sum we realize from the picture to be handed over to causes we nominate, and *then* the rest can be divided among the members, each of whom can do with their share what their good sense or self-interest dictates. But I'm bound to say in all decency, as well as in the pious hope that we shan't come off looking like a bunch of avaricious old farts, that someone who would have been the legitimate owner of one of the world's unique art objects, if it hadn't been dumped on us by accident, should get a slice off the top.'

'My goodness, she must have got under your guard.'

I met her at King's Cross. When you're waiting for someone off a train, a variety of things run through your mind – well, through mine, anyway. It's the wrong platform; it's the wrong day; she missed the train; you've come to the wrong station, stuff like that, plus a feeling of strangeness in looking for one person when there are so many – supposing you don't recognize her (as a matter of fact, I was already having difficulty recalling her features); supposing she doesn't look the same when she's dressed differently; supposing she doesn't recognize *you*. Once, when I came home from school, my mother was waiting on the platform and looked past me as I got out of the train, and only secondarily looked back and said, 'Oh, it *is* you!' Rather silly, but railway stations have that effect on me: everyone a stranger, until one person turns up and tells you you aren't.

So I walked Letty Barlow out of the place, finding yet again that the anomie induced by places of arrival and departure clings on for a minute or two after you're back in the usual world where things are predictable. Though that day was going to be an exception.

'What train back?' I asked, as we walked towards the cab stand.

'Four-ish, I think it is.'

I told the cab Fetter Lane.

'I've been looking him up,' she said as we turned into Gray's Inn Road, towards Holborn. 'He was my great-great – oh, about four greats, I think – uncle. We've got a pile of old papers in the attics. To be quite honest, he doesn't say anything about the Leonardo, but if he'd hidden it away behind the picture he *did* give your club, perhaps he didn't want anyone to know.'

'I don't think he knew it was there. If he'd hidden it under the other picture surely he'd have given us a hint. Man leaving his club anything as handsome as that is going to let them know what they're getting, isn't he? Unless he was a frolicsome old bird and wanted to tease.'

'I don't think he could have been. Someone whose abiding interest was a boring old club doesn't sound much fun.' I was waiting for her to say 'Sorry', as though the aspersions she cast on her forebear might seem to apply to other, later members of the club. But she didn't, and I was rather pleased.

'Which makes me think it wasn't Thomas Percy Anstruther who concealed the Leonardo,' I said, taking up the thought planted by Ted Mirfield, our chief clerk. 'It was the previous owner.'

'Actually, I dug out an auction slip – Christie's – date was some time like 1830 something. He paid three hundred guineas for the John the Baptist—'

'Did it say who was selling?'

'Can't remember.'

'A deceased estate, probably, which would mean the seller had picked it up thirty or forty years before, end of the eighteenth century, beginning of the nineteenth, Grand Tour time – probably got it from some Italian middle-man who'd had it stolen from a church, maybe to order!' I was quite thrilled. But then I'd felt jaunty since breakfast-time. 'Look, before we see the thing, let's stop off at Christie's. Can you be sure of the date?'

'Not really. May have been 1834. Poor old Christie's, that'd be a bit too vague, wouldn't it? I could give them a ring at home. The sale thing's on my desk.'

Them. At home. I told the cab-driver to make it King Street.

'Fine.'

We got to King Street and Letty Barlow used one of the phones on the wall by the reception place. I handed her a bit of paper from the desk and a ballpoint. She spoke to 'Them', scribbled something down.

'Got it. 12 June, 1834. No mention of the vendor.'

Who had checked the details on the sale slip for her, I wondered, as I waited to get the ear of the classy middle-aged dame behind the desk. A helpful woman. Catalogues back to the foundation of the firm. She'd send someone. And a lad in an apron returned in a surprisingly short time to hand me the catalogue in question, and I said 'Thank you' and he said 'No problem', uttering the words in such a well-bred accent that he had absolutely no excuse for using them.

We sat together on a little sofa as the ugly dealers, dressed in clothes which appeared to have been stolen from the wardrobes of others, thronged by.

'There it is.' I passed it to her. Sale of various properties. The remaining contents of such a house and such another, by order of the Duke of Somewhere, the Lord Etcetera, and other people. Then the lots that came towards the back of the catalogue.

'A study of John the Baptist, signature 'Leonardo'. Just "The Property of a Gentleman"!'

'They didn't think it was worth naming him. Or the estate didn't want it known. And the signature in quotation marks – a joke.'

She wasn't much concerned. Well, neither was I. We gave the catalogue back, with thanks.

'Worth a try,' I said cheerfully, as we climbed into a taxi, and I told the driver to go to Fetter Lane. I felt the day was already full of incident, compared with my usual days. More was to come. Turning out of King Street into St James's, I said, 'We could lunch at the club!' I did an exclamation mark, or laugh. Then I was a little forward. 'Goodness me, they'd give me marks.' I looked away from her, out of the window of the cab, and she said, 'Great. Whatever.' After I'd said the bit about getting marks, I found I meant it. I meant. Well, I meant. What I meant was, it was good to be in her company, and men would know that. But I meant – I meant something else. But lunch was postponed.

We turned down Piccadilly, up Shaftesbury Avenue, across Cambridge Circus, then through the narrow passageways by Covent Garden, and out into The Strand. The man dropped us just beyond the Law Courts.

'There it is.'

On the corner was a silversmiths. You had to press a buzzer, and the door opened. Someone was making a delivery from a white van parked across from the shop, but as the driver's mate came over with his cardboard box, he politely nodded us ahead, and I showed my credentials. Behind the counter an assistant was dealing with a customer, and we went ahead of the delivery man, while the manager figure led us towards the stairs which took us down to the strongroom. I was expecting one of those doors with wheels on you see in films, but it looked a pretty ordinary sort of door, though solid. Moreover, the manager simply pushed it open, though this was explained by the fact that someone else was already inside the strongroom, intently studying our Leonardo. This was leaning against a wall of strong-boxes, and seeing it propped up like that I thought the arrangements seemed a bit casual. Of course, they'd pulled the picture out from somewhere more secure, so we'd get a good look at it. The man in charge said, 'This is Mr Carl-Heinz Wemdinger, from America, who has come to inspect the picture.' I said who we were, not using a prefix for Letty, but handing him the full Letitia Mary Barlow, with a faint idea that Americans found three names more satisfying than two.

'Glad to know you,' Mr Wemdinger said, dropping what looked like a pair of lorgnettes on a chain round his neck which he had been using to stare intently at the picture ftom close range. 'How seldom it must be that one can stand so close to a work of genius that has lain unheeded and unseen for so long.'

Repressing an impulse to explain that if you couldn't see it the question of it being unheeded was redundant, I said, 'Yes,' hoping some happy addition might occur to me to furbish this somewhat bleak assent. 'A couple of centuries, at least. Perhaps a little more.' This seemed a mite literal. I asked, 'Are you thinking of buying it?' then felt the brightness of the query might have been more suited to the purchase of a bicycle. But Mr Wemdinger gathered my question into a sort of embrace.

'My sponsors are of the opinion, and it is one I wholly support, that this unparalleled work would make their collection, which is already among the six major art bundles of the world, the front runner.'

Art bundles conjured up a man going from door to door with rolls of carpet under his arm. Mr Wemdinger told us he was from the Museum of Timeless Art in Dallas, and he then enquired, 'May I ask, sir, are you a member of the fortunate sodality upon which this great work was bestowed?' If I'd understood the word correctly, I was, and I said so. Mr Wemdinger went on, 'Our governing body, the Timeless Art Conveners, has empowered me to make necessary arrangements. We are hopeful that a figure of fifty million will put us ahead.'

'Er – pounds?' I asked.

'We have access to virtually unlimited funds, Mr Owlish, and the particular denomination would not create a problem.'

Then a problem was immediately created, for two further figures appeared in the strongroom, one of them holding a sawn-off shotgun and the other, the shop assistant, with his hands in the air.

'On the ground,' said the man with the gun, but the manager was already getting down on his stomach. So that's what the rest of us did. I lay parallel to Letty, whose handbag burst open, coins and keys and a vanity mirror spilling out on the floor in front of me. No one said anything, the man with the gun did no shouting or screaming, and the manager had been down on all fours almost before he'd been told to do it, no doubt used to the procedure. Was I frightened? Very anxious, I'd say – very anxious that the man who was here to steal rather than kill wouldn't pull the trigger by accident. Wondered if the gun was really loaded.

'You get up nicely and help him carry the picture,' the man with the gun said. 'Me?' I heard the shop assistant ask. 'You and him,' said the man, stepping forward slightly and kicking Mr Wemdinger's foot as he lay prone on the floor. As he stepped forward I saw he'd moved to where his feet were inside my own. Saw it through Letty's little mirror, which had ended up against her handbag. 'What you do, you take the picture out to my mate in the van, then he watches you come back in. No one gets any grief that way.' 'Me get up?' I heard Mr Wemdinger ask. 'That's it.' I thought, beware delivery-men carrying cardboard-boxes with shotguns inside.

I heard Wemdinger scrambling to his feet, and out of the corner of my eye saw him and the shop man get hold of the Leonardo. What happened then, as they lifted the picture up, I still can't properly attest. I know my foot moved, and I know by the mirror that the man with the shotgun had his own feet forward of my instep, but whether I hooked him over deliberately or whether it was an accident – something involuntary, a convulsive movement, pure nerves, well, can't say for certain. He fell backwards and there was a terrible crack and I thought for an instant the gun had gone off, but it was the back of the man's head hitting the stone floor of the strongroom – a loud, nasty sound. Then I heard the assistant's feet running up the stairs. Wemdinger said, 'He's out cold!' So we got up too.

Bending down, I scrabbled for Letty's handbag and put the miscellanea back into it. Wemdinger had the gun. He didn't look very happy, holding it. 'May I?' I took it ftom him and thinking to check whether it actually had been loaded, broke it open and two No. 6s jumped out of the breach. Then it was I noticed I felt a bit queer. Letty was standing like a person turned to stone. Very pale.

'Is there a chair?'

The manager vanished behind the scenes, came back with a front-of-shop stool from earlier times, with a bentwood back and perforated seat, and she sat down.

'Sorry for the inconvenience,' the manager said. 'Happened before, I'm afraid. Opportunists, mostly, they just take a chance. These seemed to know what they were after. We don't like to make a great song about it.'

Then the police were there, doing their talking into lapel mikes, telling the number of the van which the assistant had got as it boomed off down Fetter Lane, and hailing up an ambulance for the man with the shotgun: one of the coppers laid an ear to his chest as he lay dead to the wide, or even dead. My God, it was my doing! I felt even queerer.

Mr Wemdinger was getting his poise back, which I thought spoke well for him. He said to me, 'Mr Owlish, I am proud to know you, sir.' And he shook my hand.

'Good Christ, what *was* all that about?' Letty spoke, her face now deeply flushed.

'Pinching our Leonardo,' I said. I found I was breathing rather fast.

Wemdinger was giving me credit. 'Madam, this gentleman floored the bastard. The neatest bit of footwork I ever saw outside of the coach of the Boston Red Socks doing a demonstration run. This, madam, was for real. If Mr Owlish hadn't hooked him to the floor that great picture might well have disappeared for ever, and us along with it!' He shook my hand again, and Letty turned her distraught face towards me. She stared.

'I say,' she said at last, 'you *are* a chap.' I felt curiously weak, and suddenly almost tearful.

We all went up the stairs into the shop. The police had the narrative from the assistant, said they'd be in touch with us in due course. We gave them our details, and in the case of Wemdinger and me, our fingerprints, since we'd handled the gun. I said, 'Don't forget the cartridges.' I'd brought them up with me. The ambulancemen arrived and carted the unconscious thief away on a stretcher with a policeman in attendance, and another policeman wrapped the gun in a piece of cloth and put the cartridges in a bag from the counter.

'Feeling pretty shaky, I expect,' said one of the officers. 'Would you like to go in the ambulance for a check?'

No one wanted to. The manager produced a bottle of whisky and some glasses from what looked like a safe, and we all had some, the assistant explaining that he'd been jumped before he could get a toe to the panic button.

'How on earth did they think they could get rid of it?' Letty asked.

'It wouldn't be for sale,' said the manager. 'Not to any legitimate buyer. It'd be for ransom. To the insurers.'

They were on the spot at just the right time – how did that happen, I wondered? Carter – Carterton. Knew the name but not the man. Carr? One of them had telephoned to ask where the picture was stored – at least, Prince said he did. Prince? What possible advantage—? Well, if you set up an insurance job and you shake the insurers down for ten or twenty per cent of the true value— And then there was the manager. Very prompt about getting on the floor – and the assistant, no, he was too visibly frightened. And goodness, there was Letty and me, but we were innocent, I knew I was, I knew she was— As well believe Wemdinger had rigged the whole thing!

By this time a three-handed squad from television, with their electronic news gathering equipment had pitched up.

'And how did you feel?' said the young man with the microphone and the bad suit.

I was on the verge of saying what I always hoped to hear people say, namely, 'Use your imagination', but it would have been owlish. Because I didn't immediately answer, the man nodded, as though nodding held at bay the ultimate evil, which was silence.

'It was a nightmare?' – feeding me the answer.

The very word!' I solemnly said, and grabbing Letty by the arm, we were out of there.

'What happened next?'

I looked at Randolph.

'Nothing happened next. What can happen, after things have happened?'

'No, but I mean, what did you do then?'

He really was threadbare.

'When something is complete, that's it. What happened next is another story. Another thing altogether.'

'Well tell it to me,' he said.

We were lunching together at the club, and I felt uncomfortable. Now and again a member would come up and smile and pat me on the back and indicate he approved of something he didn't make entirely clear, and of course this was because there'd been a report in the *Standard* about the event at the silversmith's strongroom, based on Wemdinger's ecstatic account in which I figured as hero. This was all right, except (as I have indicated) I may have been a hero by accident. Anyway, I was on view, and that wasn't my style, but being on view, perhaps I'd started behaving like those performers who become 'stars' overnight, and find themselves irritated by any little derogation from their new-found status because they feel the status may not be deserved.

'Well the next thing was something quite different.' But Randolph was such a duffer, how could I tell him? 'She was trembling like a leaf, so I took her back to Kew and handed her over to Margery.'

When we'd hurried out of Fetter Lane into Fleet Street we stopped suddenly at the corner, because we didn't know what to do. I gazed at Letty and she seemed blank in a way people aren't, usually, and I asked her, 'What does anyone do after a thing like this?' and she'd said, 'Oh, I wish I was at home.' But we went into a pub and ordered cottage pie and a bottle of red wine, and I know I felt wambly, but after we'd ordered apple pie and custard and a cup of coffee I said to her, 'We can't feel so terrible, if we ate all that, can we?' Though we'd only ordered the pudding because we hadn't eaten any of the cottage pie, and when the pudding came we didn't eat any of that, either. But then I saw she looked so wan, and I said, 'Look, my housekeeper is a nice woman, it's a house with a lot of rooms, let her put you up, and you can get back to Suffolk tomorrow morning.' My lightheadedness meant I didn't feel shy, and perhaps she was in the same condition.

When we got to Kew I didn't need to explain, only had to add a bit to what Margery had already seen in an early edition of the *Standard* and being a good soul she was not only pleased to be on the periphery of dramatic events but more than pleased to be able to help.

'You need to ring? Phone's in there.'

She telephoned and came back. 'Fine,' she said. 'Oh, my God, I'm tired.'

'Sleep's the thing. I'm off to the office,' I prevaricated. 'I'll just show you—' Following them upstairs, I said, 'Here we are,' and Margery throwing open the door, I went in after them into the big panelled room with its nice old-fashioned bathroom where we'd lodged visitors in the days gone by. 'You're quite private, here.' The windows looked out over our garden at the back, and beyond that to the Orangery of the Gardens themselves. Margery turned down the bed and went out, and, as I was about to follow her, I said to Letty, 'See you later', then thought of something. 'Oh, by the way' – pointing across the passage – 'there's all sorts of stuff you could use, if you'd like to. It's all in here.' It was another big, light room, where my wife had borne our children, and where her things were kept in the walnut wardrobe with the raised carving, and in the eighteenth-century bachelor's chest. 'Anything you want, all in there. Do take anything you want.'

In a few seconds I had explained.

'You see, I know she'd have wanted you to, if she'd been here.'

I felt a huge lump in my throat. Letty said, 'Thank you.' Then she bent forward and kissed me gently on the cheek. 'Thank you for this morning, too,' and as I got myself in a sort of scamper down the stairs, she called, 'Thank you both.'

But this wasn't for Randolph.

Driving her to the station that morning, I'd had it in mind to probe a little – who were 'They', the 'They' who'd answered when she'd phoned her house to ask them about the old Christie's sales slip. I went at it roundabout, telling her what a good sort Margery was. You knew she was there, I said, but she didn't get in the way, and above all didn't try and 'mother' Tom and Adelaide. They wouldn't have put up with that, and her matter-of-factness was unobtrusive – by which I meant she joined in conversations if you promoted them, but didn't bother otherwise – and she kept the house and did the cooking. 'And we have a woman who comes in and cleans, and they get on together.' I was seized with impatience. 'This sounds like someone else's life.'

'Well, yes,' she said, 'because you're telling it.'

'And you?'

'Oh – boring. You know.' Then she said, 'No, nothing. Long time boyfriend. He took off. Sorry. So dull.'

'Someone lives in?'

'No, no. My daily.'

Pulling up at the King's Cross side entrance, no parking, I parked. Walked her to the platform. The train was in.

'Well – bit of an adventure, you've got to allow,' I said.

'And you the hero of the hour.'

I just looked at her. I was smiling.

'I'll tell you what,' I said, 'I'm damned glad you were there.'

She looked at me.

Then she nodded. Walked off down the platform, then halfway along raised her hand, without turning round. Climbed aboard.

When I got back to the car I'd been given a ticket. I just laughed.

Randolph was rejoicing about the Ihara incident. 'You know,' he said, 'I think the man's a howling snob. Japanese, and a snob!'

'Aren't they allowed to be?'

'My God, you should have seen the boss's face when Ihara and I walked into the office together, all smiles. Ah – and it seems it was the stockbrokers' files that touched off the Revenue enquiry – no third man in that bit.'

Randolph had described the Ihara business and I'd told him I thought there was no harm in keeping the man posted about the bidding – indeed, I brought him up to date with Wemdinger's figure and said he could pass it on. What harm could it do? You'd have to be very lace doily to sacrifice a decent job on the grounds that it was forbidden to help the boss.

'Yes, but he's hugely devious. I'd dearly like to find out who Ihara's man is, the one who tipped him off about me being suspended. His sneak, he calls him.'

Carr, the St James's picture dealer, came over, smiling.

'The way you interposed your body between the ravisher and the maiden no one would guess you want to give it all away.'

'Oh, the bloody man just tripped. But listen, Carr, did you telephone, asking where the picture was being stored? Phone the club, I mean?'

'No – why?'

'Well, Prince tells me he had a call from someone – Carter, Carterton, name like yours, he didn't quite get it. Might have been someone passing himself off. How did they know the thing was going to be on show at just that time?'

'Don't suppose they did. Hang around, chance their luck.'

'Well, very lucky.'

Carr said, 'They're put off by real shops, all my stuff's on view, everything, and that's the great protection, they can never be sure they aren't being seen. But once they're inside a strongroom they're as snug as you please. What I *would* bet on,' he added, 'is that they were stealing to order.'

'For the insurance?'

'Oh yes. But carry that further. You're in the market for a Leonardo, along with umpteen other bidders. Let's say – round figures – twenty million—'

I was able to update him. 'Fifty, at the last count.' I told him about Wemdinger. It was rather satisfying.

'And you *still* want to give it away!'

'Not so sure.'

'What I'm getting at – well, all right, the bidder is willing to go to fifty. Now I know you have to have it available, but if you can get a discount of twenty per cent, won't you take it?'

I was slower than Randolph, but after all he is an accountant.

'Twenty per cent. Right? That's ten million—'

'The percentage could be higher,' Carr intervened, I suspect excited by the figures.

'You sell it back to the insurers for, say, ten million. OK?' – oh, those redundant interrogatives! – 'You pay off the thieves – a million. And whatever you hand over for the Leonardo you've got it for nine million less!'

'You mean the Dallas Museum of Timeless Art, or one of the others, is going to hire a bunch of *thieves*?'

'Where it's high value trading, there's always someone wanting to break a bit off the edge for himself,' Carr said. 'They'd have intermediaries, and the intermediaries would have intermediaries. International Corporations fund museums, and at the outer edge of *their* activities they use people they certainly wouldn't invite to dinner.'

'Sounds very fanciful to me.'

'Oh my dear fellow,' said Carr, as he drifted away, 'I sometimes think that anyone not dealing in Old Masters in Duke Street, St James's, must be living in a convent of good women.'

SEVEN

The turn-out for Routh's EGM was pretty well a full house, and the meeting was moved to the ballroom because of the numbers. This elegant venue was used for the Club's Christmas ball and could be hired for parties, but the unfestive atmosphere of the morning made it seem too bright. Men seemed under-dressed as they mounted the curving double staircase, entering the grand salon under a ceiling hung with chandeliers and painted in silvery shades of white and blue – indeed, one member said to another that the place made him feel shabby, and another said it was the sort of place you expected to meet George Sanders. The little gilt sitting-out chairs had been gathered into the centre of the room, and a table covered with green baize, furnished with a carafe of water and two glasses, had been placed under the long windows at the end. Arthur Ledward, as chairman, presided, and the Club secretary sat beside him and took notes. Routh spoke first – he and his meinie had summoned the meeting, and it behoved him to address the members. What follows is an abstract of the secretary's notes. Where a member made a longer statement, he is named, briefer interjections are unidentified.

The Hon. Mr Humphrey Routh: apologies for giving members the inconvenience, though it was a matter of importance. To emphasize that fact, he was able to be brief. He would make three points only: That the monies realized from the sale of the Club's picture belonged to the Club. That every member of the Club was each entitled to an equal share of those monies. And that no majority vote of the members could dispose of any single member's share unless that member as an individual so desired it; the further dispositions of those equal shares were the sole responsibility of the individual member.

A member: Does Mr Routh include honorary members in his proposal?

Mr Routh: No, sir.

A member: What is the legal position?

Chairman invited Mr Richard Owlish to comment.

Mr Owlish: Did not wish to speak except under privilege. It was his belief that Mr Routh's view was sound, but would not vouch for its legal validity.

Mr George Prince, committee member: He believed each member of the club was responsible for his share of the assets or his share of the debts of the club. There was no mutuality.

The Earl of Olney, committee member: Would just like to say he was bewildered by the rush to give these highly valuable assets away.

A member: Why did we all vote for it, then?

A member: Because we were humbugs!

Members interjecting. Chairman called for order.

A member: Are we now saying that we will give no portion of these proceeds to good causes?

Members: No, no!

A member: Who is to decide what those causes should be?

A member: And how much – what percentage?

A member: Could we not use some of the money to refurbish the card-room?

Chairman: I think it is understood that the Club's debts and certain maintenance requirements take priority before any distribution is made.

Members: Hear, hear!

Mr James Carr: There was an important underlying principle in Mr Routh's proposal. That monies belonging to the Club were not to be disposed of on some general whim or impulse. Members were perfectly capable of deciding individually what they felt the priorities were in the light of their personal circumstances, and it was a grotesque intrusion for any other member or members to seek to usurp that right. The proceeds of the picture sale were the property of members and to dictate to anyone what he should do with his own assets was like entering a man's house and telling him how to arrange his furniture.

Members: Hear, hear!

Mr Rupert Forbes, committee member: Saw virtue in Mr Routh's proposals, so forcefully endorsed by Mr Carr. But felt a word of caution would not be out of place. No sale had yet been agreed. Would the chairman let the meeting have a note of the number of bids so far received.

Chairman: There had been seven bids or offers. The first was an offer of £10 million, but this morning I received a note revising this to £30 million. The other six bids range between £20 million and £50 million.

A member: Have we any means of knowing how firm these offers are?

Chairman: In due course, I shall circulate a list of the figures to all who have entered the auction, and invite each to make a final bid. I have no reason to believe the offers are not all made in good faith, and a substantial sum on account will be required as an earnest of that when final bids are made.

A member: Was it ever considered that a public auction at one of the major houses would ensure the top price?

Chairman: Yes, and rejected. It was felt that bidders for the picture would announce themselves, and that to put it up for public auction would be wasteful of the money paid out in commission.

Mr Cosmo Barrington: Can I ask the chairman to tell us what accommodation we have arrived at with the restorer? As his unwitting agent in this matter I should like to assure members that the figure he asks for was none of my prompting. The labourer is worthy of his hire, but frankly ten per cent of many millions is a piece of impudence.

A member: Ten per cent of £50 million is absurd!

A member: Yes, but on what grounds?

Members: Too much!

Chairman: No arrangements have yet been made. I agree, the figure seems preposterous. Are we in his hands, or is he in ours? Perhaps Mr Owlish has a view.

Mr Richard Owlish: There is no doubt we have to pay the man a reasonable fee. But what is reasonable? Ten per cent of the total is his estimate, but as purchasers of his services we take a different view. After all, his finding the picture was as much an accident as us having the thing.

A member: I am doubtful of the logic in that statement. Will he not say it was his skill which uncovered the Leonardo, without which the Club would never have known it was there?

A member: Someone would have found it.

A member: It's ours, not his. It's up to us to strike a price.

Mr Richard Owlish: These speculative points are germane, if hardly conclusive. There was no contract, unless inviting him to submit his invoice is held to be agreement with his terms, which I believe would not be upheld in law. But there's the nub of the matter – to establish an appropriate fee, where both parties are at loggerheads, is to invite a legal process, and that would be expensive. Expensive for both parties, of course, and I doubt if even the best-paid picture restorer would be in a position to fund such a case – unless he was gambling on the outcome, and hoping that costs would be awarded against us. My instinct is to pay the man what we feel is right, and see what happens. One hundred thousand pounds would respect the skills he brought to bear, and would be seen as a reasonable reward for work he had in fact volunteered for and persuaded us to undertake.

Members: Hear, hear!

At this point the meeting was adjourned, the chairman suggesting that he would formulate motions on the proposals suggested, and that in fifteen minutes the meeting would reconvene to agree those motions, and take the votes.

There was a grinding and clatter of chairs being pushed back and men stood in twos and threes to talk over the points that had been raised.

'I don't know if members have fully considered the significance of export licences,' one man said. 'It's all very well the Getty or the Frick putting in their bids, but if they can't get the picture out of the country they won't be too happy.'

'Ah, that's a point,' someone else said. 'The top bid isn't the best one if it's qualified. A good bid is the one that sticks.'

'But is anyone in the auction domiciled in the UK? I suppose we won't overlook that. Would narrow the market, wouldn't it, and a narrow market narrows the price.'

The chairman then announced the meeting to be in session.

Chairman: If we can agree the motions. I have three to put before you. One, to give all the proceeds of the sale to good causes. Two, in the event of that motion failing, what proportion is to be given to good causes. Three, that after necessary disbursements to club requirements and an agreed payment to the picture restorer, the remaining funds be divided equally among the members. Are there any objections? Then I shall proceed.

A member: May we discuss the matter of how the best bid is to be determined?

Chairman: Yes. That will come under Any Other Business after the votes have been taken. Number one, the first motion that the total proceeds of the sale of our Leonardo be given away to good causes. Those in favour?

Votes in favour: 16.

Chairman: Those against the motion?

Votes against: 176.

Charman: The motion is defeated. Second motion: what proportion of the proceeds should be given to good causes, those causes to be determined hereafter. To simplify the procedure I will offer three different percentages, in descending order, and take a vote on each. First, those in favour of giving ten per cent of the proceeds to charities, or similar?

Votes in favour: 27.

Chairman: Those against giving ten per cent?

Votes against: 165.

Chairman: Those in favour of giving five per cent?

Votes in favour: 87

Chairman: Those against giving five per cent?

Votes against: 105.

Chairman: Those in favour of giving one per cent?

Votes in favour: 189.

Chairman: Those against giving one per cent?

Votes against: nil; those abstaining: 3.

Chairman: The motion in favour of giving one per cent of the proceeds of the picture to charitable causes is carried. Third motion: that the proceeds remaining after necessary disbursements are to be divided equally among the membership. Those in favour?

Votes in favour: 163.

Chairman: Those against the motion?

Votes against: 26; those abstaining: 3.

Chairman: The motion is carried. Any other business?

Mr Richard Owlish: With reference to the matter of the one per cent of the proceeds which it has been agreed should be set aside for worthy causes, may I draw the meeting's attention to the intervention of a third party, namely the lady whose lawyers claim is the rightful owner of the picture now in our possession. At the chairman's suggestion, I interviewed this lady and am of the opinion that she will carry her claim no further. However, since it is quite clear that in the ordinary course of inheritance the picture would now be in her possession, may I recommend that as members of this club we should in all decency offer her a share of the one per cent of the principal which is annexed for deserving causes?

Chairman: May I have an informal response to that suggestion?

Members: Aye!

Chairman: So minuted.

A member: Am I to understand that the committee will report back with reference to the prices finally offered, and the firmness of those offers, before acceptance?

A member: There may be reservations on the part of the bidders, particularly in the question of an export licence. May the Club be kept informed of the process of such negotiations?

Chairman: The club will be kept abreast of all such developments. The meeting is closed. (12.45 p.m.)

Forbes watched fondly as Edward auctioned the gifts that had been donated to the church bazaar. He was wearing his new suit and conducted the business in a clear decisive voice that combined amiability with authority. Everyone smiled, especially the ladies, as the young man did his stylish turn as auctioneer.

'Can't let it go at that price, water-colour of the Market Cross by a distinguished member of our art group, great deal of skill, lot of work went into this delightful picture, surely someone will say twenty pounds?'

In this Surrey village, the middle-class residents supported the church whether they were regular attenders or not. It was the sort of ancient gathering place whose site on a grassy knoll was adjacent to a mellow red-brick house or two, and where the churchyard with its cypress trees was neatly mown. Gravestones from the seventeenth and eighteenth centuries still stood upright at attractive angles, their mild inscriptions weathered by wind and rain. On this chill November afternoon, there was a smell of woodsmoke in the air, and people crowded into the porch. The church was packed, all the pews were occupied, and it was standing room only in the rear by the sacristy and along the aisle. At the further end of the nave, raised up above the congregation, Edward as auctioneer occupied the pulpit. Those present had a feeling that this was a place where people had always come together, and that irrespective of any purely religious rite, what people had always done in this place was well done.

'He's a credit to you, Rupert,' smiled the vicar, standing at Forbes's shoulder at the back of the church.

'Oh, it's a shame to take the money, padre, the ladies can't resist him.'

'Well, I'm ready to shout the banns when the time comes.'

'It's not for want of encouragement, I can tell you. Time he was out of the house.'

'You've made him too snug.'

Forbes laughed. His laugh was the well-seasoned baritone of a man who knew the world and was unspoiled by it.

'Do you know, I have a feeling the chap's shy. He magnetizes the girls, but I'm blessed if I think he knows how to make the most of it.' He laughed again. 'I mean, in the nicest possible way, Charles.' And the vicar matched the laugh, antiphonally.

There were traces of red ochre wall paintings in the transept, fleurs-de-lis and faded thirteenth-century figures surfacing dimly in the plaster-wash of time long gone. The roof beams had been renewed in the Victorian era, and a brass plate commemorated the incumbent, rich and well-born, who had funded the work. Along the walls, memorial tablets, swagged about in marble folds as by a curtain-maker, spoke of the piety of the dead. In the dusky recesses beyond the font, the woolly ends of bellropes hung down from the bell-tower like lambs' tails, and the smell inside the church was fusty and consoling.

The picture was sold and, as Edward descended from the pulpit to make his way through the crowded church, Forbes thought how well the regimental tie went with the grey chalk-stripe suit. Edward was genuinely entitled to the tie, having been turned out of the Scots Guards as a boy soldier for importuning. When Forbes had picked him up in a pub in a mews at the back of Knightsbridge, he'd been amazed at the way Edward had immediately taken on the persona he felt was required. Edward fitted in wherever he found himself. He was one of those chameleons who took on the colouring of any background without effort – his style, his accent, his clothes fitted the circumstances they were appropriate to for as long as it was in his interests to maintain a presence. It is a curious fact that people of his kind pass muster in real life, whereas on a stage the mimicry would be too broad to convince an audience – the face-values of real life protect the con man, since nobody is expecting to be deceived.

They walked back home under the bare November trees, and Forbes showed Edward the letter he'd tucked into his wallet. It was now some days after the encounter in St James's Park.

Dear Mr Forbes, it began, *I'm writing to you on behalf of the friend I saw you with in St James's Park* – there followed date and time – *and I'm taking the liberty of putting his address on this message (Mr Jasper, No. 23, Wycroft Avenue, near Tooting Broadway station). He and I met just after you left and he was able to tell me what a boon it would be if he could get from someone a few hundred pounds – I think £500 was the figure he told me would get him clear – to salvage a business that up until now was going so well. As one who loves our open spaces as much as you and he do, I know you won't take my request amiss. If as I hope you can see your way to helping him I understand he would prefer the money in cash as it will simplify matters for him if he doesn't have to put it through his bank. I hope it won't seem arch if on this occasion I withhold my name (not wishing to advertise a helping hand extended to someone in need, and knowing that as a prominent member of the Civil Service you will appreciate the need for discretion).*

Edward said, 'Make you laugh if it didn't make you cry.' After a pause, he went on, 'He recognized you, then? I mean, you aren't a public face, to speak of, are you? So how does he know who you are?'

Forbes shook his head.

'Two of them.' Edward studied the sheet of paper. 'The address being the nonce's you did it with.' Edward paused. 'I could put the frighteners on him.'

'What use would that be? Still the other one.'

'So what you going to do, Rupe? Pay him?'

'What's the alternative?'

'Seems confident you won't go to the police.'

Forbes gave a short laugh.

'Well,' said Edward, 'you could ignore it.' He stared at the paper as they walked on, past the laurels and the chestnut trees. 'See, actually,' he said, 'he wouldn't do anything. I don't see him being able to prove a thing, even with his mate's help. And he'd only incriminate himself.' Then he added, 'But he knows you won't call his bluff because you daren't risk it.'

Forbes said, 'The slightest hint of scandal would put paid to the chances of anything decent in the way of a job after retirement next year – who'd hire anyone bringing lousy publicity with him, when they can hire someone else?'

They walked on in silence.

'Pay him the five hundred,' Edward said. 'Give us time to find out who he is. Then, well.' He handed the letter back to Forbes. 'Do a bit of arranging.'

They turned in at the gate of Oldacres.

As they crunched up the gravel drive, Edward said, 'There's only one way to put a stop to blackmail.' Forbes didn't reply. Right from the start, drinking in the pubs round Beauchamp Place, eating in restaurants along the Old Brompton Road west of South Kensington tube-station – haunts which had been Edward's natural habitat and which had been well away from the homeward-bound routes of Whitehall colleagues – Forbes had sensed that no consideration of right or wrong ever entered Edward's calculation of a course of action: the essential faceless-ness which allowed him to fit in anywhere, to be the person he thought someone else might want him to be, was part of some larger vacancy in which hurt or harm to others, even to himself, did not figure. And this – Forbes pondered what the word should be – this 'absence' was allied to an obsessive single-mindedness which lay behind the success of their domestic masquerade. It was unwavering. And made Edward very useful to the people he worked for. He was one of the creative team at a firm of computer designers, whose strategy was to look ahead the three months necessary for the modification of existing technology so that the big companies like Microsoft and Apple could maintain their ascendancy.

There were dozens of such small cottage think-tanks on the fringes of the southern conurbations round London, freelance satellites of their patrons, jumping ahead of the competition with electronic dodges that weren't exactly discoveries but pushed current convention outward until the line reached its limit and, hitting the buffers, was forced to take another direction. Edward was a member of a small group in a shacky little assembly of Portakabins outside Guildford that was constantly trying to find this new direction before the existing route reached its terminus. His temperament suited him to the task: the native narrowness of his vision meant that concentration was a reflex with him, and since the co-ordinates involved in the work, though numerous, could be precisely assembled, all he needed was diligence. His ability to bring his attention exclusively and without distraction to bear on the matter in hand gave him clout at Quantum Solutions, so much so that his hours were unregulated and the morning following the receipt of the letter he set off for London with freedom to get back to work when he felt like it.

At Waterloo he used Forbes's debit card to withdraw £500 from a cash dispenser, then took a tube to Knightsbridge. Handing in his ticket, he looked to see if there were telephone books on the wall by the phones, but finding none, went across the road to the post office. He looked through the Js in the South West London book – there was no Jasper, 23 Wycroft Avenue. So the number wasn't listed. Then Edward hurried out, crossed the road by Harrods, and on the corner of Yeoman's Row pushed through the swing doors of the Grapes. The man he'd arranged to meet was standing at the bar.

'Well, it's the boy.'

'Tom. Haven't got the number yet but I'm seeing the bloke and I'll give you a bell when I've got it.'

'Consider it done. I owe you one.'

'Ace! You'll let me have a tape?'

'No worries. Send it where?' Edward gave him the address of Quantum Solutions.

Then Edward made his way to South Kensington and the tube to Tooting Broadway. Friends in low places sometimes did more for you than people higher up – less to lose: the ex-copper in the Grapes had friends in the Met who'd tap a phone for him, and since Edward in the past had played go-between in little deals involving drugs stored at police stations (it was why the man was ex), he'd repay the favour.

Edward came out into Tooting Broadway and turning west towards Colliers Wood, made his way down the fly-blown high street, stopping in at a Halal butcher's to ask directions. Wycroft Avenue was one of countless terraces of houses which twenty years before the First World War had obliterated the market gardens of south London, skeins of small villas thrown across the landscape to house a labour force of clerks, turned out by the board-schools able to read and write, and then recruited in their thousands by the counting houses of the City. Between Tooting and Merton, the gentrification of such streets had still some way to go, but the whirligig of time had so far extinguished the memory of the serfs for whom the houses had been built that young middle-class wives with husbands on the lower rungs of advertising or PR now wheeled their double pushchairs along these bricky groves with the purposeful air of people whose eye was already on Esher.

No 23 was in the vanguard when it came to enlightened refurbishment: the original astragal glazing above the sash windows had been kept when all the other houses in the street had lost it and the wooden porch with its short vertical rungs in the canopy, and the front door itself, had been sanded down to the softwood beneath.

'Phyllis! Phee-lees!'

Edward heard a high fluting male voice ringing out from the interior of the house when he rang the bell, and the door was opened by a matronly woman in dungarees.

'Come in, sweetie,' the voice from the interior warbled, and Edward stepped into a space that ran from back to front, and from side to side of the house: something not envisaged by the jobbing builders who thought Nature had intended their dwellings to feature a front room, a back room, a passage and a kitchen. A willowy man in black trousers, open-necked black shirt and with a chain round his neck, flickered down the staircase into the room – flickered as a certain sort of actor does, who comes to the end of his dialogue, then agitates his head to indicate he is about to move out of frame in a television close-up.

'Ducky, how nice to see you. Phyllis! Phee-lees! Coff-eeee. She's such a dear. Wish she'd wear the mob cap I gave her. She *balked*. Such a fashion accessory. *Do* sit down.'

Edward sat on what looked like a chair by Charles Rennie Mackintosh. He began to say, 'Look, my name's Edward Forbes, I've brought you the loan you needed—'

'Of *course* you have. I knew, I simply *knew* it would be brought by some nice person.' The man sat down on a three-legged stool, holding his knees together as though he were an ageing schoolmistress. His hair was grey, cropped very short, revealing a bald spot like a tonsure on the crown of his head. 'The sandwich bar – well, you and I know it isn't going to be the Princess Margaret set' – he let out a yodelling laugh – 'lets you know my age, ducky – but you know *quite* nice people patronize it, and when my friend – not that I know him *that* well' – he simpered – 'suggested he might be able to arrange a little loan, well, I said, I'd never have the *nerve*—'

The woman came in with coffee and a plate of biscuits.

'Lovely, darling. Mother will pour. Decaff?'

The woman went out and the man passed Edward a tiny cup seated in a frilly metal holder.

'Oh my, where's my manners! I'm Billy Jasper and it's ever so kind of—' He looked enquiringly at Edward.

'My uncle.'

'Nunky. Sweet of him. But I really can't say I know his friend at all well.' Lowering his voice slightly, he said, 'Bit cheeky of his chum, really. That's what I thought.'

'He didn't say who he was?'

'Ooh, no, ever so close-lipped. Gave him my address when we met in the park, but he didn't give me his. And then it wasn't till he telephoned a couple of days ago that I had any *idea* about the loan. More coffee?' He moved across delicately, and refilled Edward's cup. 'I can tell you were at a good school, stands out a mile.'

Edward never decided beforehand how to play things, his strategy was to graft himself on to whatever style the third party presented him with. Now he picked up on the man's hint and in his cavalry twill trousers and hacking jacket he became entirely the upper-middle-class boy. For a moment he thought of calling the man 'sir' but decided it was over the top.

'Well, my uncle's in the same position, since the man didn't sign the letter. Of course, he may not have wanted to advertise himself as doing someone a good turn, but I couldn't help thinking it was a bit peculiar. Of course, the fellow knows who my uncle is, otherwise he couldn't very well have written to him, could he?'

Edward did some simple, earnest blinking as he asked the question, and Billy Jasper gave him a solemn look.

'Hadn't thought of that – hadn't thought of that. Perhaps he's a colleague at work.'

'Mr Jasper,' Edward said, 'something doesn't seem quite right to me.'

'Oh, call me Billy – *please*.'

'You know, what I can't quite fathom out is whether he has any personal interest in the money. Apart from doing you a good turn, I mean.'

Here, Mr Jasper telegraphed embarrassment.

'Now Edward – may I? – I don't know what your uncle has told you—'

Edward was ready for this. 'Oh, that you and he had done something foolish – he didn't specify – I assumed it was something to do with your business – and this mysterious other chap –

well,' – Edward seemed to struggle, as though overcoming a public-school reluctance to impute bad motives to anyone – 'as well as wanting to do you a favour, well, might have been rather holding it over you both. Sorry if that sounds a bit cynical.'

Billy Jasper pursed his lips and did a Widow Twanky nod or two, as though there was more he could say but he didn't quite like to.

'Uncle knows best.' He proffered the biscuits. 'It's not illegal, not now, anyway – but it *could* be embarrassing. Quite frankly, I agree with you. The whole arrangement seems a bit iffy to me.'

'Uncle wonders what the other chap's game is. Oh, here it is, by the way' – Edward pulled out the bundle of notes – 'do hope it helps you to straighten things out. But isn't the other fellow running a risk? I mean, I don't know much about these things, but if the police heard about it, it might look rather rum, don't you think?'

Billy Jasper darted a look at the pile of notes on the table.

'I mean, I don't want to interfere, but when you see him, do you think it might be as well to point out—'

Billy Jasper said, 'He did say he was a bit strapped for cash himself. You say he didn't sign the letter?'

'No, just left it for you to deal with – your address and everything. That's why I was able to find you.'

The man sipped his coffee and looked over the top of the cup at Edward, rather watchfully.

'Nobody knows who *he* is. But he put my name up front. Right?'

'Oh well, of course, he had to do that. He was wanting my uncle to help you. Must give him his due.'

'Oh, yes,' said Billy Jasper, 'we must.' Then he got up and hooted again. 'Phee-lees! More coffee.'

Edward said, 'Not for me, thanks. Must be getting along. Look, would you awfully mind if I used your phone? Girlfriend – I'm going to be late.'

'Lucky girl! Hope she looks after you.'

Edward went across to the phone which was draped in a frilly dress, like a child's doll. Started to dial at random, then put the phone down. 'Oh lord, I'd forgotten. She's out shopping! Must dash.'

He shook hands with Billy Jasper.

'Ooh, what a fierce handshake! But thanks ever so.'

'You might mention to your colleague what I suggested.'

'Definitely. As I say, it's all a bit of a mystery to me. Best to uncle. Keep in touch.'

You bet I will, thought Edward, as he turned down Wycroft Avenue and took out his mobile. 'Tom?' And he gave him Billy Jasper's number. When he got the tape, there'd be something to go on. They'd have the other man's voice. It might help.

EIGHT

A public row now started. The attempted theft had put the picture back on to the front pages for a day or so, and hacks were saying that in hiding the thing away as though it was simply a pile of loot rather than one of the world's great masterpieces the Club was behaving like a lottery winner who didn't want the neighbours to know.

The Club is auctioning it to the highest bidder, wrote a tabloid columnist, *and they are splitting the take among themselves. There had been high-falutin talk about handing out the cash to good causes, but the tightfisted members have had second thoughts.*

Charity begins at home, they crow, as they tuck into their oysters and Chablis in the ornate dining-room at their St James's Street premises (the building is valued at upwards of £30 million). Millionaires and blue-bloods make up the membership, and with their Chelsea mansions and second homes none of them is short of a bawbie or two.

Good luck to them. But before they sit down cross-legged on the carpet to share out the swag, what about letting the rest of us have a sight of the golden goose, before it's buried in some rich man's trophy room, or gathers dust on the wall of some American museum? The common gaze will not affect the gilt on their gingerbread.

And there was a correspondence in *The Times*. *Sir – I am not a member of a 'club'* – one correspondent wrote, well aware of the power of a pair of inverted commas to imply the discreditable – *and the members are welcome to the arcane rituals with which they seek to prolong their schooldays. But great masterpieces belong to the world, and for some small self-selected group to refuse the people sight of a great national treasure is surely a matter for Parliament. This is the mean spirit which put paid to the statue of Princess Diana. Yours etc, E.J. Bamford, Leamington Spa.*

Sir – I wonder if your correspondents, in their understandable interest in the picture bequeathed to us by the generosity of a past member, have considered the security problems involved? It is common knowledge that the picture was imperilled, even under the strictest surveillance, and this must give any sensible person pause when they urge that it be put on general view. However, I know that my fellow members would like nothing better, and any practical suggestion as to how this might be contrived without jeopardy to the heirloom which, by great good fortune, belongs to them, would be welcome. Yours sincerely, Arthur Ledward, Chairman, The Club, St James's Street.

Sir – I was amused to read that your correspondent from Leamington Spa refers to the Leonardo picture as 'a great national treasure'. I have no doubt that the citizens of Florence, where Leonardo began the picture, or of Milan where he almost certainly finished it, would agree. Does he therefore suggest it should be returned to either of these cities, which would involve no more than a brief touch-down by the cargo plane carrying the Elgin Marbles back to Athens? Yours obediently, Erica Burton, Wells-next-the-Sea.

Sir – Envy is not a pretty emotion. What the Club does with its own property is the concern of the members and nobody else. I seem to hear a note from far-off childhood days in some of the sentiments, expressed by your correspondents – 'Why didn't I get a present too?' To which the answer is simply, 'This time, it wasn't your *birthday!' Sincerely, John F. Murtough, Welshpool.*

Sir – In response to Mr Arthur Ledward's query about security, I can assure you and him that whatever the premises and however valuable the contents, this can be arranged, tested, and guaranteed, fully insured, with the minimum of disruption, and usually within the day. Yours very sincerely, J.R. Mountfort, Mountfort Security, Edmonton, London.

Sir – How many orphans from Rumania would the many millions accruing to the Club from the sale of their Leonardo picture save from the squalor and misery and starvation of their present condition? These kids need the money, I doubt the Club people do. I do understand that we can't all devote our time to ferrying supplies to those who desperately need them, but those who stay at home can always put their hands in their pockets. Ama Jones, Mission to Rumania, Cockfosters.

So it went on show. Between the hours of four and six o'clock the public could walk up the now roped-off stairs – roped off for no better reason than that those who shambled in weren't to feel the actual staircase was open to them, only the bit that led to the ballroom where the picture was on view. There'd been a hotly debated session about what the hours should be, and it was finally decided that members who were playing snooker or asleep at four wouldn't notice any intrusion, and that round about six when other members were dropping in for a drink, the public would be gone. The security arrangements had indeed been deft, and there were two guards on duty, day and night.

But the row now took a rather surprising turn. One apparently anonymous member of the public turned out to have been the Swedish art historian Lars Jochimsen whose speciality was Italian masters of the late fifteenth and early sixteenth century – indeed, it was Jochimsen's analysis which had definitively identified the kneeling angel on the left of Verrocchio's *Baptism of Christ* as by Leonardo – of course, Leonardo was Verrocchio's apprentice, and such assistance would have been in the course of things, but it was Jochimsen's painstaking assessment which set the seal on what had often been surmised. Jochimsen's word carried enormous clout in the world of high art, and a cautious nod or a smile of agreement from the grey-bearded Swede was worth any amount of gasps of admiration from lesser fry. But a gasp of admiration was precisely what Jochimsen sent up when he came to write an article about the *Leda*. The piece appeared first in the Swedish cultural magazine *Artis* but reached out world-wide when it was reprinted in *Time*. Members who wouldn't have known a Swedish art historian from a man who trained seals picked up *Time* in the Club reading-room, and knowing it was their picture the man was going on about, felt they were in the swim.

Not one of the museums from round the world had questioned the authenticity of the picture, their anxiety was to possess it. All the bidders had received photographs, and when it came time to put cash on the table they would send their representatives to look beadily at the actual object, but as the Bury Street dealer, Carr, enjoyed telling other members of the Club, authenticity was almost wholly in the eye of the beholder – if you wanted it to be the real thing, it was. The lust to possess was what closed the deal. The purchaser became so involved with the desired object that it began to reflect his own authenticity: if it wasn't the real thing, what did that make him? Carr was a highly professional dealer, and therefore as a psychologist perhaps a little self-serving.

The discovery of a Leonardo, hitherto unknown, would have excited museums throughout the world, but perhaps it hasn't been sufficiently emphasized that this particular Leonardo *had* been heard of, but never seen since Leonardo's own time – it had been classed as 'lost'. In writings by contemporaries of the artist it was often spoken of, but the quality of the picture could only be guessed at when you considered the copies made by other artists. Jochimsen had in his time examined all the *Leda* copies – the 'free' copies as the jargon had it, copies made by artists who had seen other copies – and paid them the respect they deserved, which in some cases was scant enough, but in others (particularly in the case of the *Leda* painted by Bugiardini that hangs in the Borghese) was more than dutiful. But (so Jochimsen pursued his theme) it was in comparison with the best of these that he knew when he saw the Club's *Leda* that here was the real thing. He scouted the notion that the original had been burnt in the eighteenth century by Madame de Maintenon when she had become old and prudish – there was not a scrap of evidence that she had done any such thing, this was hearsay that had become mythologized. *Some* version of the picture had been seen at the Château of Fontainbleau in 1625, by a traveller passing through, but he, Jochimsen, would not be the first art historian to discount this casual reference on the part of a tourist, more especially because the picture had reportedly been in such a poor state of preservation it would have been impossible to judge it.

Jochimsen's analysis of the composition of the Club's version of the *Leda*, along with the technique of the brush strokes and his detailed account of the posture of the naked woman, had been edited down in the *Time* article. They left in the bit about the swan's neck as phallus, and Jochimsen's survey of the picture's imagery: the constellation of The Plough picked out in the darkening sky, the lush red fruit on the bushes, the *putti* rather bizarrely bursting out of eggs on the grass at the lady's feet, these were emblems of fecundity, achieving their apotheosis in the warm, sensual depiction of the naked figure and the tumescent swan. Jochimsen's trumpet-blast of admiration was clearly based on scholarly understanding, and because the picture was now on the world stage as a prize in terms of money and prestige, his piece, somewhat simplified in the *Time* version, thereby commanded deference from the learned and the vulgar alike.

Among the latter was Cosmo Barrington, whose friend Firethorne, the restorer, had made the discovery. Barrington was dimly aware that Jochimsen's endorsement wouldn't do any harm to the price and by this time very few members could lay their hands on their hearts and say they weren't dividing the figure by 250 (the number of full members the Club restricted itself to, and which accounted for its very long waiting list) to find out what their shares were going to be. Take £50 million as a nice round figure, that meant each member received a cheque for round about £200,000. 'Pay your bus-fare home,' said Barrington.

And then an article appeared in the London *Evening Standard*. It was a shrewd and well-aimed shot at promoting a controversy. The paper printed an excerpt from Jochimsen's *Time* piece, and then printed the other article – wry and contradictory – underneath. But here was the queer twist. The piece questioning Jochimsen's judgement was written by Firethorne, the man who'd discovered the picture.

'What on earth is the bloody man thinking of?' fumed Barrington. 'Talking down the picture, talking down the price! My God, it's like Livingstone going round telling people it wasn't Africa he discovered, it was only Basingstoke!'

There was his by-line – C.W. Firethorne – along with his credentials and a puff for his brilliant detective work, and his piece had been sardonic and detached. At the time of the discovery the journalists had only been concerned to get him to describe how he'd dug the hidden picture out of the frame, the question of authenticity being taken for granted, and now that he was going to the mat with Jochimsen he didn't exactly say the picture was a copy, but implied that the criteria for establishing otherwise had not been met.

Jochimsen had made reference to the left-hand corner of the mouth turning into the shadow of the cheek, so that it might or might not be a smile – reminiscent of the *Mona Lisa*. But Firethorne pointed out that this use of *sfumato* was so much a Leonardo trademark that it would be the first touch that a craftsman with the necessary skill might fasten on to. Hard to judge, since of course Leonardo had created his own special version of that technique from hints absorbed from the work of, among others, Masaccio, the father of Florentine painting. But to press the point, consider that same effect in the best of the copies which he, Firethorne, took to be the one by Cesare da Sesto at Wilton House; this would have been painted in Leonardo's own workshop between 1507 and 1510, and if da Sesto had not hit the mouth off to admiration – done it as well as, or possibly even better than, Leonardo himself – then he, the writer, was a Dutchman. Or possibly a Swede.

This sour little parenthesis indicated that something rankled. Was it Firethorne's status as a restorer – something of an artisan, Jochimsen might have said? And though Firethorne could class himself as an art historian – the strap-line above his piece made this clear – his reputation in that category was a good few rungs below the other man's; in setting up his own opinions against those of the star he was a bit like a member of the chorus stepping forward to volunteer a solo. But the single most aggravating factor for Firethorne would have been Jochimsen's proprietorial tone: unavoidable, in someone whose professional enthusiasm had been so engaged, and whose word was law, or ought to have been – he may not have discovered the picture, but in claiming it *for* Leonardo, he was claiming it for himself. No wonder the junior contender was irked – it was his *nous*, his work, his doing, and then the senior figure steps into the limelight which the subordinate has unthinkingly turned on for him. The attempt on C.W. Firethorne's part to switch this off again wasn't going to work – limelight follows those who attract it, and knows nothing of sharing. That Firethorne's feelings were strong is amply attested by his willingness to cast doubt on his own discovery – his was the eye which had first spotted the possibility latent in the signature, and whose diligence had revealed the hidden picture for what it truly was or, according to him, what it truly *might* be. But though one man's opinion is said to be as good as another's, it never seems to work like that.

'And furthermore,' said Barrington, 'I don't believe we kept on the right side of him by telling him he wasn't going to get the commission he was after. Pay him a flat rate of a hundred thousand when we get the money, and he doesn't give a damn about keeping the price up.'

His article turned up the volume, no doubt about it, it promoted a debate where there hadn't been one before. But the effect may not have been what Firethorne had been looking for. Instead of scaring the institutions off, it seemed to whet their appetite. To have someone of lower rank jousting with a man whose reputation was second to none in the field, a man whose pre-eminence underwrote the authenticity of the picture, had added depth and dimension to the discovery. Firethorne's views were seen as those of a younger man – he was indeed that, though not by much – who having got lucky in stumbling across the picture, now put his name forward as someone who was to be taken into account, holding his hand up for a meed of attention, but by no means being able to wrestle the senior figure away from the ground on which he stood; indeed, leaving Jochimsen's reputation enhanced, by making it clear it was worth assailing. One man's opinion is not as good as another's.

So the practical consequences of the Firethorne intervention were as follows: a week or so after the *Standard* piece appeared The Museum of Timeless Art in Dallas improved its offer by a further £10 million – this was the implication of the note signed by Carl-Heinz Wemdinger which was received by the secretary of the Club: it made a total (provided certain conditions were met) from Dallas of £60 million. And the day following that, the President of Pacific Rand increased his own offer by the same amount: which made a total bid from the Japanese of £40 million. The general impression was that other interested parties were simply holding their fire, assessing their own positions in the light of what their rivals had revealed of their own game: the Frick and the Kunsthistorisches and the Getty, and now in addition, the Louvre, had e-mailed the Club office, asking to be kept abreast of the state of play, and the committee had been ready to sanction this.

There was also a sense that the commercial realities of the situation were much closer to the surface in the Club than they had begun by being. Men were discussing the likely outcome of what was now openly referred to, in plainer terms than they would have used at the time of the first EGM. Then it was that the money was first apprehended by the committee as a presence, but now it had made itself thoroughly at home: it was almost as much a member of the Club as the members themselves. The idea of millions had become familiar.

In the bar, I heard some conversation.

'Won't change things, will it?' one member asked another. 'And yet,' he went on, after a moment's pause, 'why do I ask such a question, if the possibility hadn't occurred to me?'

'Come on. It's only two hundred thousand apiece.'

The first member nodded. Then said, 'Not sure about only.'

'What I mean, two hundred thousand doesn't change things,' his companion said. 'It isn't stuff like oil-wells or a gold-mine, stuff that turns men into something they weren't before. Listen, a couple of hundred thousand corrupts nobody. It's there for the – well, curtains, if you like, or school fees—'

'Well, come on yourself. School fees be damned, you could put ten kids through school for the money.'

'Yes, I know, I may be exaggerating a little to make the point. What I'm actually saying is, that sort of handout doesn't give you power.'

'God help us, power, no, there I agree, but depends what you mean by power. No, no, don't tell me, let me tell you – you mean power over others – ah, yes, yes, you do! – but real power is power over your own circumstances, and I say a couple of hundred thou may well help you towards that happy state, when before you were only reaching for it.'

'Rich is rich.'

'True enough, and you hear people in the papers letting on they're rich because they've got four or five long ones. Power over their own circumstances, perhaps, but not what I'd call rich.'

'I see we're agreed!'

'Ah – um – oh dear, you may be right.'

Such a conversation was impossible to imagine before the millions had walked into the place and taken the best armchairs. Curtains, school fees, a new kitchen, landscape the garden. Did everyone have such modest ideas? I wondered what Routh would do with his share of the money he had ensured would now be at the disposal of each member. Spalding could shower it on his wife. My brother-in-law would welcome it unaffectedly. But I was vaguely disquieted by two aspects of the matter: Randolph's association with Ihara, and my own bid at the EGM for a slice to go to Letty Barlow. On the face of it, neither of these considerations should have been a source of worry, but they made me feel faintly uncomfortable. Randolph had accepted Ihara's intervention in getting him back his job, and the quid pro quo was scarcely something he'd have to consult his conscience about – as I'd told him; still less, now the bidding was pretty well out in public, with the papers running paragraphs as the numbers moved upwards. But I felt that having a foot in both camps probably wasn't the attitude in which most people would want their portrait painted. When I'd reassured Randolph, had I been reassuring myself? For the thought of making a plea for Letitia Mary Barlow to have a share of whatever percentage would go to good causes was already in my head when I'd lunched with him, just after the failed heist. Did this put my own feet in both camps? Certainly not on the premise that my argument at the EGM was spurious – as I'd said, the picture was only ours by accident, in the ordinary course of events it would have come down to her via the estate of Thomas Percy Anstruther. Wasn't she deserving of consideration, especially since it looked as though she wasn't going to drag us through some costly legal action? So why the unease? I found it hard to hold this question in focus long enough to find an answer. Fleeting impressions of the woman – rolling up the sleeve of her cashmere sweater, or pale with shock after the robbery, or walking down the railway platform and raising her hand to say goodbye. And her gentle face at the door of my own guest-room, thanking me with a kiss for my care, a kiss whose tenderness was a courtesy to the person she knew I wished had been there. But I hadn't done my stuff at the EGM as a sort of bouquet, a present, a gallantry. And even if I had, it didn't invalidate anything. Yet it made me moody. The Club knew I'd met her, knew what my professional opinion was, knew – well, it knew damn all, actually. Or perhaps I really meant *I* knew damn all. So far, I hadn't told Letty about the events of the EGM, I was not at all sure that our two meetings entitled me to suggest a third, though I was certain a third was something I didn't want to do without. And then it struck me she might only agree to such a thing because I'd kicked over the bastard who'd made her lie down on the floor – she might agree to visit me as Mrs Miniver might visit some war hero in a hospital, to be kind. This was a demoralizing thought.

But an impulse to be kind to the disadvantaged is sometimes on view in a club. The impulse is often impure and has much to do with a member's frame of mind. He sees there isn't anyone else about, he wonders how to pass the next ten minutes, is confident the encounter won't be prolonged, and is fairly convinced the man he would avoid sitting next to at lunch – a meal offers no opportunity for escape – will be grateful. At the back of his mind, he is in the mood to condescend. So after the two who had been talking of money left the bar, I walked over to Spalding who was the only other person present and asked him what he would like to drink. I am pretty sure the way I suspected he must feel forever one down because of the public assault he had suffered at the hands of his wife on the evening of the Leonardo party, underlay my action.

'That's very sporting of you. I'll take a small whisky.'

The phrase 'I'll take' smote the ear like an echo from the tumuli of saloon bars of long ago, and I found myself thinking even more patronizingly of the man – I might have been on some sort of anthropological safari and my unforgiveable descent upon poor Spalding was equivalent to Margaret Mead sitting down at a camp-fire with a man who had a bone through his nose. Be assured that the operatic style with which I describe my feelings is a measure of the shame I feel at having to report them. And there is no such thing as a 'small' whisky in the Club, the measures are uniform.

'Here's how,' Spalding said to me, as he raised his glass.

Casting about for a conversational gambit, and recalling I'd seen Spalding at breakfast with Routh after the Leonardo dinner, I said, 'I was just wondering what use Routh might have for his share of the money. After arguing that we should all get it, I wouldn't be surprised if he gives his part of it away.'

'Great man,' said Spalding, and I suddenly realized how false his moustache looked. I hadn't taken it in except as a feature that was not out of place with his general address. It was a Franz-Joseph affair, white, disagreeably flourishing, and so bogus in every sense I felt he might not mind if I stretched out my hand

and pulled it off, making him laugh. But the next thought was: it's real, but somewhere inside he doesn't think it is. And the feeling I'd had that my approach would be taken as a kindness started to diminish.

'Great man, Routh,' Spalding said, in a suddenly important voice. 'Don't know when I've ever met such integrity.' His tone enjoined agreement.

'I don't know him, of course, but I'm sure you're right.' My dislike of Spalding had hitherto been a simple prejudice, but his prescriptive tone made me feel there were going to be grounds for it. I also recognized I was getting what I'd asked for.

'Are you disinterested in religion?'

'Disinterested?'

This is the last time I give myself the pleasure of patronizing anyone, I thought. I'll never do it again.

'Look, why don't you tell me what—'

He held up an important hand.

'I understand, I understand, not a question you hear much these days. But your man Routh is different.'

Your man! It was very difficult to suppress a yelp.

'No show, no display, just good old dedication.'

'I thought he put the case very succinctly.'

Spalding gave me a full-frontal eye-bulge.

'Not so, but far otherwise.' It occurred to me Spalding may have had a whisky or two before the one I'd so officiously bought for him. 'I do not speak anent Routh's endeavours re division of the spoils, I just want to go on record as someone who appreciates the man for the efforts he makes. Don't get me wrong. Myself, I'm not a religious man, but I do not believe anyone could see Routh in action without being impressed by the man's one hundred per cent sincerity.'

Spalding's solemn tone sounded familiar, but I couldn't quite place it. And then I had it: a disc-jockey being serious at an awards ceremony.

'Religious?'

'Not the flavour of the month, is it, not top of the charts just now. Wouldn't you say? But those old-fashioned values still persist here and there. I'd say Routh and those of his persuasion keep something alive that is in great danger of withering away and perishing from the earth.'

'Look, Spalding,' I said, 'I'm not at all clear what you're driving at.'

He clicked his fingers at the barman, and when he did it I was mystified again how he could ever have been elected.

'Oh, thank you, nothing for me. But tell me – what is all this about religion?'

'That's exactly what they said at the office. Religion. It won't play. We take this account, we take that account, we are not, I repeat *not*, in the tendacious business of picking and choosing. All right!' He snapped out these last two words as though imitating someone in authority, and then I thought, no he isn't, he's imitating someone else's imitation. And wasn't the word 'tendentious'?

'All right. So be it. We're in business to show a profit, and I am not going to deny that. But if we turn down an account simply because it's going to be uphill work, well' – Spalding drank some of his whisky, then turned his face towards me as though the moustache were a dowser's rod that had helped him winkle out many a skiver before – 'then all I can say is, we are a nothing people.'

What I realized then did neither of us credit. I recognized his portentousness had no bottom, and I recognized that this was what had impelled me to accost him; he was no challenge.

'Do you know, I don't believe I know what it is you do,' I said, prevaricating, and taking up his self-approving allusion to his own occupation.

'We help people to make the best of themselves. I think that puts it in a nutshell.'

'Oh – PR, of *course*,' I said, my tone combining admiration with worldliness in one fraudulent emulsion.

'That's a rather old-fashioned concept,' he said, 'a rather limited view—'

'Well, I *am* a bit old-fashioned, I daresay. I never got used to complaints being called customer relations.'

'But my dear chap, that's exactly it! Call it complaints, and that's what you get. But customer services means How can I help you.'

'I never got used to that, either.'

'You see, a man invents a bagless vacuum cleaner but does that mean his skills include self-presentation?'

'Oh that chap. I thought he was rather good at it.'

'That's simply a for instance. No one wants to see anyone up there in the high winds of publicity, not knowing how to trim the aircraft. When it comes to marketing, I don't care whether it be a combine harvester or a political agenda, at the people level we offer a helping hand.'

'You put the best gloss on it. Without actually lying, of course.'

'Richard' – I suppressed a wince – 'this is a people industry. Being people friendly is not perjury.'

'So they have to like *you*. You get the people to like you first, and then it follows they like your clients? I mean, the ones' – I hesitated for the phrase, then got it – 'your clients are pitching to.' I followed this with a lot of nods and he saw I'd got the general idea, while suspecting I didn't have any real notion of the higher maths of the thing.

'There's a moral dimension to everything, and I don't mind telling you,' and here he lowered his voice, 'that when we were approached by certain mid-East interests to run their policies past the satraps who count in our sector, well—'

'You turned them down?'

'We thought very long and very hard. And we only accepted the account after getting agreement to certain adjustments which allowed us the freest possible hand.'

'Commensurate' – I nodded understandingly – 'with their interests being forwarded. Of course. Couldn't be otherwise.'

'Richard, people skills involve a knack of keeping an eye on the ball without looking beady – absolutely indispensable. And an open mind.'

'But not so open that the door bangs.'

'That's right,' he said, surprised by a pupil who was proving more apt than he'd suspected.

I looked at my watch. 'Well—'

'And Routh. We took his people on board, and frankly, I think you'd find they've never regretted it. Look, you said you were interested.' Spalding fished in his jacket pocket. 'Here's their next venue.' He looked at the card he'd drawn out. 'Church of the True Reconciliation.' He handed it to me.

I stared at the card.

'You mean, Routh is a – what do you call them – fundamentalist?'

'And fundamentalist means basic. Back to basics.'

'No, no, hold on, is that one of those jumping up and down outfits?'

'They let their feelings appear.'

'A holy Roller? I mean, I thought they were black—'

'No, not black, the foundation is American, of course, and their enthusiasm is something to behold. If you were to look in at their next rally I'm not saying you'd be converted, but I fancy you'd be surprised.'

I was already that.

NINE

When Edward came home from Quantum Solutions he waved the tape at Forbes. 'Got it.'

He went over to the drinks table.

'Nice and clear. I had a quick listen.'

Forbes said, 'Discreetly, I hope.'

'My little office is sound-proof. Has to be.'

It was a mild evening for a winter month, the double windows were open and the soothing murmur of traffic rose up to the house high on the flank of the hill. Forbes strolled out on to the terrace and smelling the air, thought of spring. The cars were a moving chain of lights in the valley below. Behind him, the comfortable square armchairs and the sconces on the walls in the long room, the portrait by de Lazlo of his mother in a clinging blue evening dress, holding a cigarette, her blonde hair in a Twenties shingle, the baby grand with the framed photographs, the dark-red rugs on the parquet floor, the log fire crackling behind the broad hearth – Forbes had always felt that no other sort of house could be quite so real as this one, its gables and its red scalloped hanging tiles, the diamond panes in its wide bay windows, even the garage masquerading as a stables, with its neat little belfry, had always seemed to him from his earliest days to be the house in any children's story that he read – the sort of house a boy came home to in a school story (his father had copies of *Chums* and the *Boys Own Annual* from his own childhood) or set out from, as in *Swallows and Amazons*, a house more real than any other because it seemed to him like a story he was being told, rather than a place he was living in – a story told by his mother, as he sat on the stairs in his pyjamas watching the guests arriving for one of her parties, or ate breakfast at the sunlit table under the window in the dining-room while she decided on her menu for the day, or rambled importantly along the narrow lanes with his books as a day-boy to Charterhouse; even his father (and his companion portrait by the same artist hung at the head of the first flight of stairs, three-quarter length, in the full dress uniform of a major of the Blues – 'the Galloping Grocers', his father would laugh, recalling the old jibe), even his father seemed complete in the way someone in a story is, and Forbes's lifelong conviction that he was part of an unalterable tableau vouched for by his mother had left him with an unthinking allegiance to appearances: if those were maintained, the story could not falter.

Edward poured them both whiskies. 'Let's give it a go,' he said, and pushed the cassette into the machine. He pressed the 'Play' button.

'It starts here,' he told Forbes. 'The relevant bit.'

'Hullo,' came the camp voice of Billy Jasper. 'Hullo.'

'Hullo.'

'Yes?'

'Mr Jasper?'

'Oh, it's you.'

'Yes.'

You feel amused when you get a crossed line, but how swiftly the dullness of other people's conversation quenches all expectation – telephone conversations in which you take no part are banal. But then Forbes and Edward heard this—

'It worked?'

'I've got it.'

Forbes sat forward, the one person this conversation was not intended to be heard by.

'Nice young fellow. Five hundred in twenties.'

There was a silence, a pause.

'How do you want your half. I mean,' – this was Billy Jasper – 'It's a bit awkward. How will you get it?'

'No worries,' said the other voice. 'We'll get that sorted. He ask any questions?'

'Well – he was sort of wide-eyed. Seemed to believe about it being a loan.'

'Yes.' There was another silence. 'Well, tuck it away. I'm writing another note.'

Then Billy Jasper was heard to say, 'He was wondering about the police.'

'In what way?'

'What they'd think.'

'An act of kindness. A loan.'

Silence.

'But your man doesn't know me. Does he? I don't even know *you*. Do I?'

'Friend of a friend.'

'I mean. I'm not sure about any of this.'

'Well – another couple of thousand wouldn't be unwelcome, would it? Who's going to tell the police?'

Silence.

'Has he got money like that?'

'Oh, he's got it. A very senior civil servant. With everything to lose. Didn't I mention that?'

Another silence. Then the man speaking to Billy Jasper said, 'Everything being so unfair.'

After another pause, Billy Jasper said, 'Well, look, my name's the one that's known.'

'I'm trusting you with the cash, you trust me with the game plan. I'll be in touch.'

Forbes stared at his glass, then picked it up and drained it. Then he said, 'The voice struck a chord. Perhaps it wasn't the voice, more the way of speaking—' He broke off. 'I'm sure I've heard a man whose style – and then the voice too – that bit about everything being unfair. When he said it I thought I recognized something.'

Edward said, 'Someone with a grudge?'

'Can't think of anyone. There are men I left behind, overtook, in the Service. But this one's manner. Doesn't sound right. And if it was someone harbouring a grudge, surely he'd enjoy bringing me down. Asking for money seems somehow too bloody mere.'

Edward said, 'Don't leave out anyone who wouldn't mind bringing you down *and* taking the money.'

Forbes walked across to the drinks table and poured himself a second whisky.

'Is your man still tapping the phone?'

'Yes.'

Forbes asked Edward to turn the cassette back, and heard it through again. Something was familiar. The voice or its style. Some cadence. What would he look like? Forbes could evoke no image. A faceless enemy.

'See, it's no good proceeding against the other one.'

'No, no,' said Forbes, brooding. Then said, 'What do you mean – proceeding?'

'Don't you worry about that, Rupe.'

They played the tape a third time.

'Something's there,' Forbes said, 'almost like an echo.'

Edward got out the Scrabble board, and shook out the pieces.

'It's obvious he knows you: so it's obvious you know him.'

They picked up their tiles.

'But – he might know me because a lot of people know me. Since I'm at the centre of things. But I don't know them.'

Edward said, 'He's in the same world, the same swim. And what he's done has changed things. Changed them for him, I mean. He'll be feeling the tension, between him and you. Believe me, he'll be sending out radar signals. And now you know the voice' – they each chose a tile, and Edward's was the highest, so he went first – 'you'll pick those signals up.'

Forbes, still musing on the voice he had heard on the recording, nodded. There was something almost maternal in Edward's confident tone, and Forbes remembered an earlier version of the game they were playing. His mother and he would sit on the hearth-rug and deal out a pack of cards with the letters of the alphabet. Lexicon. But it was duller; it was not piquant, as Scrabble was.

Edward said, 'A day or two, and you'll have him. And then' – he placed his tiles carefully over the centre square, running them downwards for his double-letter score – '*I'll* have him.'

Forbes looked up sharply at Edward.

'What does that mean?'

'Don't ask, Rupe,' Edward said.

It was Forbes's turn to play. He shuffled his pieces along the rack. Looked at the board. Saw Edward's word was GRAZE. He laid out his own tiles. He ran his word out from the A and got rid of four letters.

ANGER. Edward wrote down Forbes's score. Then he put a B in front of Forbes's word and made BANGER. 'That's nice,' he said.

A car from the Ministry picked up Forbes next morning and drove him to Gatwick. His 'master' – the Arts and Culture Minister – was to leave the airport *en route* to Bruges to prove the Brits knew something about art by opening an exhibition of Flemish paintings to which the National Gallery had contributed a dozen of its own. A half-hour had been set aside before the flight to discuss the question of an export licence for the Club's Leonardo. A greeter at the airport led him to the conference room set aside for the meeting.

Those involved had the air of men to whom rising at 4.30 for a meeting at 6 was something they lovingly embraced. All eyes were bright as their owners piloted cups of coffee, mustered sheafs of paper, unzipped briefcases and gave the impression of being up-front without committing the solecism of seeming too eager. The civil servants present knew their place. The minister himself was *hors concours* – the Minister's presence licensed the proceedings, he held no rank. But those who have eminence without rank depend upon favour, and those perched on their ledge in a hierarchy do not. Everyone present on that morning felt pleased with themselves, and uneasy also; for the civil servants knew that if you perch on a ledge too long you are marooned, and the minister knew that eminence has a tax, and the tax is the precarious nature of the tenure.

But they were all in the swim. That united them.

'Now Rupert, do we have a position?'

'Yes, Minister. Export licences are a very blurry area, but a rough and ready question always asked is whether the work of art in question is distinguished enough to warrant us hanging on to it. Distinguished in this context simply means very expensive. And, of course, the Leonardo exactly fits the bill.'

The minister nodded. His own house was full of covetable works of art and this meant his view of the matter came in two sections: first, you hung on to stuff, because hanging on to things was instinctive. It was the animating principle of his ancestors, otherwise he'd have had an empty house. But second, this principle meant the stuff was his and he ought to be able to do what he liked with it. When his father died they'd taken a Van Dyke from its hooks in the long gallery, a couple of Gainsboroughs and a Raeburn from the main salon, and sold them to a railway heiress in Washington to help with the death duties.

'Well, it's a fair rule of thumb, I suppose.'

'But,' said Forbes, precise as the mandarin he was, 'it has to be said that at bottom, the argument *against* letting works of art go to the highest bidder rests on a sentimental premise that nobody ever bothers to spell out – that we've got to prove we aren't just a nation of pork butchers.'

One of his juniors was minuting all that was being said. He waited for the pork-butcher reference to be taken by the others as a preamble to Forbes's opting for a more realistic view. But the amanuensis knew Forbes's style better.

'Which is why I am for it.'

The others may have felt they had been about to step on a stair that wasn't there, but a sequence of nodding begun by the minister and then augmented by his PPS, allowed the moment to pass.

'Export licences aren't on the statute book, they are an instrument which operates by precedent – no one is bound by it. But I am of the opinion that such conventions are ignored at our peril. Not everything can be determined by logic, instinct is almost always a better guide. Politically speaking, that is. Our advice is to cleave to precedent, and withhold the export licence.'

The minister scratched his chin. Hanging on to things was in his blood, but then you only hung on to them because you knew what they were worth. And one day you might want to get the best price. On the other hand, precedent was almost more binding than any actual rule that *was* binding. And if you let someone sell it to some high-rolling foreigner, you were giving away the 'national heritage'. No votes in that. Forbes got things right, shrewd fellow, shrewd on his own account too because he didn't have the deciding of it – that was for the politicians: the compromising classes. But wasn't Forbes a member of the Club? Pretty self-denying of the man.

The minister said, 'Have to admit my gut feeling is let the thing go to the highest bidder. Get the best price. But you're right, precedent is a hell of a sleeping policeman, can't go bumping over it, break the chassis. And people without money only think in terms of heritage – can afford to. But they're the ones with the votes, and we're answerable to them. Quite properly.'

'I think,' said Forbes, judiciously, 'the feeling might be that if everything is up for sale, then ultimately as a country you lose face.'

The PPS chimed in severely, 'And once you open the bidding outside these shores, the next step is for someone in Brussels to decide all art goes back to its country of origin.'

This was somewhat far-fetched, but the PPS, whose face was as narrow as the slit in the castle wall they used to fire arrows from, liked to endorse the resemblance by firing a few himself. 'It might be interesting,' said the junior civil servant who was not doing the minuting, after waiting a moment to see if anyone more senior was about to speak, 'to work out under that arrangement how many pictures we'd have to surrender, and how many we would get back.'

But no one thought it was interesting. He was ignored, except by the minister whose instinct was that you never knew when an odd vote might come in handy. He gave him a nod, and what was more, used his name.

'Brian's right. Once you start handing things back, God knows what the bloody people in Brussels are going to start asking for. Heard a man the other day saying some separatists in the Dordogne were after the Statue of Liberty.'

None of this had precisely been Brian's point, but he looked modestly at his knees in case his satisfaction should seem manifest, while the PPS felt his ground had been taken. He might have let off an arrow in Brian's direction, if he could have picked the right one without seeming to.

'Now, Minister,' said Forbes, looking at his watch, 'as I made clear to you at an earlier meeting, I have an interest in this case.'

'Of course – the Club. You laid the details before us, as I recall, and declared yourself – I remember perfectly. You expressed no opinion, one way or the other, about the desirable course of action, on that occasion. We hadn't thought it through.'

'It was early days, and a view was only in the process of being developed. As to the Club, you know that I'm a member of its committee – it was minuted at the time of that discussion. If an export licence is granted, then the Club is able to sell to the highest bidder and will do well for itself. I have not excluded myself from examining the issue, since it is my duty to proffer my advice. But it goes without saying that when you come to decide the course of action you deem best in this matter, I shall have no further voice.'

'Well, of course, Rupert, but you've already given it as your view that the licence should be withheld. Can hardly play it more correctly than when you give advice that goes against your own interests. Who the devil does your club sell it to if it doesn't go abroad?'

'Frankly, I've no idea – unless some philanthropist puts his hand in his pocket. But that happily does not concern us today.'

Greatly daring, the junior civil servant who had been doing the minutes said, 'I wonder if it matters where a great work of art resides. After all, if it ended up in California, we wouldn't be able to see it here, but if it ended up here they wouldn't be able to see it there.' He just managed not to add, 'Would they?', and was rescued from a dead silence by the minister who said, 'Gerald is thinking of the National Gallery, but you see' – and turned to Gerald as though to one he knew would understand – 'it's already had thirty million from the lottery for the Van Gogh it bought.'

'Can't bid,' said the PPS shortly, 'hasn't got the funds.'

'That's right,' said the minister, 'can't do it again in such short order – that thirty million sends them to the back of the queue. Wouldn't be on, politically. I've a dozen outfits with their hands out.'

Had Gerald been less well-trained, he might have nodded. But he knew better. Forbes brought the meeting to a close, knowing the plane was due to depart.

'Hang on to it, the country's with you. Let it go, and there's endless debate. That's the way the department sees it, Minister.'

Leaving with his PPS, the minister felt for a moment that you didn't often trip across disinterestedness of this sort very often. Didn't suppose Forbes was a rich man. Salary. Could have done with it – what had he heard, couple of hundred thousand each if they got the best offer? And yet he stood against it. The minister and the PPS were ushered on to the tarmac just before the plane was called, and though their overcoats blew about in the wind, and their hair was tousled, just as though they were ordinary passengers, there was something about going first that was clear to all and sundry.

And even when it wasn't so clear, it was part of the climate. The New Year fête. Band playing. The village ladies looking at each other saucily. Wouldn't expect to see each other in such surroundings, in the grounds of the big house, not on a daily basis. So nodded merrily. Knew they all knew they were being granted a glimpse. Had freedom of the lawn. Canadian maples standing sentinel. The lake and the pavilion in the distance, the many acres.

A peep through the long windows, but there was a marquee ('Marquee if wet', which meant you didn't get inside the house). He was plain mister. But had married an earl's daughter, Lady Iris. It was nice to say those words when you met her. Lady Iris. She behaved as though she didn't mind what you called her. There were always the two sides, the outside and the inside. Two sides, and funny enough, both sides liked it. Made things interesting. Not a real difference, no one ever felt that – what would a real difference be, since all were human? But if you didn't have the levels, the tiers, what would you find to be amused by?

The telly told these very stories, stories about the difference: laughing, of course, which meant it didn't matter. It was a play, a fantasy. Bit of a joke. But when you joined in, you did it as though it was real. Well, real in the way you greeted people in the supermarket, sort of real, like the way people behaved to each other when in public; a play, because the real thing was hidden away, deep in everyone's secret domestic privacy. You had to have something to alleviate that. And it was nice to be in a story, to be a member of the cast, one among the rich and the not so rich and the fairly OK. Not the poor, of course, not the derelict, they had no place in a play because being poor and derelict took up all their time; except when you knew they were *being* played. By famous actors. That politician, poor Mr – what was his name? Wanted a – what did he call it? Classless. But where was he when he said it? On top. Temporarily, of course. Everyone knew he wasn't on top in any real sense, he was only there for five minutes; less. So it was just something to say.

The divisions were there so people wouldn't go mad with boredom. Without the divisions, where was luck, where was possibility? Just like prizes and lotteries, if you didn't have them, where was the unexpected? Wouldn't do just to meet people like yourself. Actually, you never did. Everyone was mostly just a bit up or down of you. And most of the time you were wondering who was which. So long as there was always the chance of being a bit up of someone else, you didn't mind, you didn't hanker after the top. Not the actual top. Or anywhere near. Made it interesting. So if there was a play, a tableau, a charade, it was always based on that, whatever else it was based on. It was the way everyone, absolutely everyone, wanted it. So long as it didn't matter. Or nobody behaved as though it mattered. And fragments of thoughts like these, that weren't really thoughts, just confetti (for nobody in the history of the world had ever been able to think consecutively for more than twenty seconds at a time, people sometimes fitted thoughts together out of the confetti, but not as a single spontaneous act if you except Bertrand Russell and Co, who took it up the way Sampras took up tennis) fluttered in the heads of those who were going from the tombola to the coconut shy to the rolling the pennies to the treasure hunt to the hoopla to the sandwiches to the barbecue to the produce stall. Who's making it all happen? Of course, this afternoon, Mr Prince. His money. His house. But he knew everyone would go home and not give him a further thought, or if they did, they'd do it just pointing, as at a novelty, another item among all the items outside their own lives; no special value. But while they were here, in his grounds, they were ever so slightly his. He held, however so slightly, sway. It counted for almost nothing. But he had it. Briefly. For the time.

Below the lawn, the land sloped away, you had the curve of the Downs, and then the sea. Mr Ihara swung the ball at the end of the string and scattered all the pegs on the skittle board. He won a bar of chocolate and gave it to a small boy standing near.

'Eat it now,' he commanded, smiling, 'or your mother will make you save it.'

The boy saw this short Japanese man as an oddity, not least because he bore gifts. But also because he had singled him out. The boy ran off into the crowd. Forbes strolled across the lawn. The invitation had come from Prince a week or so earlier. 'I know Ihara wants to meet you,' he had written to Forbes, 'and he felt this would be the nicest way of doing it. Quite what he has in in mind is something for him to make clear when you meet. But I thought lunch on Saturday, at my house, would be agreeable. The annual winter fête goes on outside – it might amuse you, but it needn't get in your way.'

Nor had it. Forbes was feeling almost as pleased as he had been the day he opened the letter which said he'd passed First into the Home Civil Service. Lunch had been a pleasure in every way. A man in a black jacket had served the food – some smoked salmon with quail's eggs, lamb cutlets that were pink and tender, and then a caramelized apple tart. Some Mâcon-Lugny, then a decent Sancerre. Everything done with ease, no sense of anyone trying. Ihara was amusing, Prince was a good listener, and Lady Iris engagingly subordinate. But this was not the best of it.

'Some of my associates want us to change our name, now that we are widening our sphere of operations,' Ihara had said. 'They think Pacific Rand has too local a ring. But I think they are confusing a logo with an identity. An identity is hard won. Which is why I am disappointed to find that the Home For Incurables in Putney has been rechristened the Royal Hospital for Neuro Disability.'

'But,' said Forbes, smiling, 'it's still what it was.'

'Not so sure,' Ihara said. 'You change the words, you sometimes change the idea.'

'So long as the idea is not changed by accident,' said Forbes, 'it may be changed for the better.'

Ihara laughed.

'Just giving it the college try, as we dry bobs used to say.'

Prince said, 'Dry bob? I thought you were a Wykehamist.'

'Yes, if you read my *Who's Who* entry it's funny foreigner stuff – "educated, Eton and Winchester". But my father took me away from Eton because he felt that intellectually it was insufficiently rigorous.'

Lady Iris said, 'I didn't think Eton was for that.'

'No, of course not, Lady Iris, but my father came round to thinking that what it *was* for wouldn't count for much in Japan, whereas being sharp would, and Winchester had the better grindstone.'

They laughed as they drank their coffee. Prince looked at his watch. The band had stopped playing, as though something else was due to happen.

'Time for you to do your stuff, Iris.'

'Oh, I'd better go and open it. I always do.'

The men rose.

'The only thing is, you aren't allowed to win anything, if you open it,' Lady Iris said. 'You have to give it back. Anything worth having, I mean.'

'You did win a cake-stand once,' Prince said.

'Oh, I didn't mind giving that back. And then, do you know,' Lady Iris said, staring seriously at Mr Ihara, 'I won the bloody thing again.'

'You two finish your coffee. We'll see you later.'

Prince and his wife went out and Ihara and Forbes sat down again.

'I'm glad to have you to myself for a few moments, Mr Forbes,' said Ihara. 'I'd like to sound you out on something. I referred to the expansion that Pacific Rand has just started, but we have plans for a more ambitious presence in the UK, and then in the next eighteen months or so we hope to find ourselves in Europe. But the UK is to be the centre of the enlarged operation and as chief executive – as president – my concern is to find the right man to be my chairman.'

Driving over from Godalming, Forbes had wondered what was in the wind and, assuming it must have something to do with the Leonardo, was suspicious. Was the man after some hint as to the way the export-licence decision might go? Surely even a bloody Jap wouldn't think he'd get that out of him. But then he thought there's no reason for Ihara or even Prince to know that I have anything to do with licences – the ministry dealt with the arts, but as far as anyone outside knew, licensing came under some other head, Trade and Industry, say. Prince hadn't had the slightest indication from Forbes. Inside knowledge? Unlikely. They might have made a guess, but they couldn't know.

Forbes mused. Nothing final had yet been decided about the licence, but the way the decision was going was clear enough – nothing had changed since Forbes had advised the minister to withhold the licence at the airport. But he was obscurely irritated.

This Japanese gent was in the same boat as all the other bidders – they were all on a loser, if the licence was withheld.

What Forbes hadn't expected was to be offered a job.

'I beg your pardon, Mr Forbes, for taking advantage of Mr Prince's indiscretion – in passing, in conversation, he had mentioned that next year you are to retire. Ridiculously early.'

Forbes said, 'Yes, it's the way the Service works.' And as he spoke, he was suppressing a sudden blitheness.

'Well, now, my chairman has of course to be someone who knows the political levers, who has access to the right ears, one who is not only native – always a funny word – to the idiom of what J.B. Priestley so aptly called Topside, but holds rank within it. This goes without saying, and I must ask you to forgive me the banality of adverting to it. But above all, and here is the absolute requirement, he must not simply be a man of standing, he must be of proven authority. Mr Forbes I hope you do not think it impertinent of me to offer you first refusal of this job. Oh dear me – I am forgetting I am Japanese. I should have said, First refusal of this unworthy task.'

Forbes laughed. He laughed loudly. The more loudly, in that it allowed him to conceal his delight. But Forbes hadn't passed First into the Home Civil Service by accident. He wasn't daft.

'May I say, Mr Ihara, how much I value what you've just said. It's true enough – and Prince breaches no confidence in speaking of it to you – that I shall not be *en poste* after the New Year. And mindful of how cold the winds blow in the world outside I have already put myself in the hands of those whose business it is to find places for men whose usefulness may be supposed to continue after their conventional employment ends.'

'Headhunters, you mean,' said Ihara. 'A few facts, then. Your salary would be augmented by share options and of course by yearly bonuses, dependent on our trading position – I may say that on a year-on-year basis, over a twenty-year period, our profit figures, after tax, show an increase of between nineteen and twenty-four per cent. There would be a pension equal to three-quarters of that salary. Of initial salary, if you were so unfortunate as to die while employed by me, which would be paid to your heir or heirs for a minimum of ten years. And of final salary when you decided to retire. For life, of course. Plus a termination fee equivalent to three years of that final salary.'

Forbes had no need to ask the question that hung in the air. He simply nodded, and Ihara continued.

'Money's not a problem. I would like the Chairman of Pacific Rand UK to feel as free of such constraints as do I.'

Forbes waited.

'If five hundred thousand pounds were acceptable as a basic salary, I would expect it to be augmented considerably by the bonuses I mentioned, together with the exercise of share options.'

Keep your face straight, thought Forbes. Don't laugh this time.

'A handsome offer, Mr Ihara. Subject to contract, of course.'

Ihara beamed.

'Will you think it forward of me if I tell you it is already drawn up? I could not possibly leave anything to chance, in the event that you might be minded to accept. I don't want you *poached*, Mr Forbes!'

This allowed them both to laugh, a brief sabbatical. Then Forbes said, mindful of the formalities, 'Let me reflect for a few moments in the garden, Mr Ihara.'

'Of course. I shall leave you to yourself. We shall visit the attractions.'

As they rose from the table, Ihara said, 'Your reputation does not reach my ears via Mr Prince alone, as you will have appreciated. I value your mind, and the way it combines with your knowledge of the world. This is a much rarer combination than is sometimes supposed – in the market place, it is often confused with low cunning. And that confusion has often worked to my advantage. My rivals crediting me only with deviousness have sometimes supposed me to be playing for the bottles in the cellar, when in fact I was after the vineyard itself.'

'In the office, Mr Ihara, we are very careful not to take our eye off the ball as it is being played. But the encompassing strategy is our prime concern.'

Ihara said, 'I had not supposed it could be otherwise.'

They found their way across the entrance hall and out into the grounds. Agreeing to reconvene a little later, they each went a different way.

This time Lady Iris had won a ticket allowing free entry to the Chessington World of Adventures, and Forbes watched her hand it back with a jolly smile. He had a go at rolling the pennies (the village postmistress who ran the stall had a store of pre-1960s specimens) and won 10p which he handed over to the general fund – the fête was in support of the Relief for Rumania campaign, and with the professional's disenchanted view of such matters he found himself reflecting that although almost all of his ten pence would find its way into the pockets of the brigands who ran that unhappy country, at least the business of transferring it to them offered employment to men and women who could drive a white van. But these thoughts, and others equally random, were a sort of gauze curtain behind which he rejoiced. While he sat on a tree stump and watched people eating egg sandwiches as though blowing their noses on large floppy handkerchiefs, he felt like someone who had won a prize without going in for the competition.

He caught up with Ihara at the coconut shy. A little girl was crying as she held a coconut and Ihara was soothing her.

'My aim was too good. The coconut bounced into the air and caught her on the B-T-M.'

They walked away together.

'A delightful afternoon. For me especially, if you decide in favour of the proposition I put to you.'

Forbes nodded.

'I shall need to do a great deal of homework, familiarize myself with Pacific Rand and all its functions. But there will be time, I am sure, in the months before I leave my present job, for the necessary research. Thank you, then, Mr Ihara. On receipt of your contract, I shall withdraw my name from the agency I mentioned, and hold myself in readiness for the post you offer.'

'This is splendid news.' Ihara grasped him by the hand and was shaking it vigorously as Prince walked over and joined them.

'You can't have won the tombola, Forbes, surely?' Prince laughed.

'Well,' said Forbes in high good humour, 'I think it may be said that I've done rather better. Though of course, time will tell.'

'Whatever it is, I'm delighted you and Ihara have found your meeting fruitful.'

'Indeed we have,' Ihara beamed. 'Mr Forbes has done me the honour of agreeing to join my company when he is released from the Civil Service.'

'Bravo,' cried Prince. 'We must have a glass of champagne. We must mark the event.'

They went into a small drawing-room which overlooked the garden and the man in the black jacket came in with a bottle of Krug. All raised their glasses.

'Perhaps it wouldn't come amiss to wish you luck, also, Ihara, in your bid for our Leonardo. Did he tell you, Forbes? He's upped his stake again.'

'One has to pay. Bit of a gamble, though. The question of the export licence remains.'

Forbes felt a prickle at the back of his neck as the subject was raised.

Prince refilled their glasses.

Ihara said, 'Yes, I increased my bet – upped it another five – forty-five million. As I know, this puts me below the top bidder. But then, as I say, it's a gamble. Our friends at the Museum of Timeless Art in Dallas are far ahead of us. But they too are gambling. On the granting of an export licence.'

Forbes felt a return of the irritation he had felt in the car coming over.

'I suppose,' he said, carefully, 'as far as that goes, all our bidders are in the same boat.'

Prince had wandered over to the window, was watching the people who thronged his lawn, and heard the band as it played a tune from *The Chocolate Soldier*.

'Not quite, no. Those of us domiciled in the UK will be taking a different view of the outcome.'

Forbes found himself floating slowly to the surface of an unexamined assumption.

'And there is the principle of the thing. I confess I am no internationalist when it comes to the disposition of works of art. Irrespective of who painted them, they become part of the family. Adoptive members of the country which gave them shelter. Is that too sentimental?'

Prince walked back from the window.

'Now that Ihara is based in London, of course, he is hopeful that the licence will be withheld.'

There was confidential territory here, and Forbes had no intention of surrendering it.

He said, rather heartily, 'I'm sure Prince and I wish you well – though your luck would be the Club's loss.'

'Oh, the Club will do well, very well indeed. Ihara's offer is one it can depend on.' This time it was Prince who sounded a little hearty, and Ihara said, 'Oh, depend, depend. I should be thankful indeed if I could depend on the licence decision going my way.'

And he was looking at Forbes as he spoke. And Forbes was beginning to twig what it had all been about. Farewells were made in a spirit of great mutual congratulation, and Forbes climbed into his Mondeo knowing that Ihara's contract would reach him in a couple of days. For it had been a bribe.

Forbes usually played tapes in the car, he liked early church music, but now as he drove through the late afternoon sunshine he was too much preoccupied by the odd scenario he'd been part of to think of anything else. Unpicking the moves was like playing a simple game of draughts backwards – not difficult, not like chess, the ploy had been too crude. Prince was the impresario – he supplied the venue, and the cast. Why? What was in it for him? Ihara's interest was obvious. Doubtful if he'd have offered such a spectacular *pourboire* on a mere guess – must have known Forbes was the linchpin in the export decision. So he did have inside knowledge. His international clout must somehow have got him there. But the job he'd offered Forbes was costing him no more than he'd have had to lay out, anyway – he had to have someone useful.

As ever, Forbes resented East Grinstead – you thought you'd given it the slip, but it lay in wait for you, and you were caught in its half-baked ring-road system. But he'd gone on thinking. Ihara was looking to get the Leonardo at a discount – if he needed no export licence, he had no rival. Taking advantage of his new domicile and letting Forbes know that was the way he wanted things to go. A bribe. But – was it a bribe if you'd already decided that things were going to go the way the man wanted them to go, before he offered the bribe? Nice point. Even nicer, in the other sense, when you thought Ihara didn't know this – didn't know a bribe wasn't necessary.

But then there was a question. Unnecessary bribe – but were you still obliged to turn it down? Hold on. If this was one of those medieval debates, you'd lose marks for using an assumption as a premise. You assumed it was a bribe – but no one had said it was. It hadn't been established. And still less – another thought jumped into Forbes's mind as he turned off the A22 – could he imagine anyone suggesting that *because* of the bribe he should consider switching his vote. Vote against what you thought was right, simply to thwart anyone who might benefit from the outcome? Perverse! As he traced the pattern of the argument, Forbes began to feel that little more had happened than that – well, than that he, Forbes, had got lucky.

It was none of his doing, it had come his way. He had not raised so much as a finger to further anyone's cause, he had acted in scrupulous good faith – even to the point of moving the decision towards a resolution that was not at all in his own interests as a member of the Club. And if he came out of it ahead of the game it had been the purest good fortune. In the course of a career spent devising intelligent compromises, Forbes had come to respect strategies that worked. Ihara's had been crude but effective. How cleverly he had pitched the remuneration he offered at a level which ensured Forbes would feel no pang in letting the picture go for less than it would have fetched in an open auction. But Ihara had been finessed by Forbes's own integrity. Which, face it, had caused him to pay for something he could have had for nothing. Forbes laughed out loud, and then began to whistle. As he turned into his drive, there was but one cloud in his sky: the blackmailer.

TEN

The concert grand came swooping in over the roofs as it did every year, a flying piano, something you didn't expect to see up there in the sky, dropping down through the opened glass roof of the Club's top floor, swinging into place at the end of a cable that hung from the snout of a great crane. Think of doing something for the first time, and the heart quails, but once it's been done and done again, only the bystanders are awed. 'Touch it left a bit, Ray,' one of the men in the hard hats said through his mobile, just loud enough for the passersby to catch his easy tone. 'Now down.' And flown in from Chappell's, the great black Bosendorfer landed on its points in the ballroom, as delicately as a ballerina.

Our annual concert was quite special. We didn't mind paying, and we got the best. Kiri or Placido or Alfred or Vladimir. An orchestra, small and distinguished – the Mozart Harmonia. Tickets £150 a head, including dinner. Black tie. Someone floated the idea of having the dinner before the music, but common sense prevailed, since you didn't want men dropping off. It was something you could reasonably ask anyone to, because it was *premier cru*. The broadsheets sent critics.

So I invited Letty.

'Do you like music?' I rather crassly enquired. I think I was nervous.

'Doesn't everyone?'

We had drinks in the drawing-room of the Club, and Letty looked stunning in a glistening sheath of green silk. Green suited her. I thought the members in their black ties furnished the room appropriately. Like one of those drawings by Francis Marshall, long gone. But their companions had a faintly crumpled look; this was something I often noticed at the Tate Gallery or the Albert Hall or the Chelsea Flower Show, the distinguishing mark of the middle-class older woman in places of cultural resort. As though they had been dragged out of the wardrobe at the same moment as their clothes.

Letty said, 'Well, don't *you* like music?'

She had turned down champagne, and we were drinking – my goodness, I mostly keep track of things, but I'm blessed if I can remember.

'Yes and no, I mean, I don't have to have it. I can do without it. I also find it gets in my head and keeps me awake. Repeats itself, over and over.'

'You make it sound like pickled onions.'

'Yes. Yes, of course.'

I didn't grasp what she was saying. I was listening and I wasn't listening. I was awfully nervous.

'I mean, what's it about?' I said, swallowing whatever it was, and ordering two more. 'Music. Is it ah, telling you something or is it ah, something – something in itself?'

The walls of the drawing-room are dark red leather, the chandeliers sparkle. Our staff weaved round with trays of drinks, hither and yon. They smiled, enjoying the occasion, as did the members and their guests. How glad I was to be there with Letty, tucked into a nice corner, able to see the whole room in its full fig, with a little wine-table in front of us.

'It's more accurate than words, anyway,' Letty said.

'Music is? How can it be?'

'Well, words are like bricks, they come in lumps, and they can only say what they've always said.'

I noticed she snorted quietly when she tipped up her glass and took a drink from it. That was nice. Don't know why.

'Or you can dismantle the lumps and rearrange them. But,' she said, 'the detail of everything is so much smaller than any word can be, or any arrangement of words can be, so the words can only identify anything pretty generally. Don't you think so?'

'Er – well, I follow you. Don't know that I agree.'

'When the words point to something they only point in a blunt sort of way, even when you've combined them as wonderfully as oh, those authors, Shakespeare, there's no word or arrangement of words small enough to point precisely, the detail will always escape the words, however they are arranged.'

I knew I loved her.

'Poems remind you about this by nearly managing it. Whereas music doesn't come in bits, it's a single continuous flow. Music isn't made of lumps or breeze blocks, clumps, particles, it doesn't break up into lumps, it can't. It's like a wave.'

I wondered if she would always speak to me like this. Maybe it was the drink.

'It comes before the words, you know, like the noises people made before they invented words. When the world began. Music is a sort of arrangement of all that.'

'Not very precise, then,' I said, trying to keep my end up.

'It doesn't do any explaining, if that's what you mean.'

She wasn't at all trying to get the better of me. I mean, she wasn't trying to floor me. Of course, she had floored me.

'I used to think water was bits so small you couldn't see them and they'd run into each other and become one thing, but that was because you're brought up to see everything as bits.'

'Yes, you are,' I said.

'Yes you are what?'

'Well, what you said, brought up and everything.'

'Are you listening? What comes before the bits is what the bits are made out of. The flow. That's the music. Music criticism ought to be done in music.'

I scoffed.

'Pseuds Corner,' I said.

Then she laughed. She'd been saying every word very seriously, meaning it, but not to win, or anything like that.

'Does it sound that way?'

I said, 'You aren't some kind of intellectual, are you?'

She said, 'Goodness, no.'

'Well,' I smiled, as we got up and went towards the staircase, 'it's very nice.'

As I said, the music was always good. For all that Letty had said about words, I wasn't able to stop a kind of running commentary that always filled my head at concerts. The music soothed me while I wondered about the conductor sweating. This one wore a grey suit of tails, and you could see the way the sweat came first below his armpits as he swung the baton, then started to fill the V on his back between his braces. Perhaps he brought a spare jacket. Or he might hang it on a radiator in the interval, in the little sitting-out room they used as a dressing-room on these occasions. All sorts of things you couldn't tell: was he going through the motions, or was he racked with nerves? Did the band actually watch him? Was it a real job? Beating time. The band could do it in their sleep.

And I have to admit, I was thinking about dinner. When I'm at a concert I think about dinner. I wonder if everyone does. Then I thought, is it true about musicians drinking? Some of them turning up late from the pub. How do you tell the singers how to do it? They had the songs in their heads, a repertoire, took over roles in operas in strange lands at a minute's notice – just walked on to the stage, sung in their own language while the others sang on in theirs, no one seemed to mind, might like it better, a sophisticated touch. Awfully difficult telling them if they were a bit flat – perhaps the conductor has some polite way of saying it.

We had the Mozart clarinet concerto, that beautiful slow movement that brings a lump to your throat and you don't know why – Letty's theory seemed to be holding up there; Dulcamara selling the patent medicine in, *L'Elisir d'Amore*; and the quartet from *Rigoletto* (only what gets in the way for me is the old film, where the Crazy Gang dress up as the quartet, with real singers' voices dubbed on, and I start wishing it was the film). Overture to

Der Freischütz, more Mozart and a nice broadcloth length of Beethoven. A bit of Handel; you're supposed to like Handel, but when he did something for one of the Georges it went on for three nights and the George in question was heard to groan on the third night. 'There's no edge to it!' I felt the same. But mostly it was music for pleasure, stuff you couldn't not enjoy.

We strolled down the stairs in the interval to the broad first landing which was a sort of promenade, and Letty asked me about the Club. 'What's the point of it?' she said. I told her a cab-driver had asked me the same thing. He'd said, 'What's the attraction? Do you have hostesses?' Letty laughed. I said I'd told him 'No,' and he'd said, 'Well, is there gambling and slot machines and that?' So I said, 'No, although you could play cards if you wanted to.' 'Don't see what the appeal is,' he said. By this time I was fed up with his Nobby Geezer act and as I got out I said, 'There's only one reason for belonging to this club: you can be absolutely certain you won't meet anyone you don't know.'

'Snooty!' Letty cried.

'Yes it was, but I doubt if he noticed. Would you want to join? If we allowed women?'

'What bloody cheek!' she said.

'Oh, I only meant – I mean, women don't join clubs, do they?'

'Of course they do. Only I don't like the women who do,' said Letty. 'But what makes any of you old farts think we'd want to keep your company on a daily basis? You come on as though it was still Barchester Towers and all that. An evening like this is nice, but God, I wouldn't want to come back tomorrow.'

'No,' I said humbly, 'I shouldn't think you would. But I quite like dull things.'

Letty reached up and actually gave my cheek a squeeze between her finger and thumb.

'Fibber.'

Good Lord, I felt pleased.

'By the by, curious thing,' Letty said. 'The penny only just dropped. You know the man who found your Leonardo? Well, he's my cousin.'

'What, the cousin who told you you were in with a chance? Firethorne?'

'That's him. Second cousin, actually, or is it once-removed? I never know the difference. Didn't say a word about having done the discovering. Only found about it when someone showed me a cutting of the article he'd written in the *Evening Standard*. How strange.'

'You said he knew about art.'

'Wouldn't you think he'd have told me? Odd. And wanting me to put in for the inheritance. Why not him?'

'Thought you had a better chance, perhaps. You being in the direct line.'

I wasn't thinking about Firethorne, but it was his entry into the conversation that had reminded me I was going to have to tell Letty about my intervention on her behalf at the EGM. I was rather embarrassed; on reflection my representation had been at best showy, at worst naff.

'Lives in Frinton,' Letty said, 'so he must be *very* odd.'

I told her about the EGM. 'You see, if everyone had their own, you'd have the Leonardo. So you ought to have a share.'

She said, 'No, won't do. I'll write and tell them. Don't need it.'

The instant candour I'd seen at our first meeting was so much part of her temperament. She looked at me with such a smile.

'Needn't be shy,' she said and, leaning forward, she kissed me.

A waiter came up and offered a tray of drinks. Forbes was standing further across the broad landing, at the top of the next flight of stairs. I'd seen him earlier with his nephew, an old-fashioned, well-behaved youth. At that moment he was on his own, standing with a small group, and the people in the group talked to him, not to each other.

Elated by the kiss, I returned to Letty's views on men's clubs.

'See him?' I indicated Forbes. 'I have to admit that what you were saying about chaps in clubs rings a bell when I see Forbes. Permanent Secretary, or something like that. Got an air. I'm damned if you can't sense it even at this distance. Likes to give you the feeling that what he says is but a fraction of what he could say.'

I heard what I supposed was the porter's telephone ringing down below. I was studying Forbes, and I saw him turn to look in the direction of the sound. Then the porter came up from the ground floor, and passed through the crowd on the broad landing, as though looking for someone. Not finding whoever he was looking for, he started up the next flight, somewhat impeded by the crush of people standing on the stairs. I saw Forbes excusing himself and moving down towards the ground floor, rather briskly. Letty and I had been edged across the landing by other people squeezing on to the promenade for the interval, and Forbes's group having dissolved, we found ourselves at the top of the stairs leading down. I saw Forbes hovering at the porter's desk, then saw the door of the little telephone cubicle open and his nephew Edward stepping out of it. They stood together for a moment, then Forbes moved behind the porter's desk, and he was lost to my sight. I assumed he was checking a brief-case or leaving a note. Then they both came back upstairs, and we all went up to the ballroom for the rest of the concert. Some little oddity about Forbes and his nephew and the telephone and the hall-porter's desk, though I couldn't say what, registered with me, and stayed in my head until the conductor came out again to great applause. His jacket as he turned to the orchestra, was as dry as a bone, and I devoted myself to speculation concerning his character and temperament, of which I knew nothing, and that of the singers and the orchestra. What I didn't have to think about was Letty, because she was sitting next to me. Because of her proximity, because she was really there, I didn't need to.

Some days earlier, Forbes had strolled across from Whitehall for lunch at the Club. A letter asking him for a further £2,000 had arrived that morning. With prospects that had blossomed with the bizarre intervention of Ihara, the letter was like the reminder of an incurable illness, destructive of all pleasure. The possibility of ever identifying the voice of his tormentor seemed a distant one, and the next move did not suggest itself, either to him or Edward.

'I've thought of something,' Edward had said, 'but I can't start it until we know who he is.'

Seated at the big table, and facing the windows where there were smaller tables for members entertaining guests, Forbes had ordered his lunch and had fallen into desultory conversation with his neighbour who was a doctor. He found himself thinking, as his neighbour told him at some length about a patient of his, that people who were boring could sometimes be rather restful. 'He was a member of the CIA – Central Intelligence Agency, you know what I mean?' Forbes nodded indulgently. As soon as he recognized someone was no challenge to him, he could be very civil. 'And he told me his wife had a weight problem—' As the doctor spoke, Forbes was aware that someone at one of the smaller tables under the window was looking at him, or at least looking at him and then looking away: the man was sitting across the room with three others, and he was sitting sideways on to the room, and it was the continuousness of the small movement as he slightly turned his head which had drawn Forbes's eye; with the window behind them, the detail of all four faces at the table wasn't at all clear from Forbes's place at the long table.

'So I said to the CIA chap, send her along, I can set up a chart for her, give her a diet she can follow—' The conversation at the table opposite was energetic, and a word or two, or a laugh, came across the room from time to time, reaching Forbes's ear through the low murmur of his neighbour's story. 'But the chart didn't work, she'd bring it in, all marked up, but it went up and down because she wouldn't stick to the diet—' The man in profile across the room was playing his part in the conversation, but he was not so absorbed that it stopped him switching momentary glances – it was almost like a nervous tic – in Forbes's direction. 'So I told the CIA chap – your wife's not sticking to it. And he said What's she doing. . . .'

And then the conversation, the sound, hit Forbes again, just momentarily. He saw the lips of the man in profile moving and heard just a few of the words he was speaking – 'get into the market and catch it'. And he knew the cadence. While his neighbour continued his story, Forbes's ear was essentially elsewhere. 'So the CIA man said right, I'll have her followed. Actually put one of his agents on the job. Agent reported back that the wife was eating chocolate and not jogging.' Forbes laughed appreciatively. 'Will the marriage survive the surveillance?' Edward's point about the radar, the inextinguishable tension between himself and his antagonist was true. A batch of sound came his way again – he saw the lips move. And he knew the voice again. But it was the faint head movements, the glances, which had set up the communication.

His neighbour rose, and Forbes nodded him goodbye. Sat with his coffee, waiting. The four at the guest table got up, and this time the man in profile's refusal to look over at Forbes as he moved across the room to the cashier's desk seemed more obvious than his earlier glances. But away from the window, his face was in full view. When Forbes went over a minute or two later, he said casually to the lady doing the bills, 'Just remind me, who was the member who walked out of the door last?' And, looking at the account she'd just filed, 'Oh yes,' she said. 'It was Mr Spalding.'

Forbes left the dining-room, and walking past the open door of the reading-room saw that Spalding and his guests were sitting down to brandy and coffee. He went downstairs to the phone booth and rang Edward at Quantum Solutions.

'We've got him, then. What I'd dearly like to get a look at,' said Edward, 'is his mobile phone. Assuming he's got one.'

Forbes said, 'Oh he's got one. One of the tribe which brandishes them.'

'Look, can you get a sight of it? The make. The manufacturer. What it looks like.'

Forbes glanced sideways out of the little sedan-chair that had been converted into a phone booth, across the corridor to the hall-porter's desk. It was empty. 'You aren't allowed to use them here, of course. You check them in with the porter. If the porter isn't around—'

'Do the necessary. Then let me have the details.'

Forbes said, 'Look, I'll get back to you.'

He stepped across the hall from the phone booth. There were cubby-holes. The porter scribbled a name and put it in when the members left things with him – gloves, cases, mobiles. Forbes would say he was wondering whether he'd left a briefcase there. He stepped behind the desk. Scanned the boxes. Three mobiles. Each with a bit of paper tucked under an elastic band. 'Spalding'. Shape, make, size, serial number. Forbes photocopied it in his head as if it were a memorandum – old skills. Walked over to the phone and rang Edward again.

'Now,' said Edward, 'we're in business.'

Forbes, not knowing what Edward had in in mind, said, 'What are you up to?'

Edward said, 'Whatever you do, don't try and dig out his mobile number at your club. We don't want anyone thinking you have an interest.'

Forbes, more uncomfortable now that he actually knew his enemy, said again, 'What are you thinking of?'

'Don't bother, Rupe,' Edward said, 'I'm just going to give him a fright. And I'll get his number. I'll need it. But we're off the ground. We're flying.'

Arthur Ledward considered the meeting which was to decide who would get the Leonardo to be so confidential that he decided the venue should be outside the club. He'd sent a personal letter, handwritten to ensure privacy, to each member of the committee, asking them to assemble at an hotel none of them had ever heard of, in Buckinghamshire.

'All this cloak and dagger stuff seems a bit exaggerated,' Calderstone said to Olney, as they passed Northolt in the hired car they were sharing, and came on to the M40. 'You can take things too seriously.'

When they'd all assembled, Ledward spoke. 'I've asked you to convene here because I want to be sure that no one gets wind of our decision before we think it the right moment. In the club, we are too close to interested parties, and I fear that means all the other members. I simply wanted to avoid awkward conversations, and what's worse, journalists. If no one knows we've had this meeting, we can avoid all that. Unless anyone leaks,' he said, with an impassive look at his fellow committee members.

'If we all accept the confidentiality of the meeting, as I'm sure we do,' said Calderstone, 'the question will not arise.'

'Of course, of course,' Ledward nodded. 'I think the whole business is getting on my nerves a bit. As chairman. When it all started, there was an altogether different cast to it – I myself had always hoped that our initial vote to give the money to some good cause would have been the beginning and end of the whole thing. Now it seems all the members are simply waiting for a pay-out. No avoiding it.'

Calderstone said, 'Why should we want to avoid it? After all, that's the way the final vote went.'

Ledward looked bleak.

'Of course,' he said, 'it's a matter of taste. A matter of temperament. Of how one views such situations.'

No one said anything, but the faces of the rest of the committee seemed a touch restive.

'We cannot hope to conduct our affairs as an elected committee as we might like to do as individuals,' said Prince, a little grandly. 'As an elected body, we set aside such private feelings. We simply do what we were elected to do – put the wishes of the members into effect.'

Ledward nodded, though he seemed unappeased.

'Of course, you're right. No question of it. But I am damned if the situation we are presented with pleases me. It's too much like business, and I'd always hoped a club was a refuge from all that.'

'It's a special case, surely,' urged Forbes. 'We don't do deals in the club, we don't produce papers, we don't talk shop. But here's something that simply can't be dealt with in other than business terms.'

Ledward sighed.

'I'm sure you all have the right of it. But the picture. It may be ours. Of course, it is. But the style in which the club is shuffling round it has a touch of the vulture. Distinct echoes of the slot-machine arcade.'

'Have you ever been in one, Ledward?' asked Olney, apparently without irony.

'Let's get rid of the damn thing quickly,' Ledward said, 'and return to civilized living. I should be pleased if we could walk out of here and present it to the first hospital we came to!'

Prince said, a mite sardonically, 'Some of us could certainly do that without missing the cash very greatly.'

Ledward said, 'You are quite right to rebuke me. Holier than thou. Quite right, it doesn't suit me. Let's get on with it, then.'

They had been allotted one of the hotel conference rooms, featureless save for a long table and the chairs that went with it. Through the windows could be seen a paved area, classifiable as a 'precinct' since its function was not immediately apparent. They had drunk their coffee and Calderstone, having asked permission, was smoking his pipe.

'Well, now, five of the seven bidders have made substantial deposits as an earnest of good faith, the other two are considering their positions, and are effectively out of the contest. All the interested parties have made sealed bids, and have assured us they are final and irrevocable.'

'Do they impose any conditions?' Prince asked.

'Oh yes, indeed they do. All are mightily concerned that the picture may not be granted an export licence, and in that case all bets are off.'

Forbes said, 'May I ask, Chairman, what the range of bids is?'

'They run from forty-five milion to sixty million. The lowest is Ihara's and the highest is from the Timeless Art people in Dallas. Ihara is a cunning fellow, because he tells me in his letter that he is now resident in this country.'

'And he's the only one, is he?' asked Olney. 'I mean, bidding from the UK.'

'That's so. All the others have bases in Europe and America.'

Calderstone said, 'Wouldn't it save time if we took the highest bid first? Seems reasonable not to bother with the others if we don't have to.'

Prince said, 'Well, as I understand it, the disadvantage of the Dallas bid is that they don't buy unless they get the licence.'

'Not quite,' said Ledward. 'All the others are categorical on that score – no licence, no sale. But Dallas says it would risk it.'

Forbes said, 'In so many words?'

Ledward rubbed his chin. 'I'd call it an intimation.'

'Rather dodgy,' Olney said, 'to make it stick, then?'

'If they reneged? Expensive,' Prince said. 'Court case, and the picture unsold. Bit of a gamble.'

'But in that case,' said Calderstone, sucking at his pipe, 'wouldn't one of the others come forward as underbidder?'

'Not without the licence. It's the same snag,' Olney said.

There was a silence.

Calderstone puffed away meditatively. 'Looks as though Ihara has outfoxed them all – gets the thing below value.'

Forbes said, 'I'm not a businessman, but I'm sure Prince and Ledward will confirm that value is determined by the market. No market, no value.'

Ledward was reflective. 'Frankly, I don't like Ihara's style though that might just be prejudice. I've done business with the Japs, and they're awfully sharp. Might hang on and see if any of the institutions in this country topped his bid.'

Olney said, 'But they've all had plenty of time to chip in – wouldn't they have done it, if they were going to? Don't know how the membership would take it, with the picture still on their hands and knowing they could have had forty-five million for it.'

Calderstone's pipe was of the curved variety, with a steel stem. What might be called an expert pipe-smoker's pipe.

'I still like the gamble with Dallas. And if they copped out, wouldn't Ihara take it up again?'

Ledward smiled a wry smile. 'It isn't the Japanese way. Once a Jap has come second, he's out of the contest for good. Coming second is bad enough, but trying twice is admitting it. He really loses face.'

Calderstone went on, 'And another point – have we taken into account the possibility of Ihara backing out?'

Ledward's smile was drier yet. 'There again our man Ihara has placed himself ahead of the game. Where the others have made deposits he has put the whole amount upfront.'

'What? The whole forty-five million?' Olney was incredulous.

'I don't like it, I don't like it a bit,' Ledward said. 'Where Ihara is concerned my nose tells me something's off. He has surely gone to inelegant lengths, in taking up residence here—'

Prince interjected, 'In fairness, he is expanding his business into the UK – though I daresay that's reached your ears.'

'Yes, I'd heard. And like many a rich man before him, Japanese or otherwise, he wants trophies. But the fact remains that he submits the lowest bid, and at the same time ensures that if a licence is not granted, it is to his advantage. Still, whatever he's up to, the fact is that his money is on deposit, in escrow, and if the deal is agreed, he cannot take it back.'

After a pause, a silence, Ledward said, 'Well, we all know the situation. I'll take your comments and your votes now, if it's agreeable to you.'

Calderstone spoke first. 'Still like the idea of Dallas, but recognize it's shaky. So Ihara gets it.'

Olney was nodding. 'Nothing I'd like better than take the top bid, and run. But can't see it.'

'So your vote? Ihara?'

'Has to be.'

'Forbes?'

'My concern is that we do not play ducks and drakes with members' legitimate interests. A bird in the hand. It's the lowest bid, but it's the only certain one. It gets my vote.'

Prince said, 'There doesn't seem to be any argument. We've got his money. That's the clincher.'

'Well,' said Ledward, 'as a member of the awkward squad, I don't want to vote for Ihara because instinct tells me not to. But logic being against me, I suppose I'll have to. Five votes to nil. We are unanimous, and let's hope the damned business is done with.'

They lunched in the restaurant of the hotel, where all the flavour was in the menu, leaving the actual food tasting of beige. 'Dover sole,' Ledward apostrophized the dish he was eating. 'Cooked in Dover, and posted.'

Forbes was pondering the outcome of the meeting, running over those aspects to which his own responses might have been touched by considerations other than those he shared with the others. He had made no mention of the embargoing of the export licence, because that was subject to the confidentiality of his own position, and anyway if he'd mentioned it the outcome would have been even more certain: he had exerted no undue influence. And the arrangements between himself and Ihara were entirely incidental to any decision about the sale, and that decision had been arrived at – certainly as far as he was concerned – purely on the strength of the argument. There had been no dissembling. He could not feel himself compromised. Did Calderstone or Olney have secondary agendas? Prince had been cosying up to Ihara, so much was clear from the lunch at his house, perhaps he had his eye on some business advantage. Ledward's bias was all in the open. But they'd done their duty by the Club, each member would be better off by £180,000 or so and, as he trepanned his steak-and-kidney pie and stuck a fork into its portion-controlled interior, Forbes's conscience was clear.

What Edward wanted to avoid was using his ex-policeman friend to dig out Spalding's mobile number. It could be done in a trice, he knew, but then it would lay a trail between him and what he was devising. So at Quantum Solutions, with a short wave radio and a bank of five linked computers, he set about doing it electronically. Random hacking was, by its very name, an enormously time-consuming hit-and-miss affair – it would take forever to wade through a possible forty thousand names and numbers. But only if you were trying to do it by hand. Edward's setting up of the computers to work together would cut the time to half a day. Even this proved a worst-case estimate. The radio provided a sequence of beams and the five computers tittered and whimpered through the possibilities at a rate of three a second, and a scant two hours after they were set going one of them went peep-peep like a microwave announcing dinner was ready. Edward had programmed Spalding's name into the sequence, and as soon as the electronics hit it, they stopped at the number it was paired with. Then Edward faced a small dilemma. Did he check the name by ringing the number? Even with the who-was-calling amenity blanked off, Spalding's provider might maintain a record, and that would leave a trace, however slight. But it wouldn't matter if it was a call-box because a call-box belonged to nobody.

Edward drove into Guildford, stopped the car in a turning off the ring road by the cathedral, and walked on until he found a telephone box. Rang the number. 'Sidney Spalding here,' came the reply, and the voice was the voice on the tape. Edward rang off. Then walked into the despoiled centre of the town and at a Dixon's looked round the shop until he found the mobile he was looking for. Bought it and walked out with a sensation of deep satisfaction. He spent the afternoon in his office taking the thing apart, and having made certain adjustments to the micro-chips in its innards. reassembled it, and then sat with it in his hands, the expression on his face sharp-set and eager, like a child who knows where his present is hidden but also knows he mustn't play with it till Christmas.

'Now we have to find the right moment for the swap,' he said to Forbes that evening. Forbes hesitated, but very briefly. He knew he could not, would not, ask Edward outright what he had arranged. Nor would he stop him.

'That's easy enough. The Club, the evening of the concert. I know the shit is going to be there because his name was on the list. We're going, of course, and that would be the time and place. Mobiles checked in with the hall-porter, as I told you.'

Edward nodded.

'But how do we make sure the porter's not on the scene?'

'There's a phone-box opposite his desk. What you do is go in there, ring his number, ask him to find someone, and while he's away, I make the swap.'

Edward looked admiringly at Forbes.

'You know, Rupe, you can tell the tale almost as good as me.'

I said to Letty, 'You don't have to go back tomorrow, do you?' She was putting up at an hotel in Basil Street. I hadn't liked to say my house, I suppose I was a bit shy. But then I thought she might be as old-fashioned as I am.

'Have to. Meeting the chap I let a cottage to.'

Pang of annoyance.

'He's the most frightful pain. Thinks the country is a sort of Saturday morning in Belsize Park.' But I didn't like to think of her meeting him or anyone else. 'His wife's worse.' Ah, that was better. 'Want me to do something about the bathroom. Duck-egg blue, I shouldn't wonder.'

We were walking out of the Club after the concert and the dinner, and Forbes and his nephew were just in front of us, hailing a cab.

'Well, I'd got a curious expedition to propose to you. Real anthropology.'

I told her about Routh and the revivalist stuff that Spalding had bent my ear with.

'It's on tomorrow. But,' I said, 'actually it was only an excuse. I wanted to see you again tomorrow.'

We cabbed it to Basil Street. She got out. 'I only said I wouldn't want to go back to your club tomorrow. I didn't mean you. I didn't mean I wouldn't want to see you. What I'll do is wait for you to ask me out again. You know. Please.'

She waved goodbye and walked into the hotel. I told the driver my address, and sat back. Funny about feeling happy. It's about the future. About hope. I'd thought that was all over for me.

ELEVEN

I like those suburban roads which run down into Surrey. There is a quietness in the avenues that seems to be specially theirs. You come through the built-up bits, schools and playing fields and industrial estates, then you find yourself in parts where the green hasn't been entirely extinguished, and there's a golf course or two, and the green seems to be telling you the country has its uses, even though it has to be held in check. And then suddenly there are real fields, and houses that make you feel they've always been there although when you look they haven't been there long, Edwardian, but if not old, old-fashioned, with tennis courts as well as swimming pools, and a bit of land, and when you pass a white van with a logo which boasts that some plumber was estd. 1970, the houses seem positively ancient. Stockbrokers, I suppose; it was always called the stockbroker belt in old detective stories – the stereotype popped up in my head as I drove down through Richmond and Kingston thinking of places like Claygate and East Clandon, places where men with money enough, even if no pedigree, lived a comfortable notch or two beyond the gin and tonics of the bank managers and the estate agents. In the pubs and clubs and hotels at which they were regularly seen, they might feel that if there'd still been squires in these parts it could have been them.

Esher was a place I didn't know, just a name. A single street of shops. I edged through the two or three sets of lights, and kept an eye out for Claremont which I saw from the map was just beyond the town. The grand eighteenth-century house was now a school, but the grounds belonged to the National Trust, and as I walked up to the ticket place there was no one about. 'They don't get here for a an hour or so yet,' the man explained, so I thought I'd take a look at the landscape while it was empty, paid and went in.

Hard to imagine any real environment looking more like a hand-tinted print of Queen Anne's time. The lake was the central feature, surrounded by well-gardened spinneys, and there was a miniature pavilion on a small island. Paths threaded their way through this artificial pleasaunce, one of them leading up into the trees, past a ha-ha to a belvedere on a hill, possibly a natural promontory but more likely constructed in the interests of variety by the landscape artist, whether Repton or Brown, employed by the duke who had had the whole thing contrived for his pleasure (I read all this on the notice-board at the entrance), with later adjustments by Clive (who pulled down the Vanbrugh house and had another one put up, while rerouting the main road to Cobham so it didn't encroach, and still, no doubt, standing aghast at his own moderation).

The shore-line of the lake was adorned by a grotto, but quite the most distinctive item in this perfectly preserved 300-year-old fantasy was the amphitheatre carved out of the park which overlooked and dominated the fifty or so acres. It rose above the lake in a series of gentle tiers, its curving grass slopes carefully maintained, so that in the gleaming sunshine it was easy to imagine the grand ladies of the household promenading above and below, as they performed a masque. But there was a white block or plinth at the centre of the topmost tier, almost like an altar, on which a microphone had been placed, and slung in the upper branches of the tall trees behind it I could see cables and loudspeakers. Momentarily, I felt the intrusion of something at odds with this harmless fairy glade and found myself out of humour.

Getting there too early. Tiresome, when you were only mildly curious. But truth to tell I was thinking about Letty. That was where it really was. Who cared about these revivalist nutters, it *had* only been an excuse, she was the reason for such a daft expedition, but on my own, what the devil was I doing there? I crossed the road and went into a big pub and ordered a glass of Guinness, picked up a *Daily Mail* and turned the pages.

A man came into the bar, and handed me a leaflet. I glanced at it – 'Church of the True Reconciliation. All welcome.'

'It's across the road in a few minutes.'

'Thank you,' I said, and turned again to the paper.

But he was still standing there.

'I know you won't mind me asking. But are you saved?'

As I say, I was feeling bad tempered, and I should have stuffed his leaflet up his nose. But what can you do with the village idiot? Well, one thing you should never do is ask him anything. Especially anything to which the answer is more than ordinarily likely to emerge in the form of Scotch mist.

'I'm not at all sure I know what you mean by saved?'

He was delighted. I doubt if he often encountered responsiveness, in any form. So he told me what it was, to be saved.

'On what authority,' I asked him, 'do you tell me this? For,' I added, 'you offer me no chapter or verse.' Now that was quite the wrong way to put it, because he took me to be referring to the Bible, and rattled off a selection of chapters and verses. And he told me with intense pleasure that his authority was God.

I was of course in the shallowest of water, and had only myself to blame. 'How does God communicate with you?' My only excuse is that I had time to kill, but how foolish my own end of the conversation sounds. He said that God's voice was unmistakable.

'Really? And what language does God speak in?'

He said, I thought very reasonably, 'He needs no language.'

I shouldn't have started all this because there was nowhere it could go.

Finally, I said, 'Do you never get a crossed line?'

This must have just reached the place he was locked up in, since he actually asked for clarification.

'What do you mean?' he said.

'I wondered if you could always be quite sure it was God.'

He smiled.

'Oh yes. Quite sure.'

That was about it, because even though I could see I had surprised him by not ignoring him or telling him to go away, he was aware he had others to address, and I wondered if he ever met anyone willing to join him in his solitary confinement; anyone, that is, who was not already there.

He moved on and said, 'You would make a great Christian.'

And when I said, 'But I *am* a Christian,' he was already cruising away across the carpet, quite unaware that the barman felt the pub space was being trespassed upon. He gave out a few more leaflets and then he left, and I got up to go across the road and see what was happening. Perhaps I should say that I'm one of those Church of England fainthearts with an aversion to enthusiasm of any sort – I simply don't care for spontaneity. I like to think that if you're doing religion at all it should go very quietly, and mostly be made up of hymns and church bells and parsons who have dull wives. Kindness is the keynote of my sort of – well, what can you call it?

Not religion, really, more doing what my class has always done I suppose, but kindness defines it for me, and before anyone else says it I'll say it for them – sentimental is what it is: motes in the sunbeams through the stained-glass windows, and no sign of anyone being fervent. But there are as many kinds of religious feeling as there are people feeling it – as the Hindus say, each individual has a religion of his own. I don't feel any of it very strongly at all, but think God and all that is probably true, and take atheists to be as unappealingly enthusiastic as their religious counterparts.

I say all this because I don't want anyone to think I am fool enough to believe that a fundamentalist rally – and what an unpleasant word 'rally' is, especially in this context – has anything to do with religion of any sort. You get God called on all the time, in an angry sort of way, and you know God doesn't get angry, it's only people who do that. And laying God under contribution every time you say something that you feel like saying seems to me to be impertinent as well as fatuous. If God were anything like some of the people who claimed to speak in his name, I would want nothing to do with him. But such people were at the centre of all that went on that day, and in a place that had been designed for what was frivolous and amiable, something authoritarian and essentially unfriendly had taken its place.

Cromwellian was one of the adjectives I had in mind, but Cromwell wasn't pretending. Horrible old bastard, he was sincere. But then I thought, so was Hitler, and all things considered perhaps it was better that the people running this particular show were simply crooks. For that's the conclusion I came to. Guilt seemed to be the fuel that the speakers were firing on: not their own, for the way they ranted made it clear they felt their share had been got rid of in some way, and so they were in a position to accuse everyone else. And I had the feeling those accused were quite enjoying being accused.

They did a lot of lamenting. Every time the speaker shouted out something he specially didn't expect anyone to disagree with, hurling it at the audience like sling shot, daring anyone not to applaud, they all wailed loudly in unharmonious affirmation. People sat cross-legged on the grass in front of the amphitheatre, and just behind the first few rows there was a line of wheelchairs; I saw a woman with the sort of grey pudding-basin haircut I associate with St John's Ambulance ladies scuttling about and marshalling the infirm. She stopped by one lady in a chair whose head was lolling backwards. 'Have you been prayed over yet, dear?' I heard her ask, and on receiving a response she said, 'Just sit there quietly, they're all engaged at the moment.'

But before the speakers came to the podium, music was blasting from the tannoys: there was a trio decked out in beards and trinkets, energetically having at their drums and guitars, while a line of girls in jeans and trainers, all wearing Tee-shirts printed with the words *Mad for Jesus*, swung their legs left and right on the lower two tiers of the amphitheatre, singing a song about God as the electronic cyclone swept through the trees. I think I resented the T-shirt slogans because of the concocted ambiguity: yes, if you were a non-believer, they were claiming you'd think they were mad, so they shoved it in your face, while retaining the other meaning for themselves – to be mad for Jesus was to be true and good. Crude PR – but might work for a certain sort of audience. PR? Spalding. Was he here? The inmates of the wheelchairs clapped their hands more or less in time with the music.

Then the *Mad for Jesus* girls skipped down and began pushing what looked like bottle banks on wheels from the periphery of the amphitheatre on to the flat stretch of grass in front of it. Each of the carts was topped with a hoop of fairy lights which spelt out the words SIN BIN, and a big man with a moustache like the Marlborough cowboy and dressed in a white suit appeared at the top of the amphitheatre and began to speak into the microphone in an accent that might have been from somewhere like Arkansas. He could have been Bill Clinton's brother.

'God's temple is not built of brick and mortar, God's temple lies within, God's temple is the human body. But my beloved friends, God will not dwell in a space fouled by unchastity. We pray for that brother, that famous brother whose name is big box-office all over the world by reason of his *wonderful* ballads, but he should have stood up in front of the Lord and cried aloud, Lord I have *sinned*, I shouldn't never have slept with all those women. But when he gave the press conference and told what he had done and the dreadful disease that was the consequence of what he had done, he said it like it was just something he was going to have to take more care about in future. And what *happened* when he said this? The shares of the condom companies shot up *overnight*!'

There were scattered cries of lamentation and despair from among the audience. Shouts of 'Shame, shame!' 'Turn to the Lord!' 'Halleluja!' This was when I concluded the people who were running the show were con artists – perhaps the most effective sort of con artist, in that they very nearly believed what they were saying, even as they deployed the arts of lying in all their theatrical splendour: an unbeatable combination. And being accused of the wickednesses of mankind stirred the emotions of the audience in ways that were far from straightforward, for the words of the preacher brought them close to those sins of the flesh that they had not committed and made them feel as though they had, and while this provoked their guilt, the guilt attested to the attractiveness of what provoked it, and the combination of remorse and pleasure was what everyone was there for.

'I say to you today and every day guard your purity – guard it from the Evil One who is crazy jealous of that purity, who wants to take that purity away from you and fill the space with lewd imaginings and carnal desires. I say to you on this bright and beautiful day, in Jesus's *name* abandon the totems of pollution, drugs and cigarettes and drink and sex magazines. I call upon you to put these things from you – I call upon you to rid yourselves of them for ever. I call upon you here and now to *bin* your sins – to cleanse yourself of your moral garbage by pitching it into the Sin Bins as they come among you, lest you are *hurled* into them yourselves on the Day of Judgement. Take the smallest coins you have about your persons on this bright clear winter's day and as tokens of your desire for total cleansing, pitch them in as the Sin Bins come by.'

The American idiom would have added a spice to the show, all entertainment was now American, so it must be the right way to take your religion. The *Mad for Jesus* girls were singing as they pushed the Sin Bins through the crowd. The tune was 'The Love Bug Will Get You If You Don't Watch Out' brought up to date by the electronic thump of the accompanying music.

The Sin Bin will get you
If you don't watch out,
And when it gets you,
Why you scream and shout!

Ho ho di ho!
Hi hi di hi!
THAT'S *what sin is all about.*

Everyone was throwing pennies into the bins, and I judged the manoeuvre was just a preliminary, to get them used to parting with cash. Where would Spalding be? I strolled on the outskirts of the crowd as the music continued and the next speaker was awaited. Perhaps Spalding didn't have to turn up to the actual rally, his after all was a backroom task. I had turned away from the podium and was looking out over the lake where a single small rowing-boat was moored to a finger of jetty running out into the glassy water. And as I gazed I could scarcely believe my ears. The voice was unmistakable, though oddly distorted, whether by the tannoys or by the occasion. I turned round.

'We all know that the virus of AIDS is the virus of sin. But disease is the outward sign of inward malignancy so often – of the warped and degrading desires that feed like the cancers they are on the perishable material of our weak and enfeebled humanity.'

There he stood, in his tight little double-breasted suit, Routh, with the words welling from his bleak unopened face as from some hidden spring, some dark undeclared source, perhaps as unknown to himself as it ever would be to those who met him in other circumstances.

'I look below and see our brothers and sisters in their wheel-chairs and I ask: is it only our bodies which are disabled, or is the outward disfigurement but an image of the deformity within? The halt and the lame carry their burden for all to see, but what of those who conceal the rottenness that eats away their immortal souls? Who show a smooth unblemished face to the world even as the worm of perversion is feeding in the corrupt darkness of their lustful hearts.'

Now there were eager cries of 'Forgive us' and 'Praise the Lord' and 'Halleluja'. Was this who Routh really was? He meant every word, he was not dissembling.

'But remember that every atom of your corrupt depraved bodies belongs to Jesus. And he will come among us as Jesus the avenger with his terrible sword to cut down the wanton and the unrighteous. Well do the unclean have cause to tremble, for Jesus's eye X-rays every soul, you may hide your shameful fantasies from your neighbours but you cannot hide them from Jesus. He sees into the filth and grime of the human heart, he tears aside the curtain and reveals the sordid tableaux that offend his gaze. He is God's *spy*! He knows where those surreptitious glances at the top shelves of newsagents leads, he knows the lustful pictures of naked women in tabloid newspapers are but the deadly preliminaries to the abuse of children by satanists in black-magic rituals and orgies involving teenage girls who are used as brood mares to produce the foetuses for sacrificial rites!'

Now there were cries and groans, and a man in a wheelchair shouted, 'It's true, it's true! Repent! Repent!' The *Mad for Jesus* chorus started to sing to the tune of the hymn, 'Glorious things of thee are spoken' –

Jesus, Jesus, Prince, Messiah
Save us from our wicked sins.
Thine the rod and thine the fire.
Now our penitence begins.

Routh was still at the podium. I wondered if it had ever crossed his mind that speaking like that to the weak and credulous was a form of assault. He made Jesus sound like the writer of poison-pen letters.

'Too late! Too late! Those fatal words! In a day, in an hour the choice is taken from us and the filth and impurity in which we have luxuriated are exchanged eternally for the agonies of eternal damnation. Too late to howl for the fire to be quenched – the fire will burn the sinner to the bare bone – the torture will be everlasting, the pain endure unendurably as the seared flesh falls from the blackened bones and is unconsumed, that it may burn again and again and again.

As Routh was speaking the ullulations of the crowd increased in volume, responding to the words he uttered almost as a lynch mob might have done. What horrified me was Routh's naked relish.

'Let the blood of the Lamb wash your sinful wounds. Let your sinful soul be stained in the blood of the Lamb. A blood sacrifice for the wickedness of mankind.'

As though he would have shed that blood. The mob howled. I was sick at heart. Once we had been touching on religion in the Club and a rather solemn old buffer said the Jesus story must have something in it, something that answered a human need, otherwise it wouldn't have persisted for so long. He said he supposed suffering and pain called for ambiguous representation, for though the primitive desire to hurt could be repressed, and the feelings of guilt that went with it could be stifled, both were still there. 'Hence that filthy gibbet with the man hanging on it.' I thought his words extravagant. But listening to Routh and the crowd which howled back at him, I saw again those savage Crucifixion scenes so hugely popular in their day and felt what I'd felt many times: Jesus didn't have a chance. Routh walked off and the big American came back. It was a great relief.

'Praise the Lord. Halleluja. I thank the Lord *Jesus* for the testimony of Brother Routh. God bless you, Brother. OK, now, Brothers and Sisters, the Lord says there is one thousand pounds fifty-four pence that is here today to be taken up for his holy work, and God's word never fails. If God tells me that money is here, it is *here*! Say Aymen, say Aymen!'

What had been a simple excursion to satisfy my curiosity had turned into something darker. I wish I'd never heard Routh doing his dreadful stuff. Hearing him inflame the crowd.

'Now that's a lot of money, Brothers and Sisters, but believe it or not there is four people here who will open their hearts to the Lord and be the first to pledge ten pounds each of that one thousand pounds fifty-four pence exactly. Holy, holy, cry Aymen!'

I had walked away a little distance, into the trees, still listening to the pitch-man as he worked the crowd.

'How many believe the Lord is telling the truth when he says there is four people here who is going to be the *first* to pledge ten pounds for the one thousand pounds fifty-four pence that will be gathered up today towards the hydraulically operated choir-loft that is to be installed in our house of refuge for beloved evangelists who have been overtaken by age? Who believes, who believes? Hold your hands up high!'

Men wearing blazers and carrying buckets labelled GIFTS FOR GOD had taken up positions flanking the speaker on the topmost terrace, and, of course, they had to be up there so the first of the donors to come forward could be seen by the rest of the crowd.

And good enough, a young man, and then a few moments later a young woman, began to climb up the grassy tiers, and after a short pause a middle-aged couple followed them, and the man in the white suit crowed triumphantly into his microphone.

'Isn't that wonderful? God's holy word is fulfilled! Pray for them, Brothers and Sisters. The angels sing! The girls in the *Mad for Jesus* T-shirts were swaying in unison, and the guitar-and-bongo brigade strummed moodily, the tableau a more developed version of a mock auction in Oxford Street. At this point I saw Spalding. He was moving down one side of the amphitheatre. I retreated a little further into the trees.

'I cannot believe the Lord's word will be denied here today, Brothers and Sisters, I cannot believe there is any folks here who would blaspheme and deny the Lord's words. Let not the word of the Lord be denied, for the wrath of the Lord is terrible. He is dreadful in battle, he slays the infidel, the doubter. He mows *down* the mean and evil.'

Now the men in blazers, the bottlers, had come down from on high and were moving among the crowd with their buckets. There must have been a thousand people present, so at a pound a head maybe the ringmaster's prophesy wouldn't be so far out. Spalding had strolled to the sandy edge of the lake and was looking out across the water as though giving himself a bit of a break.

'Bless the Lord, oh bless his holy name, that you may par*take* of his loving plan to endow those courses in Hawaiian guitar, Psalms, Homiletics and Divine Healing that will give our students the skills and strengths to take his holy word throughout the *world*.'

Then I saw Spalding climb into the little rowing-boat, pushing himself away from the wooden jetty, and edging slowly out into the lake. Unshipping the oars, he began to scull slowly towards the middle as a light breeze ruffled the surface of the water. I rather wished I'd thought of doing it myself.

'He will not *spare* the mean and the ungenerous, he will force open the fists of the tightwad—'

All the time, I was idly watching Spalding, speculating on the degree of his cynicism – after all, what did he or his firm care what cause they promoted? It was legal, and it paid, and who could say it was his business to worry about the message they were selling? As well expect an actor to eat the margarine he did the voice-over for. Spalding had shipped the oars and was drifting gently towards the island with the little pavilion. He was no real distance from the shore, and I could see him clearly. He took out his mobile phone from a top pocket – I knew that's what it was, because he pulled out an aerial as I stood beneath the trees watching him. I saw him concentrate on the thing, holding it in his left hand and beginning to prod in a number with the other.

'He will *smite* the ungodly—'

An explosion filled the universe. The noise rocked and echoed and reverberated, and was orchestrated by the screams of birds and the shrieks of the crowd. Across the lake a pillar of smoke 150 feet high had risen into the air where Spalding and the rowing-boat had been. Fragments and shards of wood were pattering down into the water and the crowd scattered, dissolving into random particles under the influence of panic, accelerating in all directions.

I had felt the blast whip past my head. Horrified, I raced round the edge of the lake towards the blue column of smoke, but raced towards nothing as the debris floated down from the sky. I looked behind me, and the crowd as an entity had disintegrated, some this way, some that, along with the men in the blazers and the man in the white suit and the girls with the T-shirts and the bearded musicians. I stared at the water and saw nothing but debris. My heart pounded, my breath came in gasps. The column of smoke lost its shape, resolving into wisps and tendrils as it drifted across the lake and rose up and was lost in the upper air as though it had never been. There was a smell of burning.

People were scattered in ones and twos, some crouching behind the trees, all with an air of frozen expectation as though awaiting some further dreadful visitation. But the theatricals of a moment before had been whipped away: a man in a rowing-boat had been blown to pieces and real fear had stripped the crowd naked. I got to the gate, but the doorkeeper was already telephoning the police and an ambulance. No one knew what had happened, most people's backs had been turned to the lake, and they were chattering nervously, not listening to each other. Was it an Islamic terrorist group, revenge for the American air-strikes on Iraq?

When the police arrived I buttonholed one of them and said, 'If you'd like to know what happened, I saw it and I can tell you.' And I did.

'You were watching the boat, were you, sir?'

'Yes. I knew the man.' I explained how I knew him. 'His name was Spalding, Sidney Spalding, and I believe he was doing the PR for this rally.'

'And you saw the explosion.'

'I saw Spalding row out. I saw him using what I took to be a mobile phone. And then I saw and heard an explosion.'

He wrote it all down, and took my name and address and my occupation. Then looked out at the lake.

'There won't be much to go on. All in bits and in the water. We'll drag it, of course. Excuse me, sir, but are you a member of this organization?'

'No, I was here out of curiosity.'

'And do you know whether this Mr Spalding has family?'

'I know he has a wife, but I don't know more than that.'

Then he said what I'd been dreading.

'Of course, we can send someone over to break the news, but if there was anyone who was known to the lady—'

'I don't know her, I've met her.'

'Might be better coming from someone who wasn't a complete stranger, sir.'

I knew I had to do it.

'Yes,' I said, 'you're right. If one of your colleagues could telephone my club, I can ask them for her address.'

He spoke into his lapel mike and I gave him the club's number, which he passed on. Then we waited, and he said, 'They're on the line now, sir. If you'd speak into this.' So I got the porter to tell me the address without saying why I needed it, and the policeman wrote it down as I repeated it.

A rubber dinghy used by the keeper of the grounds had been inflated, and he and two policemen and the ambulance men were rowing across to the scene. A matter of form.

'What we'll do, sir,' said the officer I'd been speaking to, 'is keep the information to ourselves until you let us know the next-of-kin has been informed. Just ring this number.'

'It'll take me a couple of hours from here. If she's in, of course.'

I took the card with the number, nodded, and left. It crossed my mind that Routh might have been a more appropriate messenger, but I didn't see him, and anyway I couldn't have spoken to him, even to land him with this appalling task. Sometimes you had to do things you didn't want to do. I checked the *A–Z* and got to Camberwell, turned up Camberwell Grove, very gentrified, and out on to a hill with a view of Crystal Palace – why call it that, long gone, it only awakens expectations. Down the road to a roundabout called Goose Green – was the battlefield in the Falklands called after it? No, many goose greens, once. I found their street. Terraced houses with bay windows, not very big. As I recalled her saying at the club dinner, there was a space in front for the bins, not quite a front garden.

I knocked on the door but there was no answer. A momentary pang of relief. Was I going to be able to avoid this? No. So I went next door, and told the woman I had an urgent message for Mrs Spalding, and the woman, a pleasant woman, said, 'Oh, I know just where she is. She's up the lotty. They have an allotment, you know. She won't mind me telling you, I'm sure. She's always there on a Tuesday. Nothing the matter, I hope?' And she told me in some detail how to get there. I went through some side roads that worked their way upwards of the high streets, and I found myself going by hedges and gateways and fences that seemed to have been let alone by anything that had happened across the last seventy or so years, and at the top of the hill bumped out of a lane into a rough sort of parking space that was surrounded by allotments – not a usual word these days, not many such spaces left behind by the international concrete.

When I got out of the car I made my way between stands of runner beans and tomato plants and tiny cherry trees and little ploughed pocket handkerchiefs of earthy dug-up plots that hadn't yet been planted, past a beehive or two. And the grassy path, narrow and one of many, was hummocky, with here and there a standpipe and a small cistern, and now and again a little shed such as a child would dream of living in. The allotments were high up, on a long broad slope. I stopped for a moment amid this little wilderness, a clutter of small natural, very private places, so personal that each seemed to bear the features of its owner, making it impossible ever to mistake one plot for another. I looked out through the tangle of wheelbarrows and onion sets, and saw at the bottom of the long slope a playing-field, and then beyond and below that a perspective of London from east to west like a cyclorama that almost seemed to rotate for you when you turned your head. There is a picture called *A Clown and an Angel Before a City*, and when I see it I cannot decide whether the figures will enter the city, or turn from it. While I stood in the tussocky grass, on this high unconsidered spot, I wondered again.

Mrs Spalding's neighbour had said their allotment was on the west side of the slope, and I was moving in that direction. I would recognize her, I hadn't forgotten her weatherbeaten countenance, and when I saw her delving away at the earth with a spade, at the end of one of the paths, I walked even slower, and then without considering what I might say, approached her. She looked up and I greeted her.

'Don't I know you?'

'We met at the Club dinner. To celebrate the Leonardo picture.'

She jammed the spade into the earth.

'But what a peculiar place to meet again.'

'You weren't in. Your neighbour told me you were here.'

'Oh. Why?'

'I have some very bad news.'

What else do you begin by saying? She came across the clods she'd been turning over, then on to the little track that ran between her plot and the next one. I saw the sun glinting on the tall towers of the city far away. Then we stood together, and I said her husband had been killed.

'Killed? You mean he's dead?'

There were two deformed plastic kitchen chairs that someone had abandoned.

'We'd better sit here,' I said, and we did, the spiky legs of the chairs sinking into the grass and tilting sideways. And I described what had happened.

Because she couldn't allow herself to be confronted by the hugeness of the event, not immediately, she said, 'So we won't get the pay-out from the picture.' It was a utilitarian note, and I was glad of it, because you can always make a response to that kind of thing. 'Your interests will be safeguarded. Be assured. The Club would want it.'

She was wearing wash-leather gloves.

Then she said, 'He was a dreadful fellow. I don't know how I shall live without him.'

My idea was to let her speak.

'All front. But you see, I knew him. Knowing someone. It's everything. I've never known anyone else.'

After a pause, I said, 'Is there a friend or neighbour—?'

'Oh, Mrs de Cruz. She must have been the one you spoke to. I suppose the insurance he took out with the mortgage will pay it off. Will I ever know what happened to him?'

'The police—'

She asked me to tell her again what had happened.

'You mean, in an instant? A whole life. Blown up, you said.'

We sat in the grass-smelling allotments. The sun declined.

'Ashamed of Peckham. You've got to live somewhere. He had no redeeming feature, but he was mine. Do you understand that?'

'I do. My own wife. She was killed in a car crash.'

'Oh, you poor man.'

She put her wash-leather-gloved hand on mine.

I said, 'Memory. Which never dies.'

We sat in silence, on the sideways chairs.

Then, as we looked across the little tousled place where people so modestly brought a touch of order out of the shouting business of being alive in a universe which doesn't care, I said of the 'rally', 'I was there out of curiosity, and I believe it was not right for me so casually to see your husband die. But better for someone who knew him to see it, perhaps.'

Then I lied.

'I thought he had a special something. Could never quite put my finger on it.'

Mrs Spalding shook the gloves off her hands, dropped them in the grass.

'It's nice of you to say it. Hard to believe, though. He was so cynical. Nothing mattered to him, except things that don't matter.'

Then I said what I truly did believe.

'My own feeling is it doesn't matter what we thought of anyone who was close, that close. The closeness, the fact of it, the fact that they were with us, is the thing. I don't myself think anything else much matters, you know. It's the fact. It's so much more than anything you could say about the fact.'

She wept.

I said, 'Shall I ask the lady next door—?'

'No, I'll go in to her, later on. Thank you. I think it would be rotten to hear this dreadful thing from someone who didn't know what it was themselves. It gives you a right to bring the news.'

I nodded.

'I wonder who did it? Terrorists? But why?' The largeness of the event, and also its dreadful particularity, must have been running through her mind.

'I do a bit of secretarial work, that'll go on.'

'And,' I said, 'be sure whatever share he would have had from that picture—'

She nodded. And said, 'I like Peckham, actually. But poor old Sid, I don't know who he thought he was. Well, I do, but it won't go into words.'

When we got up, I led the way through the individual private places, past an occasional person who was dwelling on an arrangement of sweet peas or tying up some raspberry canes. They didn't know what had happened, and when I'd telephoned the police and told them I'd broken it to Mrs Spalding, the people in the allotments would hear all about it on the news, where it would be turned into something characteristic of the news, something the news was there to be filled with. So that it wouldn't sound like anything that had happened in an individual private life, would seem to be miles away from the hands that made little holes in the earth to plant seed potatoes or stretched string from one side of the plot to the other to make sure the baby carrots would come up according to plan, in the due season.

TWELVE

The newsreader said, 'So far no one has admitted responsibility for the explosion, and it is known that Mr Spalding had no affiliations with parties either side of the sectarian divide in Northern Ireland. The possibility of involvement by Islamic terrorist groups who are opposed to the recent air strikes by the American Airforce in Iraq, has not been ruled out. Forensic experts say the explosion may have been caused by Semtex, but have little hope of establishing this since the debris recovered from the lake is waterlogged.'

'So it was a bunch of bloody wogs,' Edward said. Then laughed raucously. 'Wonder how they set it up!'

But he was alone in the car. When he got back from Quantum Solutions he went into the house and shouted, 'Roo-hoop!' Went into the drawing-room and found Forbes with a drink in his hand. 'You heard? Our troubles are over.'

Forbes handed him the whisky and poured himself another.

'We weren't the only ones who had it in for Spalding, then.' Edward took a swig from his glass. 'Shouldn't have got mixed up with those American tub-thumpers, what do you call them, evangelists? America – the Great Satan, don't they say in those faraway countries of which we know little?' He chortled. 'It's over, Rupe – we needn't have bothered.'

Forbes said, 'You didn't say what you had in mind with the mobile.'

'Oh God,' Edward said, 'you know, indoor fireworks, electric shock, funny snake jumping up his nose. But the Islamic brothers seem to have been more serious.' He finished his drink and went across and poured himself another. 'No, well. Nasty business, if you prime it with Semtex. Didn't they say Semtex on the news? But of course no one will ever know.' He took a suck at the whisky. 'Beauty of it is the weapon – if weapon there was – was blown up too. No trace, no leads, no nothing. Everything in little bits in the water. Couldn't have been a better venue.' Then he looked at Forbes. 'Come on Rupe, why so solemn? Listen, you've heard of spontaneous combustion, might have been that. Or look – perhaps the bastard's conscience got to him, and he committed suicide.'

Forbes said, 'The less said, the better.'

Edward replied, 'Don't you think I know that as well as you? My face is straight, my lips are sealed. But one thing remains: I want that five hundred quid back.'

Forbes looked at him hard. 'What does it matter?'

'Not a lot. But I don't want your bit of rough trade deciding he'll take over where his pal left off.'

'What are you going to do?'

'Put the frighteners on him.'

Edward telephoned Billy Jasper and said he'd drop in the following morning. Hoped Phyllis wouldn't be there, as he was a bit anxious doing business with a third party in the offing.

'It's her day off, anyway,' Jasper told him.

So, bright and early the next morning, Edward knocked on the door of No. 23 Wycroft Avenue. Billy Jasper opened the door.

'Hullo,' said Edward, doing the public schoolboy.

'Edward!' whinnied Jasper. 'It's you, dear boy, come in come in, it's just us – Phyllis is visiting her aunty and uncle. And how is your own dear uncle? Ah – wait, I bet I know! – he's sent you with the readies! Enter, enter.'

They walked into the open-plan sitting-room.

'Coffee?'

'Got no time.'

'These little chats. Very cosy. And I'm not saying I can't use the money.'

'What money?'

Edward's public school manner was falling away, and something else was showing through. Billy Jasper hadn't noticed.

'Two thousand. It's going to be a big help.'

'For what?'

'Oh, you know. Things. The business.'

Edward went over to the television which was sitting in a corner. It was a big one, with a large screen. He took hold of it with both hands, and jerked it over. The works spilled out on to the carpet. Billy Jasper went white.

'What are you doing?'

'Can't you see? It'll need repairing. Or it might be cheaper to buy a new one.'

Edward walked across to the chimneypiece. It was a marble one, with a centre plaque featuring cherubs, something the owner had had put in, and on the mantel, below a plentifully gilded Florentine-style looking-glass, was a nineteenth-century French clock with white marble columns and ormolu mounts and classical figures holding up the dial. 'Catch,' said Edward, and threw it at Jasper. It smashed on the floor. 'Hope you're insured.'

Jasper sank down on a chair. 'What do you want?'

Edward said. 'Oh, I've got what I want. I've got two blackmailing letters from your mate, both of which for all I know you wrote yourself—'

'No, no—'

'And thanks to some old friends in the Met who aren't all that particular when it comes to doing a pal a favour when a blackmailing poof takes a liberty with him, I've also got both your voices on tape, talking about the scam you were trying to work on the gentleman I share a house with. But it looks as if you haven't heard the best news.'

Jasper was staring at Edward, terrified.

'You didn't hear it on that telly of yours? You must have missed it. Your friend got his just deserts. My God, I wish I'd been there. Lot of work must have gone into planning it, and the end came out beautiful. He was blown to smithereeens.'

'I – I didn't know him – didn't know who he was—'

'Bollocks,' said Edward, 'you knew he was Sidney Spalding, and from what I hear it may have been some other friends of mine, some nice Islamic friends, who take it very unkindly if people don't stick to their idea of the straight and narrow, who whacked him. You wouldn't want *them* coming round to give you a seeing-to, now, would you?' Edward walked across the room as Jasper cowered on his chair, and pulled a picture off the wall. It looked as though it might have been an Arthur Boyd, and he put his knee through it.

'Well, when I say I've got what I want, what I haven't got is the money you stole from me on my first visit, and I'm having that now. Quick, or I might get violent.'

Jasper got up and edged towards a small desk with inlays and veneers. With a trembling hand he turned a key in one of the drawers. Pulled out a pile of notes.

'You're very lucky I don't ask for interest.'

'I never meant to harm anyone, it was him—'

'Ooh, that's what they all say, don't they? When they're up against it.' And Edward took Billy Jasper by the throat and shoved him against the wall. 'You're a scumbag and no one misses a scumbag.' He hit him across the face with the back of his other hand. 'You miserable shit. I've a mind to finish you now. Guess who did for your friend?' He hit him again, and Jasper sank into the fireplace, clattering the fire-irons.

'Don't know, don't know.'

'You're getting off light. I hope you know *that*.' And this time, kicked him.

'I've got you by the balls, though the idea fills me with repulsion. I've got the letters, I've got the tape. And if you wake up in the middle of the night and hear something down below, don't bother wondering, it'll be me. Then you'd better worry.'

He pulled Jasper back by the collar, so that he was face upwards, gibbering with fright.

'Do you understand?'

Jasper squealed, 'Yes, yes.'

Edward said, 'I hear a word about any of this, I'll really be out of patience with you.' He wrenched the looking-glass from above the chimney piece and held it over Billy Jasper. 'See? You wouldn't want that horrible face of yours decorated with one of Phyllis's kitchen knives, would you? So see you behave.' And the glass fell out of the frame in slivers as he crashed it down on the brass coffee table.

'I advise you to clean up before Phyllis gets home.' Jasper lay on his back with his arms round his face. 'Just tell her one of your rough friends got a bit out of hand.'

And Edward left, closing the front door quietly behind him.

A notice went up at the Club, announcing that the sale had been completed, that the Leonardo had been sold to the Chief Executive of Pacific Rand for £45 million. Members would be circularized with the details of the sale, the contingent expenses arising, and after the necessary deductions agreed at the Extraordinary General Meeting, cheques would be sent out at the earliest opportunity.

'Very satisfactory.' said a member.

'Come in handy,' said another. 'We didn't get the best price, though, did we?'

'Mustn't grumble. Something about export licences, I gather. Let me buy you a drink.'

Upstairs in the library, Ledward was saying. 'That's it, then. I received a rather charming note from Miss Letitia Mary Barlow renouncing any claim on the proceeds. Said she felt that since her forebear probably had as little idea that he was giving away a Leonardo as the Club had that it was getting one, she didn't see that she had any part in what she calls this rather peculiar business. Peculiar indeed! Says she much appreciates Owlish's interest on her behalf – you recall his intervention at the EGM and has told him what she's decided. You know, I have an idea Owlish is rather taken with the lady, and I may say having seen her at the concert I admire his taste. But if there's any development in their relationship he'll be relieved, I daresay, that now there won't seem to be any conflict of interest.'

Other members of the committee nodded approvingly.

'How does it stand with the restorer?' asked Calderstone.

'Oh, Firethorne. Well, I had a slightly less charming letter from *him*. It's in the file here, if you want to read it. Put briefly, he thinks we're cheapskates. But Owlish was right – when I wrote to him I sent him a cheque for the hundred thousand we thought we'd try him with—'

'Post-dated?' Olney asked.

'Oh, dear me, yes, I don't think it makes you a cheapskate to be sure the proceeds are in your own hands before you start handing bits of them out,' Ledward said. 'But as I say, Owlish had the right of it, because though Firethorne sends us this rather disobliging letter, he somewhat undermines his position by not returning the cheque.'

'Mm, not too sure about that,' Forbes said, in rather judicial mode, tapping his fingers together as they made a steeple in front of his nose. 'May be hanging on to it, but doesn't mean he isn't finding out his legal position meanwhile.'

'Ah, Owlish again,' said Ledward. 'He's been into it and the long and short of it is there was no contract. We've paid the man what we think is fair and what he thinks isn't enough – but, according to Owlish, there isn't a case.'

'Hope he's right.'

'When does the Ihara figure take delivery?' Calderstone asked.

'Oh, he's got it. But not a moment before his money was on deposit with our bankers, who are getting overnight rates from the money market. Nice return. And it starts from the day it was first in escrow.'

'How much?' Olney asked.

'Should be eight per cent, give or take a fraction of a point.'

Calderstone's pipe made a whiffling noise as he drew on it.

'A little over ten thousand a day. Not bad.'

Forbes said with a magisterial smile, 'I admire your instant precision, Calderstone.'

'Comes of actually being made to learn my twice times table, Forbes. Stands you in better stead than playing games on a computer.'

'Of course,' Olney said, 'that's before tax.'

Ledward said rather sharply, 'Of course it is. But bear in mind the capital sum is wholly tax free. What we sold was a chattel. No CGT.'

They were silent.

'My God,' Ledward exclaimed, 'I shouldn't like to go through such a bizarre scenario ever again.'

'Oh, I don't know,' Olney said. 'Broke the monotony.'

The rest of them laughed, but Ledward said drily, 'May you live in interesting times, as the Chinese curse goes. Give me monotony every time.'

They rose.

'Prince not with us, then.'

'No, sent apologies. He's rather tied up.'

Prince was in what the previous owner of Ihara's house had called his library. This was a room some forty feet long, containing all that appertained to a library in the way of library tables and lecterns and chairs with reading-stands and large circular magnifying glasses attached to them, indeed all that a library requires in the way of ancillary equipment, but no books. The walls had been covered with *trompe-l'oeil* bookcases filled with the *trompe-l'oeil* images of books, and it was with a sense of being in a picture by Magritte that one might have climbed up any one of the pairs of library-steps to view more closely on the topmost shelves the spines of books that did not exist.

'I kept it as it was,' said Ihara, explaining this to his guest, 'it is surely a curio, and probably unique. In a way, it would have been a desecration to alter it. And as I do not intend actually to inhabit this strange place very long, it won't have a chance to pall. Now, what is our next move?'

Prince rose, and wandered round the walls, running his fingers over the spines of the 'books'.

'Every attention to detail,' he said. 'These are only spines, but every one of them calf-bound!'

'An extraordinary man. He was principally in oil, and that is a field where you often find the maverick, the oddity. Now hugely rich, where before he would have been a peasant. As is the case with all those Sultanates. So vulgar, but when vulgarity is on such a scale it becomes interesting.'

Prince had seated himself again.

'More than a few such people, I shouldn't wonder, among the benefactors of The Museum of Timeless Art. They please themselves, so long as it is tax-deductible. Anyway, we know Dallas is definitely on. Their Mr Wemdinger has the confidence of his board – the Convenors, as they are called – and they look on the matter of an export licence as Ruritanian nonsense. When I spoke to Wemdinger he made it clear that many of the most prized pictures in the collection were there with the wholehearted consent of those who had sold them, but not necessarily with the approval of busybodies who felt they ought to have some say in the matter. So long as the title is good, that was Wemdinger's point. And that we have. We have unimpeachable title.'

'We have indeed. And the price has been agreed with dear old Dallas.'

'Neither of us supposed they would go to the full sixty million, since the circumstances entail a discount. Are you satisfied with the final figure? I ask, because I know you were reluctant when we last discussed it, but since then I've been on to Wemdinger, and am convinced he won't budge.'

'So it's fifty-five million? Well, I'd hoped to screw a little more from them, but as entrepreneurs I think we may be satisfied.'

'I'm glad to hear you say it, because a turn of something more than twenty-two per cent seems to me to be acceptable on figures that are not insubstantial – leaves ten million net on an outlay of forty-five million. I can't offhand think of an investment I should have preferred to have put my money in. Especially allowing for the time-scale, which is brief, and the risk factor, which is very slight.'

Ihara, who was seated at one of the library tables – inlaid with brass and tortoiseshell, an ebonized boule table of the late nineteenth century – was fidgeting with a quill pen that lay beside an inkpot. It was of the sort that would have appeared in nineteenth-century illustrations of lawyers' offices. He looked down at it.

'Of course, we all like to surround ourselves with furniture that will let people know who we are,' he said, 'but really, all this stuff is like the decor for a film set.'

Prince looked at him. 'And for a film that was never made,' he said, absently.

'Anyway, as I say, what next?'

Prince got up and stretched his legs.

'Two options: you're moving, so you can take your possessions with you – take them anywhere you like without asking anyone's permission; or second, you could simply crate up the picture and get it out without anyone knowing.'

Prince, who was walking round the vast room, stopped to peer through one of the magnifying glasses, pulling a credit card out of his wallet to see what the enlargement was.

'Now, frankly, I like the second option best. Yes, you could bundle everything up, have it shipped out, but when I say you don't have to ask leave to do this, I've got no firm legal ground for saying it. I could easily get advice, as could you. But when you ask advice you create a window through which people can get a look at your affairs. There would be enough scope for someone who felt like it to alert such authorities as there may be.'

Ihara nodded, felt the end of the quill pen with his finger. Dipped it into the inkpot, but the pot was dry.

'*Sub rosa*: the Leonardo is quite a big item.'

'Oh, I don't think we should think of wrapping it up in a bit of brown paper and trusting to luck,' said Prince. 'We don't want any risk of the thing being confiscated. Equally, we don't want to multiply the downside by going in for hired aeroplanes or the like. No, I think I have a better idea.'

Prince returned to his chair. 'You recall how we came by the picture – the Club, I mean?'

Ihara said, 'The restorer found it. What was his name?'

'A man called Firethorne. What happened was that it had been hidden underneath another picture. It had been framed and then the John the Baptist had been clipped in on top of it. As you know, the Leonardo is still in that same frame.'

Ihara had taken a penknife out of his pocket and was cutting the end of the quill to make a new nib.

'Now Firethorne is an expert in all this – lifted off the old John the Baptist picture and left the Leonardo in the original one – well, we both know that. But what I'm getting at is this: let Firethorne reverse the process. Put him on to finding a picture for us of the right size, something of no real account, and he can slide it into the frame as he slid the other one out. And then the Leonardo is in purdah again.'

Ihara scratched the end of his nose with the quill pen. He mulled the idea over, not entirely convinced. 'Leaves him able to infer rather more than I would wish,' he said at last.

Prince reflected. 'That had occurred to me, but I think it's the lesser risk. If we sought legal advice on exporting the thing and got the answer No, the water's over the dam – whoever we consult will consult others, and the word is out. Then whatever we try and ship comes in for scrutiny. I say Firethorne is first choice. Pay him well, but not so well that he thinks something's up. You're just wanting to protect your investment by concealing it – as the original owner did.'

Ihara, unable to do anything with the pen he'd cut, laid it back in the groove in the table, alongside the dry inkpot.

'Who approaches him?'

Prince said, 'It doesn't much matter, though it can't be me since no one knows I have any share in this. So why not one of your men?'

Ihara got up and rambled round the room on his little bow legs.

'My men – I have a goodly number. Do you mean my Japanese men?'

'Why not?'

'They are good for very specific tasks, carry them out to the letter – I remember saying as much to Lord Olney – but if you get them involved in anything that might seem to be touched by, ah, ambiguity then their oriental faces immediately suggest duplicity. To the Western eye, that is.'

Ihara moved over to one of the long windows on the side of the library which looked out over the Thames.

'It is strange to think you couldn't stand at this window with a book in your hand unless you happened to bring one in with you. Truly surreal. No, I think an approach to Mr Firethorne should not be made by a cunning oriental. I have a young man in mind who conceives himself to be in my debt. As you suggest, I will leave him with the impression that I am concealing the Leonardo for those reasons it was concealed in the first place – as a device against thieves, and as the whim of a rich man, who shows his trophies only to those it pleases him to.'

Ihara went back across the room and picked up a telephone that stood by the empty ink-stand.

'I daresay our messenger would be on the make quite as readily as anyone from the Land of the Midnight Sun, but a certain *naïveté* would make it uphill work for him. Though his simple Anglo-Saxon face might well disarm his victim.'

He had dialled the offices of Crawfords, the accountants, and in a few moments was speaking to Randolph Wells.

THIRTEEN

Which is why Randolph found himself on a train to Frinton-on-Sea. The train clattered along the estuary, then went inland into the bits of Essex that seem remote from the Essex that has jokes made about it, and where real villages have old names like Tolleshunt Darcy and Gay Bowers, then after Chelmsford and Colchester the line turned down through the bungaloid flatlands towards the sea, and the train took the branch line to Frinton, leaving the possibility of Clacton to lesser mortals. Randolph had just about heard of Frinton, had read about it in the papers when someone wanted to open a fish-and-chip shop there and the residents wouldn't have it.

It was a bleak enough place on a winter's day, and he seemed to be the only human being. The grey metal sea and the wide sandy shore fronted a long road full of what he took to be empty hotels, but as he passed one of them he saw it had a brass plate describing it as a Rest Home. The seagulls screamed overhead. Between a variety of gabled Gormenghasts, in one of those gaps that seem endemic to sea-fronts – perhaps created years ago by a German plane unloading a bomb or two as it flew back across the North Sea – there was a double-fronted bungalow which was the residence and studio of C.W. Firethorne.

He was a tall, loosely assembled man with a beard and a bale of hair that looked as though it had been parked on his head as a temporary measure. He opened the door, holding a mug of something in his hand. Randolph announced himself, and they went inside. Firethorne, who was wearing a floppy, paint-splashed cable-knit sweater, led the way into the studio area of the house, and without saying anything, mixed another mug of the something and handed it to Randolph. There were two easels, various chests of long shallow drawers of the sort print-sellers in Covent Garden keep their wares in, a bench, a couple of trestle tables, pots of paints, and three or four canvases leaning up against the walls, all of a classical or antique aspect, which the visitor assumed had been run in for repair and renovation – two tripods, each with its camera, were no doubt used to record the various stages of restoration. There was a strong smell of turps, and an old-fashioned gas-fire blazed and hissed. Firethorne perched on a stool, as though he wasn't much used to sitting down, and then indicated what looked like a large wicker waste-paper basket turned upside down, upon which after a second's hesitation Randolph seated himself. Firethorne had greeted him, but in the ensuing preliminaries hadn't said anything further, and Randolph had been making conversational noises which didn't add up to much, in the way people who were waiting for someone else to say something sometimes do.

Then Firethorne took a long draught of his Horlicks – it was only afterwards that Randolph decided it was Horlicks, having first supposed it to be something he had heard his mother call a 'coffee dash' – and said, apropos nothing, 'Ah well. Yes.' Randolph nodded. He'd had an elderly uncle from the north who scarcely spoke during actual conversations, but would break silences in which people might have been reading books or looking out of the window, with the single exclamation, 'Aye!', as though some galactic revelation had crashed in on him.

'What Mr Ihara is wanting is a nice picture to fit,' said Randolph. 'To fit the frame of the Leonardo. It doesn't have to be all that nice, but nice enough.'

'Nice enough for what?' asked Firethorne.

'To be sort of real. Not some absolute dud. You know? Because after all, it's going to be on top.'

Firethorne scratched his head, and for a fraction of a second

Randolph thought he was going to remove the hair and place it somewhere more secure.

'Well, that's easily enough done,' said Firethorne.

'Because,' Randolph said eagerly, as though Firethorne might not have caught on, 'he doesn't want the Leonardo to become a target for thieves.'

'Doesn't want it on view.'

'Right. And knowing how skilfully you dug it out' – was dug it out quite the phrase? – 'the way you discovered it, he thought you could hide it again. And the other thing,' Randolph had been primed in detail by Ihara, 'he's well off and I suppose he doesn't want everyone to feel they have a right to see it.'

'That's curious,' Firethorne said, 'because if I was rich I'd want everyone to see it.'

'I don't think he's like that, Mr Firethorne, I think he feels so secure in the money sense that it doesn't occur to him.' Then thinking what he'd said might be thought to reflect on his host's social perceptions, Randolph added, 'But my God, I do agree. I'd invite the neighbours round.'

Firethorne placed his empty mug behind him, in the sink where Randolph supposed he washed his brushes.

'So he's ante'd up, has he? Money's been paid over?'

'Oh yes, yes, yes. He's got the picture, and we've got the cash.'

'You're a member of the Club? So if you've got the cash, I suppose I'll be getting mine. For services rendered. Be able to present the cheque they sent me.'

'Oh – the committee. They're going to send round a circular, giving us the details. No, the money hasn't been divvied up yet.'

'There wouldn't be anything to divvy up without me.'

'Oh – ah, absolutely.'

Firethorne got up and opened one of the shallow drawers and brought out a packet of digestive biscuits. They had chocolate on one side. With his fingers – no sign of plates – he handed a couple to Randolph and sat back on the stool, holding the packet.

'Very parsimonious, your committee. However. Where's the picture now?'

'Dear me,' said Randolph, 'that's not something Ihara tells me. Oh, and of course, if you take on this little job for him, he wants it all kept absolutely dark. Doesn't want anyone to know.'

Firethorne asked, 'What do you do in Ihara's organization?'

'I'm an accountant in the office he bought into. Crawford's. You've heard of it?'

'No,' said Firethorne, 'I've never needed an accountant. But perhaps that makes you the right person to ask. What are the terms?'

'The terms?'

'For finding the right sort of picture, and refitting it.'

Randolph shook his head, as someone out of his depth.

'Yes, I'm an accountant. But not his accountant. And that's why, I'm sure, he wanted me to ask you to telephone him at this number.' He took out his wallet and handed a printed card to Firethorne. 'His personal number.'

Feeling a little hemmed in, Randolph rose from the wicker thing and walked over to the pictures leaning against the wall.

'These here for renovation? Listen, what was it like – I mean, sounds a rather funny way of putting it – I mean, what did you feel like, suddenly finding you had come across a Leonardo that no one had seen for hundreds of years?' Randolph hadn't much idea of the kind of conversation that went on in artistic circles, and hoped he was hitting the right note.

Firethorne took another biscuit from the packet.

'Like' – he paused, then went on – 'like reading a very favourite story yet again. There's a story by Scott – *Ivanhoe* – and I must first have read it when I was very young, and ever since I've read it continuously, all the time, and every time I read it it's so much a part of me that I can hardly believe I'm not the author.'

'You know,' said Randolph, 'that's strange, I have just the same feeling about those Jeeves stories by P.G. Wodehouse. I got them as a birthday present when I was ten, and you know, what you said about *Ivanhoe*, every time I read those stories they're so real to me I could just as well have written them myself.'

'Exactly,' said Firethorne. 'I'd always known the picture – the copies – in the way I'd always known *Ivanhoe*, and it was as though I'd written the book and painted the picture. I don't of course mean I'd have been *able* to, just the feeling that they belonged to me. So that's how I felt when I uncovered the Leonardo. And Leonardo' – he gestured towards a shelf of books above the bench – 'has been my lifetime's study.'

'I do understand.' Randolph smiled, delighted to have found a community of interest with such a rare sort of bird. 'That feeling of ownership, as though in a funny way I was P.G. Wodehouse and you were Leonardo.'

Firethorne laughed. 'Well yes,' he said, 'I suppose you could put it that way. Assuming the picture *is* by Leonardo, and that still remains somewhat hypothetical.'

'Ah, yes,' Randolph responded, getting on like a house on fire. 'That article you wrote in the *Standard*. Makes you wonder.'

'You read it?'

'Oh, absolutely.' This was true, because Mr Ihara had sent him a photocopy, so that he could bone up.

'It's just that the man Jochimsen was going a bit further than the evidence warranted. I wasn't impugning the authenticity of the Leonardo so much as querying Jochimsen's way of going about it. His forensic style was so categorical, you'd have thought he'd been at Leonardo's elbow while he painted the thing. But there, I daresay my own interest in painterly techniques makes me protective of them.'

'I think it was very' – Randolph was about to say 'sporting', but altered it – 'straightforward of you to broach the possibility that it might not have been the real thing – it being your own discovery, and all.'

'Well, as I say, I was trying to protect Leonardo from the likes of Jochimsen. If we start confusing scholarship with blind enthusiasm, we lose all credibility.'

'Jolly difficult to prove it wasn't a Leonardo,' said Randolph, hitting on what he felt was a positive contribution to the exchange.

'There'd probably be no conclusive proof,' said Firethorne.

'But proving it wasn't wouldn't be nearly as difficult as proving it was. And that's what I was getting at.'

'Absolutely. Anyway, the buyer is happy, and as I say, if you'd simply give him a bell, you can strike a deal.'

Firethorne ushered him to the door and Randolph set out for the station along the windy promenade, feeling that as a messenger his duty had been done.

When Mr Ihara's personal number rang, it was Mr Moto who answered it. But as soon as he heard Firethorne's name, he handed the mobile over to Mr Ihara, and left the room.

'Thank you for your call, Mr Firethorne, I am most grateful. I hope my young man made the requirements clear.'

'Oh yes, of course, quite. I'm sure I can find the sort of picture that fills the bill.'

'Fills the bill and fits the frame. Ha, ha, ha.'

'Might take a week or so.'

'At auction?'

'Oh no. Trade outlets. Lots of big pictures.'

'But you won't advertise your purpose?'

'No one ever does, round the dealers.'

'And of course you know the dimensions.'

'If the dimensions are out by a little, that's easily adjusted.'

'Now, as to terms. May I suggest what I had in mind?'

'Please do.'

'The expenses arising – travel and so forth, money to fund the purchase of a suitable picture – are, of course, to be paid in advance. Then the fee. There's your time, and above all your skill. And I believe something in addition for confidentiality. Does five thousand seem reasonable to you?'

There was scarcely a pause from Firethorne's end of the line.

'No, not really.'

Then there was a silence from Ihara's end. It was Firethorne who took it up again.

'You see, as far as the confidentiality goes, you're already into that, aren't you?' Ihara, who was not a man to pretend when there was no mileage in it, laughed.

'My dear sir, I am in your hands.'

'Not entirely,' Firethorne said, 'or at any rate, once we agree on a price, no more than I am in yours. Once the money's right, I'm by way of being an investor. I have a real interest in seeing everything goes according to plan. You see that?'

'Goes according to plan?'

'You'll need a sheet of the right sort of fibre above and below the Leonardo.'

'Enlighten me.'

'Against X-rays.'

'But—'

'Why give Customs the edge?'

'But – my plan was simply to safeguard the picture from mutilation or theft—'

'Wouldn't it be a nice little bonus if the picture were fully transportable?'

Ihara chuckled. 'You are a man after my own heart, Mr Firethorne. Name the figure,' he said.

'Fifty thousand.'

No need to reflect – Firethorne was guessing, but he'd guessed right.

'Done,' said Ihara cheerfully. 'In the circumstances we don't need anything on paper. You will be paid a month after the job is finished, an interval which will allow for the successful completion of any further arrangements. Should such further arrangements fail, the price reverts to a basic five thousand for your labour.'

'I don't think so,' Firethorne said. 'I'm an investor in the sense that I have an interest in whatever you plan, but not an investor in the sense that I accept any risk. The risk is entirely your own. No, no, the price is fifty thousand, whatever the outcome. And I do need it on paper, in the form of a properly witnessed contract. I am willing to accept payment at a month, however.

'You do not disappoint me, Mr Firethorne. The contract will be in the post, and I know you will treat it as confidentially as you will treat the whole assignment.'

'Be assured of that,' said Firethorne. 'As soon as I receive it, I shall begin my researches.'

Ihara telephoned Prince and explained. 'So we're in for a further twenty-five thousand apiece. Frankly, all things considered, I believe we got off lightly.' Price replied, 'I agree. And it's a comforting thing to know that we have far and away the best man for the job – the money makes him something of a collaborator, and secures his silence. No, cheap at the price.'

Firethorne lectured three days a week at the Tradescant Institute of Fine Art in Bloomsbury Square, and it was from there he set out for Camden Passage on the morning his contract arrived. He disliked Camden Passage intensely, as he had the feeling it was staffed by actors. He didn't mean real actors, though of course for all he knew they might be, if anyone ever got round to hiring them as such, though most of them probably only got the chance when it came to unloading their junk on the punters. But it was the environment itself which suggested to Firethorne a tatty set in which some cheapo telly film was being shot, and since he had all the snottiness of an academic combined with the disdain of a craftsman, he didn't like shopkeepers who seemed to be above themselves.

And not for the first time he found himself reflecting that there was something second-rate about Islington itself, what with Sadlers Wells theatre being there, a place doomed to second place since you couldn't imagine Pavarotti choosing to sing at it if he could sing anywhere else. But he found this thought extending somewhat, as Pavarotti came second too, when you thought of Domingo. The misanthropic vein helped him on his way, as he scampered in his sandals across the unstylish boulevards and then flapped over the fancy cobblestones which (he thought) were as apt a precinct for an arcade specializing in repro as any council could have devised.

Firethorne had a way of ranking things; he knew which pictures were good, nearly good, not quite good, and so on. His view of art was of the excluding sort, and though Jochimsen's proprietorial tone must understandably have nettled the man who had actually uncovered the Leonardo, perhaps another impulse was also at work, a fear that he, too, was ranked: destined for that second place which he was always so swift to spot, and the article he had written as a riposte to Jochimsen, an international name, might well owe something to that aspect of his temperament. He was passing a shop with a lot of gilt items in the interior, and he went in, having caught sight of a couple of large pictures among the gaudy mirrors. His eye skittered round the walls: one of the pictures was a full-length account of a ducal figure clad in silver stockings, with a pointed waistcoat and pear-shaped slops.

'Nice little item,' said the proprietor, noting his interest.

Firethorne nearly said 'Painted it yourself?', but forbore. The flatness of the image suggested some sort of giant transfer. The other big one was of a lady with a vast spangled ruff and a triangular face. 'Circle of Bette Davis,' he muttered under his breath. 'Thank you,' he said to the man, and went out.

Sauntering on, he entered various shops, and saw nothing to the purpose. Then went down into the Underground and took a ticket for Victoria, walking up to Pimlico. The shops were posher than the Islington sort, and the shopkeepers wore suits. There was a not bad imitation of a Hillyard, full length and very decorative, and this time he thought he ought to mention the fact that the label didn't quite indicate it wasn't an original.

'Nice copy,' he said to the man, who had wavered forward in a welcoming way.

'Copy? But of course an early copy. One doesn't expect an original of something that is unknown outside the Prado.'

'I judge the picture to be by Fernans. His work isn't bad, is it? Would you agree it compares with Isissi and Caplain?'

Realizing this wasn't a punter, the shop man said, 'We're into decor, here.'

'Oh,' said Firethorne, this time unable to resist, 'of course, so many restaurants.'

Into one of which he now marched. It was supposed to be

French, but since real French waiters are never pert, this may have been an exaggeration. Firethorne didn't mind spending money when it wasn't his own, and ordered a meal that was perfectly acceptable. He then indulged one of his chief pleasures, which was that of not tipping, getting up from the table slowly so that he could relish the look on the waiter's face as the fact was registered. He put up at one of the small but by no means economic hotels in Ebury Street, and in the morning cabbed it to King's Cross. There was a vast antiques warehouse that he knew of, adjacent to Hatfield, and a local bus took him from the station to the door.

'Are you Trade?' asked a dinky little woman as he entered.

'Good heavens, whatever made you think that?'

'Oh, it doesn't matter. Please go in.'

And he went into the enormous evil-smelling hangar where the accumulation of mahogany, he thought, might put you off furniture for life. He clambered to the floor above where the pictures could be seen. Some were dim and rusty and others had been so determinedly cleaned they looked like picture postcards. He found it hard to imagine an artist standing in front of any one of them and actually painting it. He was down the stairs again, his sandals slapping. Back at the station, he made a couple of telephone calls to dealers he knew, and a man in Stow-on-the-Wold described something he had in stock that sounded as though it might do. 'Big glossy Victorian job, woman in a ball gown. Respectable bit of work, if you can't run to an Ingres.' The dimensions sounded about right, and the price – £3,500 – was high enough to let you know it wasn't going to be rubbish, without being so high that the picture ought to have been by someone you'd heard of.

'Look,' Firethorne said, 'can you fax me a photo? Send it to the Institute, so I'll have it this afternoon.' Then he got on the train.

In Bloomsbury Square the Institute was just closing, but Firethorne went in and found the fax waiting for him. Closer to Sargent than Ingres, anticipating Sargent, even, he thought as he studied it – the figure elongated in the Sargent manner, rather than the fuller shapes you got with Ingres. None of the spirit of either, of course, but workmanlike. The dealer had scribbled the dimensions on the fax – picture with frame, picture without frame – and Firethorne called him.

'Looks as though it would suit the client,' he said. 'Don't want the frame, you can sell that to someone else – client has his own ideas in that department. So if you knock five hundred off the price, and throw in the delivery, it's a deal.' With little more than a facetious groan, the dealer agreed – big pictures tended to hang about. And Firethorne returned to Frinton.

On the principle that lightning doesn't strike twice in the same place, Ihara had kept the Leonardo at the vaults in Fetter Lane where the heist had been attempted. And when Firethorne had made slight adjustments to the dimensions of the picture of the Victorian lady, and framed it according to the purpose it was to serve, he'd had it delivered to Ihara, along with sheets of carbon fibre that he deemed necessary to the purpose. At this point the *Leda* was sent to the house on the Embankment. Mr Moto had hired a Securicor van, and he and Mr Akisura rode shotgun on the way over. The picture had been crated in layers of wood under the supervision of the strongroom people and when it arrived it was carefully unloaded and taken into the main salon – the enormous room with the ridiculous hairy chairs. The men from Securicor propped it up very carefully against the wall, and though they knew no more than that it was an item of value, weren't sure whether to indicate that they were aware they had been handling something worthy of respect. They moved backwards momentarily, looking up at the crated item as though it might have had some connection with Princess Diana. They left, and Mr Ihara walked into the room, smoking a cigar. Both Mr Moto and Mr Akisura bowed.

'Leave it as it is,' Ihara said. 'When Firethorne arrives, he will dismantle the thing.' His assistants withdrew, and Ihara walked across to where the Victorian lady had been hooked onto screws which had once supported a large glass transfer print of Buffalo

Bill advertising root beer. Studying it, he thought, Not a bad picture, as Firethorne entered, ushered in by one of the Japanese who immediately left and closed the door. The picture restorer carried a small leather bag.

'You know, these clever craftsmen are still undervalued,' Ihara said, nodding at the Victorian lady.

'They are well enough,' Firethorne said, dumping his bag on the floor, 'but they can only remind us of their betters – those with the vision, the view of the matter, something utterly unknown to tinkerers like the fellow who painted that. He hits off a technique, and I'll give him credit for it. But as for signs of life – nil, none, nothing.'

'Like all experts, you're harsh,' said Ihara. 'I wish I could paint as well as this chap.'

'Precisely,' said Firethorne, as he emptied the tools out of his bag. Then he got to work on the crate, the screws coming out easily and the layers of the smooth strong hardwood piling on to the floor, until he could lift the picture itself from its protective shrouds, and carrying it away from the debris, lay it up against a blank space on the wall. Standing back, he appraised it.

'Like the sun extinguishing candlelight,' he said.

The naked woman stood poised at full length, her enigmatic smile, the swan that is not a swan, with its wing round her rump, the cryptic icons scattered at the borders of the image. Ihara pulled over one of the hairy thrones, and sat down to contemplate the picture. He said nothing for a while, his cigar burning away between his fingers.

'How the stance, the combination of spiralling axes – the *contrapposto* – makes the figure so seductive,' Firethorne said.

'What did you say?' Ihara was not listening. Then he said, 'What? Ah – seductive, yes. It is. But what a drab word to apply to so complex an image.'

Firethorne nodded his head. 'I was not attempting to sum it up. It is too comprehensive for criticism. All that can usefully be said is to hint at a context. The torso turned in one direction, the head in another, the arm reaching across the body in yet another, such contrapuntal movement informs the entire picture – that posture, the stance as of a philosopher of the school of Athens. *Figura sempintinata* – giving the figure the illusion of being visible from all sides.

'You are right,' Ihara said, 'when confronted with a work of art that is the thing itself, we must confine our comments to the tangential or historical. The picture speaks for itself.'

Firethorne said, 'It can't be otherwise. What the image is, in its endless invocation of something otherwise unknown, cannot be spoken of. The picture itself. That's all there is.'

'Particularly, I believe, with Leonardo, in that he strove to make each of his pictures the quintessence of its own genre. An apotheosis. Is it not said that he wished to paint no other portrait after he'd painted the *Mona Lisa*?'

'Just as it is inconceivable that he could have done a second *Last Supper*. And with the *Leda* we have his single venture into the mythological – of course, there are sketches, drawings, preliminaries, but the fully realized image of fecundity is achieved once, and once only. And here it stands before us.'

'Scattered with hieroglyphs, enigmas. The children bursting from the eggs seem an obvious enough symbol, but why holding flowers, and the significance of those particular flowers? Then the red-coloured fruits, the pigeon, the single constellation in the sky, the bridge over the river, the town.'

'Yes,' Firethorne said, 'not all of which appear in the copies. But one feels they could be translated, these single items, as once the Rosetta Stone was translated. But what is untranslatable is the picture itself, the whole matter, the mystery.'

'In the face of which,' said Ihara, rising, 'modesty becomes us. I'll leave you to your work, Mr Firethorne. It has indeed been a pleasure meeting you.'

So the two pictures were laid out on the floor, and Firethorne went to work with micrometer and chisel and screwdriver, and since the preliminary adjustments had already been done, in a short while there was a layer of carbon fibre beneath and above the Leonardo, the *Leda* was covered, and her place taken by the

Victorian lady in a blue ball-gown. Firethorne carefully reassembled the wood slats round the single frame, and left the package propped against the wall. He zipped up the implements in the leather bag, made his farewells, and left the house, a craftsman of the old school.

FOURTEEN

Then the framed item was crated up, and it was sent by airfreight to The Museum of Timeless Art in Dallas. There was a big X-ray at the freight terminal, through which the container passed, and nothing untoward had registered; the dispatcher was listed impersonally as Pacific Rand, the content declared ("oil-painting, Victorian"), and along with boxed computers, modern reproduction furniture, crates of Scotch whisky from a noted distillery, batches of chocolates *en route* from Belgium to Los Angeles, a stack of mountain bikes from Birmingham and a great variety of the sort of goods that are continuously in transit, such as Wedgwood pottery, hand-made shoes, recently published books, Sheffield cutlery, it was taken out to the planes on transporters and stowed.

At the Club, the distribution was happening. Cheques were in the post, and after subventions to the Club's bank-debt and material requirements, each member received very close to £180,000. Men felt pleased – Routh was not seen to rejoice, since it was understood that it had been a matter of defending the principle that had motivated him throughout. No one had any idea what difference the money might have made to individuals. The *omerta* which had always applied to members' private finances was now if anything more tightly observed, and no one knew into what vast hole anyone's share had been tipped, or to what pile of lucrative investments it might have been added. The advent of the money was the cause of good feeling, but never directly referred to.

Sometimes a member might hope that good causes had been helped, as though he might have had a hand in such transactions himself, but this sort of thing engendered very cool responses, if any. As Owlish had predicted, the slice that would have gone to Spalding had been passed to his widow; Ledward had added this fact to the death notice pinned up on the notice-board, and members felt it was the right sort of thing, and this also was never spoken of, afterwards. So it could be thought that club life would resume its even tenor, its uneventful style, its deep, its profound uninterestingness. It would fall back into that perennial slumber from which it must now hope no fairy prince would ever again awaken it.

Along with Ledward, I had felt uneasy about the events we'd all been party to. The idea that it was all over, that there were no loose ends, now that Ihara had the goods and we had the cash, was something I was glad of. But my expectation in this regard turned out to be premature. Nonetheless, I have to admit that it is the part of the story I like best. I was to be more vividly involved in the outcome than ever I could have supposed – indeed, I hadn't supposed there would *be* an outcome. But if there had to be a denouement, and someone had to put his finger on the nerve of the matter, who would mind if that someone turned out to be himself? Well, I smile as I write. It could easily be said that Letty was there before me, and that my own contribution was but a refinement. But I'm getting ahead of myself.

It was three or four weeks after the pay-out that she called me. We had been enjoying little expeditions, jaunts as we called them, many a nice dinner and outing, and though as I said I am an old-fashioned fellow, I was hoping she might agree to come on a little European trip, say to Vienna, or to Copenhagen, or to Rome, and there we would be together, and being together, we might find we *could* be together. So there it was, and the telephone rang, and how pleased I was to hear her voice.

'My dear woman, what a treat.'

'I'm not at all sure you'll think it is, when you hear.'

'What does that mean?'

'Well,' she said. Then went silent. 'Well. Here we go. First off, poor old Firethorne is dead.'

Her cousin.

'My God, oh dear, how sorry I am!'

'Run over.'

And I said, 'Run over! In *Frinton*?'

At this she laughed a little. 'Sorry – but you know, I didn't know him at all well, he was a cousin, but a stranger really. No, not Frinton, it happened in Chelmsford. Poor fellow was crossing the road outside some art shop he got things from, tripped over and the poor bugger in the van behind hadn't got a chance. Well, I mean, Firethorne hadn't got a chance either, of course. But the van was over him, and the driver's in shock, and personally I blame it on the sandals.' Then she did laugh, and said 'Oh, how dreadful, but I can't help it. If you wear those flip-flops.'

'Where are you, what are you doing?'

'Well, they contacted me, only relative, or at least he had my name in his wallet, and now I've got to do the clearing up.'

'Oh, God, what a chore for you. Can I help?'

'Yes.' she said, 'I'm awfully afraid you can.'

What did that mean?

'You're where?'

'Frinton.' Then she laughed again. I thought that however distant the relationship, she was feeling what everyone feels when someone they know actually dies. And the feeling has to come out, even inappropriately.

'Will you come down here? Now, I mean?'

'Sure, give you a hand. Now? Drive, I guess.'

'I could tell you what it's all about, but it won't do on the phone. You'll have to be here.'

'Look,' I said, 'you're not in trouble, are you?'

'Nothing like that. But do come. Will you come now?'

'On my way.'

It's a long haul through the City and the East End to get anywhere at all, but at last I got clear and was beetling off through the sprawl towards Colchester, then wiggling down towards the coast, and finding the road that turned off for Frinton. 'As fine a trio as ever was seen, since the bishop took the two typists to Frinton-on-Sea during Septuagesima'- a line from Beachcomber that had stuck in my head from childhood, when I was allowed the *Daily Express* after my mother, while my father read his *Times*. I was a solemn child, I think, but the oddity of his humour seized me as though he were a mad uncle. Why Frinton? As I drove into the place, there was nothing obvious that would make you smile. Something about gentility, hence the bishop and the two typists. These were silly thoughts, repeated again and again, like the music I'd told Letty I couldn't get out of my head. Wished Beachcomber had actually been my uncle. Or would I have got used to him?

She'd told me where the bungalow was, so I parked on the empty sea-front and walked along. I thought it looked drab, but then I think bungalows always seem a little more neglected than real houses.

'So glad you're here. Better go into his studio first.'

The place had a frowzy, personal smell. How long would it linger, now that he wasn't here? All his stuff was scattered around in the studio part. A bench, brushes, sink, easels, pots of paint, three chests of shallow drawers, a couple of trestle tables, a shelf of books – all, I noted, on the subject of Leonardo.

'So you've got to clear it all up?'

'What on earth's the point? There isn't anyone to do it for. I'll get one of those house-clearance firms round. But I'll have to do all the other boring things, like bank statements, probate, is there a will, all that. I've already dug a pile of stuff out – dumped it in a dustbin liner, go through it when I get it home. Do you want a cup of tea?'

'No. Wouldn't mind a drink.'

'I think you're going to need one.'

She went out, presumably into the other wing of the place, and brought back a bottle of gin.

'Can't find anything to go with it.'

'Neat gin.'

'Better than nothing.'

She pulled out two glasses from under the sink, then said, 'Oh look, here's some orange squash.' She slopped the gin into the glasses, then a drop or two of squash, ran the tap and dribbled in some water. Took a sip. 'Ambrosia,' she said, shuddering, and handed me mine. It must be what burglars feel like. Completely alien place, someone else's life, so private.

'Killed instantly, was he?'

'Yes, I think so. I had to see his head, for the identification. Poor bastard.'

She'd seemed a little, what can one say, not feverish, but a bit disordered, and now I thought, no wonder.

'So drink up. No, not exactly that. But what I'm going to tell you might get you looping-the-loop a bit.'

'What *do* you mean?' But I took a swallow of the gin and stuff, and felt a little light-headed myself. Letty walked over to the three large chests which buttressed one of the walls. Each of them had a number of long shallow drawers, and she pulled one open.

'This is going to cause pain,' she said, 'great pain.' And she slid out a sheet from a stack of sheets, and laid it out on the top of the chest. I went over, carrying my glass of gin and orange.

'Have a look,' she said. 'Though it won't be as clear as some of the later ones.'

What I saw wasn't at all clear. I was looking – or so I supposed at a colour photograph, much enlarged, something twice the size of an ordinary folio. The left foreground was filled with shadow, from which protruded an arm and a hand. The hand held a paint-brush, which was pointing at, or was in contact with, a canvas on an easel – the perspective didn't allow for certainty. What was on the easel was out of focus.

'It gets clearer later on,' Letty said, and slid out a couple more of the large photographs. In one of them the shadow on the left had turned towards the camera and revealed a face, or at least the lower half of a face, since the top had been cut off by the edge of the picture.

'Whoever it is, he's got a beard.'

'You'll see. Just go through a few.' And she pulled out some more of the prints. And she was right. I did see.

It was a man doing something to the canvas in the first photo, and every now and again in one of the photographs he'd turn to the camera. What wasn't clear was what was on the canvas.

'Wait a bit. Is he—'

'Oh, yes,' said Letty, 'it's Firethorne.'

'Well, I'm blessed.' I looked up, seeing the cameras on their two tripods which I hadn't really taken in when I'd entered the studio. 'He's keeping a record.'

'Yes, he is,' she said.

Then seized with the novelty of the thing, I said, 'Does the canvas get clearer in any of the other photos?'

'It does,' said Letty.

'Then I wouldn't mind betting it's our Leonardo. What a craftsman! Just the thing for his students. Keeping a photographic record of the bits he's had to restore.'

'No,' said Letty, 'he isn't doing that.'

I looked up from the pile of photos, waiting for her to show me some more. She opened another of the drawers. Looked up at me.

'So it isn't the Leonardo,' I said, rather disappointed.

'Well, yes,' she said, 'but that isn't what he's doing to it.'

'Then what *is* he doing to it?'

She looked me in the eye.

'He's painting it,' she said.

There were dozens of the enlarged photographs, some with Firethorne in focus, some with the picture in focus, some with both in focus. It was fascinating to see the picture actually taking shape, partly painted sections at the top of the canvas, then a space at the centre being filled, an outline of the graceful female figure and the swan, a shot of the *putti* at the lower edge of the canvas, the bushes in the foreground with their distinctive red fruit still to be painted. Every process in its creation – its manufacture – recorded by the cameras in obsessive detail, not once but over and over again.

There were more than a hundred prints of the process – continuous exposures from the two cameras set on automatic at those moments he wanted recorded, as he went on painting. I clipped one or two of them to an easel to get a better look. I was shocked and amazed and really only half believed what I was looking at. And then we came to photographs of a different sort: a hand scraping at a canvas, removing paint from the surface of another picture, the same hand daubing the canvas, an old canvas, with a short stubby brush dipped into a bowl, a close-up of a stove—

'Where would the stove be?' We went into the other half of the house. There was an Aga in the kitchen, but it wasn't the stove in the photograph. Then we found a stone outhouse to the rear of the bungalow, and the stove was there – a vast affair. You lifted the top flap and uncovered the baking-surface. The place also had the look of a dark-room, with its infra-red lamp, enlarger and developing trays – no taking the negatives round to Boots. Back in the studio we found a sequence of photographs in which the canvas was being lifted on to the stove; whatever picture had been on this old canvas – could it have been the picture which had lain under the John the Baptist? – had been removed, but with dim smears of colour still to be seen; then shots of it being drawn out from the stove, and some further close-ups of the canvas, naked save for the smears – the process was later explained to me, something to do with preserving the original crackle of the older picture so that it would reappear on the surface of the newly-painted one, and this was contrived by scraping off the top layers of paint but leaving the bottom layer of primer which the earlier painter would have used to condition the canvas. Then you had to daub the thing with a mixture which would duplicate the dust that would have accumulated in the crackle over the hundreds of years, then do the baking for exactly the critical length of time – 'Delicate business,' (my informant was Carr, the Bury Street picture dealer) 'but the process was documented in the greatest detail after van

Meegeren's trial. The papers in the case came out as a book. He'd only have to consult it.'

Of course, van Meegeren had leapt to mind as we went through the stack of photos, one by one. The great Dutch forger – can you have a 'great' forger? Yes, I think so, if the forgery extends beyond mere technique – had left no such evidence.

'Don't you remember him?' I said to Letty. 'Oh, you're too young. He did Vermeers. Trouble was, he sold one to Goering when the Nazis occupied Holland during the war, and after the war he was done for trading with the enemy. The only way he could get out of it was by telling them the picture was a fake – far from collaborating, he'd taken Goering for a ride.'

'What rotten luck,' Letty said. 'Being forced to explain a conjuring trick.'

'Worse than that. They didn't believe it was a conjuring trick. They thought the picture was genuine. And van Meegeren had to prove he could paint Vermeers by sitting down and actually painting one in front of the lawyers!'

She smiled. 'They can't do that to poor old Charlie Firethorne.'

We were squatting in front of a pile of the photographs on the floor.

'Something else. When one of his fake Vermeers was hung in a public museum – *Supper at Emmaus*, I think it was – van Meegeren would join the crowd gathered round it and noisily question its authenticity. Now that reminds me of Firethorne's article in the *Standard*, telling off some senior critic for accepting the Leonardo too easily.'

'Rather clever. Adds a sort of dimension to the top man's opinion – makes it more real by being disagreed with. And if you throw doubt on your own discovery it could take the wind out of anyone else's sails who felt like questioning it.'

'Oh yes, and in the thing he wrote he sounded really irritated, which was what you might expect considering it looked as though the other man was trying to steal his thunder – and then his comments about not being sure it was genuine would be put down to jealousy.'

I took out one of the large colour photos of the completed picture and propped it up on an easel.

'See, no one knew whether van Meegeren was going to have the last laugh by fooling everyone and then sticking it to them when he announced he'd faked the lot. But he did it so well, would they believe him? Firethorne documented the whole process – wonder whether he had something or other like that in mind? Pulling the chair from under everyone. Sort of paranoid thing, really.'

Letty said, 'But doing a fake is a bit paranoid, isn't it? Like you're secretly afraid you aren't much good, so you produce something to prove you must be as good as the person you're imitating, the one everyone agrees is top of the heap. I think he took all these snaps to prove he'd done it – prove it to himself.'

I was looking at the snap of the completed picture.

'The Dutchman cut off a little bit of the blank canvas he did one of the Vermeers on, and I suppose he felt he could always show how exactly the fibres fitted, so it must have been him. But not as good as photos.'

I took in the detail of the picture, saw the small symbolic objects scattered round the edges of the image, studied the pigeon, the *putti*, the fruit bushes, the constellation, the little bridge.

'I suppose he got all that from one of the copies. He must have worked from one. Is there anything that looks like it?'

Letty went through the pile, but couldn't find anything.

'He couldn't copy from anything this size, though, could he? Ah – what about in here?'

There was a single drawer that ran along the bottom of the widest chest. She drew it out, and inside was a copy of the *Leda*, photographed in sections, each one highly enlarged. I spread them out on the bench, then compared the various sections with those same areas in Firethorne's picture. I picked up a big magnifying glass that was hanging on the wall above the work area, and took a closer look. Really, the man's skill was astounding. The cracked eggs from which the babies were sprawling seemed to me to have a finer transparency in the green-veined surface of the shells in his version than in the other one – there, even through the magnifying glass, the tracery could hardly be seen. The brush strokes, marvellously clear in all the photographs, were different in Firethorne's version – of course! He was copying the copyist, but he was *Leonardo* copying the copyist! Not just the skill, but the massive lifelong study! I whistled in admiration. The books on the shelf, which I'd supposed he'd bought to assist in restoration, now took on another significance.

'You know, Letty, the word fake hardly seems polite.'

And there were slight variations, small additions he had made, revelling in his mastery. In the copy the sky was empty whereas in Firethorne's picture there was the single constellation, and in the one he was working from there were no bushes bearing red fruit or berries, he'd put those in.

The revelation came to me.

'Letty, these bushes.' She'd been kneeling down and going through more of the photographs. She got up and came over to the easel where I had her cousin's completed version. I handed her the magnifying glass.

'The bushes aren't in the one he was copying from. The bushes along the lower edge of the picture, just beneath the feet of Leda. The ones with the red berries. Any idea what bushes they are?'

She took a squint through the glass. 'They're very distinct, aren't they? Each leaf. Small, dark green, little veins. And the branches, the twiggy bits, they've got little thorns on them. Red berries. Don't recognize them – not very good at botany.'

'Well,' I said, 'I think I do.' I sounded rather solemn, I must have done, because I'd never made a discovery before. 'I know what they are.' Actually, as Letty said afterwards, I sounded portentous. Well, for once, perhaps I was justified.

'Well, yes, go on. What are they?'

Then I said,' *Pyracantha*. Spiky evergreen, red berries.'

'OK, then what? What does it matter?'

'That's the botanical name. Do you know what they're usually called?'

'Oh, come on.'

'Firethorn.'

She stared at me, then gave a great shout of laughter.

'You're a genius!'

I'm sure I smirked. But I was on a roll, there was more to come. I felt it. I looked at something else that was in Firethorne's version and not in the other.

'C.W. Firethorne, well, well, well.' I pointed at the picture. 'That other bit, up there' – I pointed at the sky in Firethorne's version – 'that's not in the copy. The arrangement of stars in the sky. What do they call it – every schoolchild knows. That particular constellation?'

'Oh yes, the Great Bear. Even I know that.'

'Now just tell me this – what's its other name?'

'Hold on, I'll get it. Got it! The Plough.'

'Right – and it too is a fertility symbol, of course. But I'm just wondering. What was it you said Firethorne's first name was?'

'Charlie.'

Now I was shambling round the studio, practically gibbering. A code-breaker who had cracked a code he didn't know was there. A denouement – and I was the mastermind!

'Just one more little bit, and I'm damned if I don't ask to join Mensa. Tell me, please tell me, what was old Charlie's *middle* name? The one beginning with W.'

'Oh.' Letty seemed stumped for a minute. 'Wait a bit, I used to know. Family name. Some uncle or other.'

'Go on.'

'It was the uncle's surname, but it always reminded me of the sort of name you shouldn't call a child. Like Darren or Shane. No, not Shane – Wayne. Only it's not spelt that way—'

'No, it's not. Let me spell it for you—'

'How would you know?'

'Because the other name for The Plough is – Charles's Wain.'

She cried aloud, 'How do you do it!'

'Natural talent. A gift. Probably never do it again. Shot my bolt. But dammit, Letty, I got it right.' I gave her such a hug, and then I stopped and held her away, and then for the first time kissed her as I'd wanted to kiss her from the first. 'No, I think it must have been that stuff you found under the sink, the gin and Harpic you gave me.

Letty said, 'God, isn't all this peculiar?' Then in a low slightly rough voice, said, 'Do you know what I'm thinking?'

I said, 'I'm certain I do.'

And she said, 'I wish we could do it now – here.'

But I kissed her again, hard, and I said, 'Let me drive you back to Suffolk.'

And Letty said, 'Oh yes, please.' And went to the gin bottle and mixed up some more orange with it, and we sat looking at each other.

'The man,' I said, 'actually *signed* it. Charles Wain Firethorne. It takes your breath away. But, oh my God, what an uproar there's going to be.'

'Glad I didn't accept your kind offer of a share of the money,' Letty said, sipping her drink. 'Won't everyone have to give it all back, now?'

'Well, I ought to know the law on that point. If something's sold in good faith it's a matter of *caveat emptor*, let the buyer beware. But I'll have to check on it.'

Then I laughed – my sleuthing and the gin, not to mention the magic moment that changed my relationship with Letty, had put me above myself. 'I simply can't find it in my heart to be sorry for Ihara. He made the lowest offer, showed everyone else a clean pair of heels, ran off with the trophy, and it turns out to be the booby prize!'

'Won't the members think it the decent thing – give him his money back?'

My laugh was now a bit raucous. 'Oh, come on. It's not as though the President of Pacific Rand is widow and orphan country, is it? He's a businessman, cut-throat stuff. *He* finessed us into not taking the highest price. One or two of the more sisterly members might think his bet ought to be returned, but where are they going to call the money back from? It's lost itself in new cars, second homes, better schools, sailing dinghies, the Bahamas. Poor Mrs Spalding, the Widow Spalding, will be about the only one with any of it to hand, on deposit at the post office, I daresay. Damned if I'd want to pauperize her, to reimburse Ihara.'

Letty said, 'Don't drink any more of that gin.'

'What? Oh, no. Mustn't.' I looked again at the photograph on the easel. 'No, Firethorne is the winner by a country mile. He painted a Leonardo, included his own signature so there'd be no doubt, and took money for it into the bargain. Oh, yes' – I turned back to Letty – 'when you go through his bank statements, check that bit out. A hundred thousand should show up, the chunk the Club paid him for the discovery – discovery! – and you'll have to add it all in for probate.'

'Mustn't send that back, then?' Letty said.

'No – probate. That means it's all got to be accounted for. Tell you what, just send all the papers to my office and I'll get someone to go through them.'

'If no will turns up, looks as though I'll be the legatee. That's when it'll be all right for me to send the cash back to the Club.'

I laughed.

'I knew you'd say that. Shall we go?'

We went, but not before we stowed all the photographs, and locked the drawers.

'Not quite sure who to tell first. Poor old Ledward, he thought he'd got the thing off his back at last, and now – dear oh dear. He'll have to pass it on to Ihara. Don't envy him the phone call. And what about the newspapers? Should I do that? Or no, they'd want to get straight to you.'

'Don't mind me,' Letty said, 'I'll tell them to fuck off.'

'Yes, but they wouldn't. They might camp out, beseige you. No, no, if I do it, they don't need to know you're involved. I could say – I could say I'd heard of the death, the accident, and had come down on my own initiative.'

'Well, I don't know,' Letty said, 'I'm not the frail old thing you thought I'd turn out to be when we met for the first time. No, to hell – you tell them, tell them how it happened, and I'll deal with them.' Then she chuckled. 'Famous for fifteen minutes. I wouldn't mind that.'

Then it was my turn to say it. 'That gin's got a lot to answer for.'

And she said, 'Not yet as much as it will.' I knew exactly what she meant, but I wasn't sure she'd got the grammar right.

The dawn in Suffolk was misty through the big windows, seen across the fields. I heard a scream – it was a peacock. She said she was always thinking of getting a mate for it. The pheasants knew the season was over because they made a noise to tell everyone where they were living. We had gone into that tall comfortable bedroom after a supper of scrambled eggs and toast and a glass of wine. And we were tired, but not that tired. And after, we slept in the big nice bed and were so comfortable I could hardly describe it – coming home, something like that. As though we had always known each other. These are, I hope, experiences common to many, known to all, for which special words are not needed – my feeling on that misty morning, with a water-colour sun falling through the long sash windows, was that it had always been waiting for me; it was not new.

After breakfast, the call to Ledward. His silence was long and pained. 'May you live in interesting times!' I heard him mutter, and then he gave a dismal groan. 'Very well – Ihara must know, and I must tell him. How do we handle the media? Is that something you feel you could take on? What with you being in at the death, so to speak.' I told him I would, and we decided I should telephone the PA and let them take it from there – it was bound to run and run, it had everything a journalist could ask for, a Leonardo sold for £45 million turning out to be a fake, the vivid photographic evidence of the forger in the act, a touch of Sherlock Holmes (me!) and a wonderful dollop of *schadenfreude* by way of custard – a bunch of toffee-nosed old farts who thought they'd won the lottery made to look silly and very possibly having to hand the loot back!

As to the last, Ledward was terse. 'Even if we aren't obliged by law, we may feel obliged by decency.'

I said to him, 'So there'll be another one of those damnation EGMs?'

His only answer was another groan, then he asked for Letty's number so he could call back, if need be, after his *mauvais quart d'heure* with Ihara.

Letty was strolling on the terrace in the misty sunshine which caught the blonde glints in her brown hair. 'Ha, ha,' she cried, and 'Ha, ha,' I cried, as we linked arms and paraded gaily, sniffing the sharp sweet air.

'We come off pretty well,' I said.

'Oh, we do, we do,' she laughed. I laughed. There was nothing else but laughing.

'What I mean, well, I mean all sorts of things, but little things too, like neither of us being bothered by the money side of all this, and though we'll be plagued by journos, it's only because we're the good guys.' And again, we had to laugh. Then the phone rang. I nipped in, and it was Ledward.

'This sorry tale gets worse and worse,' he said. 'But the question of handing the cash back to Ihara, or indeed anyone else, doesn't arise. The brute has already sold it on!' Ledward gave me the details: Dallas was holding the parcel when the music stopped, and now it was their business to get what satisfaction they could from Ihara.

'It rather cheered me up,' said Ledward. 'The thought of the wily oriental having to do all the arguing – not unpleasing, would you say? In fact, I came on a bit holier than thou with him, and though he didn't sound remorseful, by jove he did sound bloody annoyed.' We both laughed heartily. 'They don't like coming off second-best,' said Ledward, 'but of course the upside as far as we're concerned is we're off the hook. Anyone wants their money back, they can't come to us. By jove, the more I think about that scaly Jap, the better pleased I am.'

I did the stuff with the PA – was on the phone for ages: could they interview me; could they interview Letty; could they gain access to the photographs; what did I think; what would the members think; did I know Firethorne; did I think it was a sign of the times, the lowering of standards.

That last bit had me roaring, 'You mean the ability to paint a Leonardo so convincingly that the world's most expert student of his work was deceived – you're calling *that* a lowering of standards?'

'No, no, I meant moral standards—'

'I leave you to be the judge of those.' And while I was talking, Letty laughed silently.

'I liked it when you were telling him about how you spotted the ideograms – backing shyly into the limelight.' But then the phone started to ring, and it didn't stop. All the journalists in London wanted Letty, and while she was filling them in on the detail, there was a clang-clang on the front door and a camera crew from a television station in Ipswich edged into the hall and were about to set up in one of the big rooms at the front of the house when Letty came charging in bellowing at them. 'Outside, outside, I don't want to wait for you to have to pack all that up when you've finished,' and they shambled out on to the terrace.

'I'd say being famous for fifteen minutes brings out star quality in some of us,' said I, and she threw a cushion at me. 'Come on,' and we walked out to the camera as to the manner born. Three photographers from various newspapers arrived, and joined the assembly. The television people got her nicely arranged against a distant view of the park. 'That fifteen minutes is beginning to seem rather longer than I thought,' Letty said.

'Don't inhale. You might not be able to do without it.'

But before it was over, we all got fed up.

Fax machines were white hot. Papers ran updates. The telly gave it prime time. Ihara was variously represented as a thief – 'controversial' was the word the hacks used – a hard-faced thief – 'an entreprenurial figure in the Thatcher mould' – a thief who nearly got away with it – 'never one to avoid a gamble' – a Japanese thief – 'sailed close to the wind in time-honoured style' – a thief who did not count the cost to the poor and needy – 'The market was his bible' – a thief who robbed everyone – 'the unwary received hard lessons,' and finally, a thief who was caught bang to rights – 'As the Prime Minister has gone on record as saying,' one of the toadies said solemnly in the Commons, ' "those who flout the laws of any country and find themselves on the receiving end of processes which no democratic – ah – assembly can condone, have only themselves to – or – I may say, categorically, at the end of the day, the proof of the pudding"—' And the other layabouts cried, 'Yah, yah!'

I don't say Ihara was a saint, but I couldn't fathom out how he'd done anything wrong. He didn't know, because no one knew, that the Leonardo was a fake. All he'd done was take a profit. I was rather pleased by the way the Dallas people got their act together. The way I heard it, they'd begun by thinking they ought to get the money back from Ihara, but someone pointed out it was indeed *caveat emptor*, and wiser councils had prevailed; so they got Ihara to agree to stay mum, and their PR department began putting it loudly about that any knowledgeable person who took a look at the picture would see that it was hugely superior to the best of the copies, and if that was so they would leave it to the intelligent onlooker to realize that it must have been painted by Leonardo himself. What they were saying was, we don't want you to think we're mad, spending £55 million on a fake. In spite of which I have to say that I did hear that Wemdinger, their negotiator, had been fired – 'Let go' was the phrase used by the man, a visitor from the States, that I found myself talking to in the Club. 'I understand,' he went on, 'that he is now running a dolphinarium in Florida.'

Do people believe the scotch mist they read in newspapers? Everything was lost in a fog of prevarication. I even began to wonder if Letty and I hadn't dreamt our visit to Frinton-on-Sea. 'Did you enjoy being famous?' I asked her, and she replied, 'For the first thirty seconds.'

I think the Club is much the same place it ever was. And the men there don't seem a lot different. Forbes continues our link with Ihara – took a job as UK chairman of the man's outfit, and looks, if anything, even more piss-proud than he was when he was in the Civil Service – he tells me (*deigns* to tell me) that his nephew Edward is now the boss of the computer firm I keep forgetting the name of – clever young man, evidently. And if I include Forbes as an Ihara connection, I must say the same of Randolph and, indeed, of Olney. The day Ihara marched Randolph into the office and got him his job back must have done him a power of good, because he is now second-in-command – mind you, I think he's reached his ceiling, but then, I didn't suppose he'd get as far as this. And when Olney's firm of estate agents went bust for ramping a property conveyance, it was Ihara who picked up the pieces at a firesale price, and it seems Olney was unscathed – Ihara knew an earl would always be an adornment to the letter-head. Oddly enough, Prince resigned – nobody knew why (was it Olney who said he thought it was because he wanted to devote more time to making money?). Routh, well, after that dreadful evangelist thing, after what happened there, I couldn't ever be in his company, I steer clear of the man. He still drinks his one glass of dry sherry, but that's as much as I see of him. I did write once to Mrs Spalding, I felt a formal letter of condolence was called for, and also a word of reassurance about the money after the uproar caused by the unmasking of Firethorne. She was missing Sidney, she said when she wrote back, but the money was nice – she was having the bit of garden front and back done up – 'landscaped', she called it – but the allotments would still be her favourite place. '*Sid never came up there, but it's nice and restful, and I can think of him while I'm doing the weeds*' – I'm pretty certain she didn't intend any sort of joke.

Letty sent back Firethorne's hundred thousand to the Club – he seemed to have been quite well-off – and just after that we were married. We kept one of the photographic enlargements from the pile Firethorne had made to commemorate his *Leda*. We had it framed, and it hangs in the downstairs loo.

However.

The revelations had left the art *guru* Lars Jochimsen nursing his wounds. His reputation as infallible connoisseur – the Berenson of his day – had taken a tumble. But the man was no posturing hack on a Sunday newspaper, he was a scholar, and he had stamina. First, he cast up, in the form of a detailed list, those aspects of the picture which had persuaded him that the *Leda* was authentic. This came out in *Artis* the Swedish quarterly which had published his original opinion, though in the Press at large he failed to get the coverage his initial endorsement had received. His next move was to contact The Museum of Timeless Art in Dallas. Since what Jochimsen was saying was what they were saying, he received a very sympathetic hearing, and everyone on the professional staff knew that he was – or, until just recently, had been – pre-eminent in his field. What he wanted to do was to come to Dallas and submit the picture to exhaustive technical analysis. Here, the Timeless Art people were a little wary. If the analysis went their way, and supported authenticity, well and good, but if it went the other way – and the prevailing view was massively behind the likelihood of such an outcome – what was in it for them? Jochimsen was brisk. His interests, he pointed out, were identical to theirs: if technical analysis showed the picture to be a fake, his reputation was irretrievably lost. He would sign a confidentiality agreement. Any revelation would be at the discretion of Dallas, and he would bind himself to silence unless the museum gave him leave to speak. It was in his interests to do so. Seeing the force of this, the museum offered to pay his expenses, he would be their guest. No, he would not. Were he to accept, no journalist would miss the opportunity of claiming that he had taken their shilling, and was, if not in their employ, at least in their camp. His disinterestedness must be unassailable. He thanked them for their courtesy, but would pay his own way.

So resigning himself to a fortnight's diet of hamburger, Jochimsen was pleased to find that his favourite pickled herring, his Aalborg aquavit (he had always preferred Danish schnapps to the Swedish brands), and any variety of smorgasbord was readily available in down-town Dallas, as indeed was anything else, including excellent radiographers. Jochimsen knew that to uncover signs of underpainting on the Leonardo canvas would be evidence of nothing save economy on the part of whoever the painter had been – canvases were used and reused, and sketches or trials, partly finished pictures, were routinely painted over, all the time. What he was looking for – and, of course, hoping not to find – was evidence of later additions in the resins used, or any artificial accumulations of dirt in the *craquelure*, which if the picture were genuinely of the early sixteenth century would only contain the natural residues of pigments and varnish, decayed over the centuries.

The picture was examined in the museum's spectacular laboratory, an amenity only used when the museum deemed it prudent: someone comes in with a parcel under his arm saying his granny was left this picture by a direct descendant of Constable, and the lab was handy for quickly establishing that it had been sprayed-on by a Korean who did six at a time. But when a whole lot of dough already paid out had put everyone's neck in a noose, as was the case with the Leonardo, no one was in too much of a hurry to go down the corridor and get the pathologists to confirm it. The word 'pathologist' scarcely conjures up the reverence with which the *Leda* was laid out and scanned. The initial X-rays, the ultra-violet and the infra-red photography, revealed nothing – whoever painted the picture had painted it on a canvas that had been new in the early sixteenth century. This raised Jochimsen's hopes, since some of Firethorne's photographs had shown him cleaning off an old canvas, and although the primer would not have shown up under X-ray, some remaining evidence of what had been painted on it might have remained.

Nor did analysis of the dust in the crackle show that it was tainted; at the back of his mind, Jochimsen knew there was a chance that it could turn out to be Indian ink, the medium used by van Meegeren to counterfeit the real thing – he'd painted over the varnish of his Vermeers with it, and when it dried it passed as dust: it was only in hindsight that the 'experts' said that it had aroused their suspicions because of being 'too homogeneous'.

All the miniscule detritus was examined under microscopes in the most prophylactic of environments. There were shavings from the frame and the stretcher, unseeable to the naked eye, a sample of the varnish itself, removed by laser in undetectable quantity, and every stage of the process was carefully annotated and logged: they had a time-clock record of the microchemistry at the end of every paragraph.

The various processes were monitored narrowly by Jochimsen, and all of them proved negative. But 'negative' means just that – a negative finding was not an identification. Jochimsen and the museum people knew this, but knew also that if no single negative finding was registered, if there was no positive evidence that the picture was a fake, then it wasn't. They had taken samples from sections of the picture, and the whole of the surface had been X-rayed, and nothing to impugn its authenticity was revealed – there was no trace even of restoration, the picture was in pristine condition, untouched. Yet this was a picture 'proved' a fake by the existence of photographs purporting to show C.W. Firethorne painting it. But the photographs – as Jochimsen pointed out to the museum colleagues – were external evidence, nothing on the actual canvas before them had been found that authenticated it as a – well, yes, you had to use the word – *genuine* Firethorne.

It was then that Jochimsen had his own revelation. Recalling the copies, the one in the Borghesi, the one at Wilton House, each versions of the actual masterpiece by Leonardo that he believed he had under analysis here in Dallas, he realized that he had overlooked one thing. Two things.

'I need a sample,' he said next day to the ever-responsive technicians, 'from two further specific areas of the picture which we have not analyzed.'

The lasers were used to fulfil his request. The samples were placed on a slide under the spectrograph. Jochimsen's cold unforgiving Swedish eye turned to the illuminated screen. He laughed. The colours into which the spectroscope had separated the samples betrayed phenol and formaldehyde – unknown before the nineteenth century.

'Do we celebrate? I don't see why.' One of the museum luminaries put it to Jochimsen in a low voice as they ordered their Caesar salads in the commissary.

'These samples show two small areas, and two small areas alone, that were painted by Mr Firethorne, and these little additions – unknown in the other copies – are the only traces of any other hand save that of Leonardo himself.' And Jochimsen permitted himself a noisy Scandinavian laugh. 'Forgive me, my dear chap, I suppose I am a bit triumphant.'

'Just those two sections—'

'Of course, the radiography in itself could reveal nothing, chemical analysis of those small particular areas was required. I am talking about the bushes in the foreground – the firethorns – and the constellation in the sky, which is called by any number of names, one of which is Charles's Wain. All the poor man ever did was paint them on. His name, in code. Ha, ha, ha. The two additions with which Firethorne adorned – or you may say, defaced – a perfectly genuine Leonardo. Clean off the stars and the bushes, and you have the finest, best preserved, one-hundred per cent genuine Leonardo in the world!'

Then it was that the smiles on the faces of the curators were turned up to sun-lamp level, and the man who first made the facts known to the governing body – the Convenors – was actually humming as the call was put through. Here was indubitable evidence that the picture was the real thing – for if the modern chemicals were confined to two small areas of the surface, then they had been added: the hand which had painted the picture itself had known nothing of phenol or formaldehyde. And then came news indeed. While Jochimsen had been in the States a colleague from Uppsala had been studying the photographs which purported to be a record of the faker's progress.

'Oh, yes, he was a faker. But he was faking the photographs, not the picture,' said Jochimsen's informant, laconically. 'You get them under the big lamp, put them together, and it's obvious. What he was doing was masking sections of the negatives, covering them up, so that when he printed them out the white spaces looked like bits of the picture he hadn't painted yet. For example, he cut a paper shape of the Leda, covered the image on the negative with it, so when he printed it out it looked as if there was just an outline, waiting for the master to paint in. But under the lamp you can see the blanking isn't perfect. You get edges that don't quite cover what they're supposed to cover.'

The wire from Uppsala to Dallas now hummed with self-congratulation, as Jochimsen and his colleague dilated upon the curious nature of the situation.

'But the oven – the baking—' Jochimsen pondered the thoroughness of the fantasy.

'Maybe he was practising, maybe he did have it in mind to run up a fake some time or or other – fixing up an old canvas ready to paint. But the photography – you had something like it in the thirties,' said the man from Uppsala, 'pictures of the spirits of your loved ones. Veils and faces materializing in suburban front rooms. They doctored the print-outs in the same way – any suspicion in the negative of someone's arm being seen, and they masked it with sticky tape. Frauds, of course, but fantasists too, just like your man.'

'You mean,' said Jochimsen, 'he believed it?'

'Oh no,' said the colleague, 'sort of game. Don't suppose for a minute he ever meant to show the photos to anyone, no one would have known if he hadn't died. Just couldn't help tampering with the Leonardo. Childlike, really. Acting it out. A charade.'

At his end of the line, Jochimsen was silent for a moment.

'He didn't ask *me* if I wanted to play.'

'Look on the bright side. He set you up, but you tripped him up. With a little help from your friends.' And as Jochimsen put the phone down he had to admit that his pal from Uppsala was entitled to his final, contented chuckle.

In the cool salons and corridors of The Museum of Timeless Art the soberly clad curators exchanged the greetings of men and women who knew their own worth. They spoke gravely of the slight put upon them by cynics and unbelievers everywhere, and their style was that of the righteous. They praised Jochimsen, their preserver, took comfort in the cutting-edge technology of their scientists, and gathered in front of the *Leda*. No words perhaps could quite sum up what their feelings were as they gazed at the masterpiece, now fully authenticated, but if there was one comment that seemed to encompass the feelings of all as they looked up in reverence at the Leonardo which had cost the Museum £55 million, it came from a pretty young woman wearing large, studious glasses. 'He saved our asses,' she said glowingly, and the words came from her heart.

As to the cleaning-off of the Firethorne additions, someone at The Museum of Timeless Art seems to have been endowed with imagination and largeness of mind. After considerable debate, it was decided the additions should remain. Why remove the evidence of such a remarkably economical attempt at fraud! The Firestone additions were small, nicely done and unintrusive, and for visitors to the museum, they could be a selling point, a novelty. The Convenors were agreed, and, after all, the additions could be removed at any time.

And a selling point they proved to be. The visitor strolls into the long cool gallery where Leda has a wall to herself, and stands to admire. When he walks closer to read the rubric which tells you all about the picture, he stands back again to take in the constellation of stars in the painted sky, and the row of bushes in the foreground. On the little gold plaque attached to the frame, there is Leonardo's name to which has been added (in brackets) 'With additions by C.W. Firethorne'. There are some who feel the additions are distracting, and indeed there are people who say they visited the gallery not because they wanted to see the Leonardo, they wanted to see what Firethorne had done to it. This annoys the connoisseur, the serious student, but can you think how it would annoy Leonardo? He is the star, his name appears above the marquee – but it is C.W. Firethorne who pulls them in. One can only hope that in the great hereafter, they have never met.